The Doctor
of
Broad Street

The Doctor
of
Broad Street

KATHERINE
TANSLEY

Matador
9 Priory Business Park,
Wistow Road, Kibworth Beauchamp,
Leicestershire. LE8 0RX
Tel: 0116 279 2299
Email: books@troubador.co.uk
Web: www.troubador.co.uk/matador
Twitter: @matadorbooks

ISBN 9781 785892 103

British Library Cataloguing in Publication Data.
A catalogue record for this book is available from the British Library.

Printed and bound in the UK by TJ International, Padstow, Cornwall
Typeset in 11pt Aldine401 BT by Troubador Publishing Ltd, Leicester, UK

Matador is an imprint of Troubador Publishing Ltd

For
Lucy, Eddie and George

...The Medical Officer of Health ... stated the gratifying fact, that in consequence of the vast exertions of the commission, the dreadful disease [cholera] had not appeared in a severe form in any of the districts of the City, where, on former occasions, it had assumed the very worst features...

The London Standard, Wednesday 30th August 1854

Soho, London

I looked up at the building on Marshall Street, the coal-stained bricks and tattered curtains an echo of my childhood home. A sun-baked flake of black paint fluttered into the gutter. In the grey world of the poor, even on a summer's day, the blues seemed more muted, the sun more faded. As I waited three boys, walnut-brown and bare-chested in the heat, took turns dousing their heads in a bucket. They threw their heads back and laughed as round drops sizzled onto square cobbles. I loosened my necktie, perspiring, envying their freedom. I turned away as the door opened and a young woman appeared, her watchful eyes scanning the street, wary. In the gloomy hallway, the smell was of human waste.

'I'm Dr Roberts,' I said. The girl stood back to let me enter. She was eighteen or so with clear skin and striking eyes the colour of hazels. She wore a faded red dress, sweat-marked under the arms, the long sleeves surely too hot for this summer. Her acrid, unwashed body scent crept into my nostrils as I took in her long, dark curls, tethered with a scrap of old ribbon. She pushed the escaping strands behind her ear with fingers ingrained with the dirt of London. 'How can I help?'

'It's me friend, Jo Parker. Me mother found 'er on 'er way back from buyin' eels at the fishmonger.' Her full lips pursed. 'If I ever find them devils…' her eyes glinted as her hand stabbed at the bannister. It wobbled precariously, most of the spindles gone to feed the fires which made life bearable on a winter's day.

'I see.' I climbed the narrow stairway behind her, the woodwormed planks creaking beneath my shoes. Her slender ankles were bare above her old boots, split at the seams. What would it be like to be a poor young woman in the alleys of Soho? Better a doctor, a man with a purpose.

''Ere, Doctor,' she said, as we entered a small, airless room where the window admitted little light. As my eyes adjusted to the gloom, I saw a girl on a reed mattress, a woman holding a chipped cup to her lips. I was momentarily a child again, pressing a cup to my mother's lips as she lay dying.

'Emily,' the woman said to my guide.

'Mother, it's the doctor,' said Emily, and the woman looked up as I approached. The girl on the mattress was fifteen or thereabouts, her dress in a bloodied heap at her feet. Her shimmy was torn and bloodstained and a sheet partially covered her legs which were strangely white; white except for streaks of dried blood. Her head lay back on a thin pillow, her lower lip split and bleeding, the skin on her forehead ragged and her fair hair dishevelled with debris. She groaned; her eyes shut against the horror of her world.

'Oh, Doctor, this is Mary Parker's girl, Jo,' said the woman. 'This is their lodging; I brought 'er 'ome, poor lamb. I'm Betsy Bates and Emily here is my girl.' Her ruddy face was filled with anxiety as I knelt beside the patient.

'Jo, can you hear me? I am Dr Roberts.' There was no response. 'What happened?' I asked Betsy Bates.

'Set upon, Doctor; I came upon 'em in Pulteney Court and chased 'em off; two of 'em there was, the brutes. How could they? I've sent for Mary and I packed her boys off outside,' she murmured, her hand on the girl's forehead.

'Can you get some water?' I said, but I knew water would not wash away the seed which would grow inside her, defining her life of poverty before she'd come of age. Emily scurried off with a bucket without a word.

I examined the girl and found no injury bar the facial cuts and bruising and the ominous stains on her legs. When Emily returned, I cleaned and dressed the girl's wounds. I rubbed balm into her lip and bandaged her head to cover the ragged graze on her smooth forehead, raw and exposed. I'd seen it so many times, I was almost inured to the sufferings of the poor; but today I truly felt it, how unfair life was. The girl uttered no sound, like an animal stunned in a trap. I offered her laudanum but she wouldn't take it, so I poured some into a cup.

'Give her this if you can. Have you reported it to the constable?' I said, handing it to Betsy.

'No, they won't catch 'em now, the monsters.'

'Get her to drink; the wounds will heal, but her mind will take longer.' I stood and turned to leave.

'How much, sir?' said Betsy, looking up at me. I shook my head.

'I have done very little,' I said. How could I charge these people for my services? I was lucky to have escaped such a life myself. 'There's no fee.'

'Thank you, Doctor,' she mumbled, moved to silent tears by this small kindness. I moved to the door but as I was about to leave, Emily spoke.

'Will she be with child, sir?' she said, her voice tight, and I felt the room brace itself for my words. I looked at Emily Bates, her pretty features and wild, untamed hair, her brown eyes with a spark of fire in them now the shock was less acute.

'I'm afraid only time will tell,' I said. 'Good day to you, I will see myself out.' As I left, I took a last look back at the miserable scene.

Outside, the sun beat down and the three boys sat on the step, throwing pebbles into the gutter. They brightened to see me, expectant, but I shook my head.

'Stay here a bit longer, lads, until your mother returns and says you can come back.' They slumped, deflated. 'Here you are, though,' I said, reaching in my pocket and drawing out three farthings, one apiece, tossing them in the air. They fell on them with joy. As I walked away down the hot street, I could still hear them whooping.

PART I

PART I

ONE

I attend a lecture and I hear some worrying news

I sat in the oak-panelled auditorium; it was packed, a throng of distinguished faces illuminated by the oil lamps. People sat on the steps and craned for a better view. Even the large oil paintings which hung on the wall at the front, of past presidents and great men of medicine, seemed to listen. The irregular swathes of pink and red, yellow and grey captured their expressions for eternity. My mother always loved the colour in life, everywhere she looked she saw the shades and shadows, the tones and tints in the world. But it seemed arrogant to think men of the future would want to be watched over by those long dead.

John Snow was a slight man, but what he lacked in physical presence he made up for in his command of the stage. In a sombre black suit and dark tie, you would not give him a second glance in the street. Nonetheless, his quiet, husky voice penetrated to the back of the hall. As he paused, you could have heard a pin drop. I watched as my friend placed his hands on the lectern and drew breath for the conclusion of his talk. His clear grey eyes surveyed the audience and I briefly caught his eye as he gave the merest of nods to acknowledge my presence.

'In conclusion, gentlemen, I put it to you that the techniques employed in the administration of anaesthesia are not, as some have suggested, mere trickery and sleight of hand. They can be learned by any physician who applies himself to the study.' There was warm applause from the hundred or so physicians gathered. People stood, talking with their colleagues as they surged down the steps to the front, eager for a closer view of one of the great pioneers of anaesthesia in England. Anaesthesia: lack of feeling. He disappeared from view into a circle of greying heads, a well-to-do, educated grey. I remained in my place on the wooden bench watching, amused, as I knew John would not welcome the attention. After ten minutes, the crowd thinned and I went to him.

'Well done,' I said, shaking him by the hand and looking down at his flushed face, as he stepped from the lectern. 'It was most interesting to hear of your work.'

'Was it all right, Frank?' said John, as ever self-doubting, mopping his brow with a plain handkerchief as he looked up at me, suddenly unsure.

'It was excellent, my friend, they loved you. Your courses will be oversubscribed, mark my words.'

'Another interesting talk, Snow,' one of John's colleagues, a straggler, came up behind him. 'But what of ether, then; has that fallen from fashion already?'

'Ah, Dr Foreman, indeed it has, for ether displayed more toxicity and unpredictability than chloroform, and chloroform is now the favoured agent. There will be others soon too, have no doubt,' John replied.

'Chloroform's caused all kinds of problems too, I've heard: deaths and the like?'

'There will always be unscrupulous elements in our society who misuse medicines for nefarious purposes and there have been instances of criminal acts being carried out while victims are under the stupor of chloroform. But administered carefully, in the correct dosage and under medical supervision, I still believe it to be the best we have available to us.'

'Yes, yes, you know more about it than I do, Snow, I'll take your word for it.'

'Good for you, Dr Snow.' John's friend from his days studying at the Westminster, Joshua Parsons, now an eminent renal physician, came up behind and clapped him on the back. 'Are you coming for a drink, man?'

'No, no, I thank you, Dr Parsons, but I have a prior engagement with my friend, Dr Frank Roberts, here,' said John.

Professor Henry Clutterbuck, the retiring president of the Westminster Medical Society, came over, his hair a silver grey and his round metal glasses slipping down his nose. 'Well done, Snow. You are making quite a name for yourself; I hear your services are in demand all over the capital now.' I hovered uneasily, never quite used to mingling with the greats of modern medicine.

'Thank you, Doctor, it keeps me busy,' said John, with a faint blush at the compliment.

'I did hear tell you were working on the cholera again? Terrible disease,' he grimaced, deep lines forming in the loose skin of his forehead.

'I am, indeed. There is always more to learn and I try to fit in my study around my other commitments.'

5

My heart plummeted in my chest at the mention of the cholera but the subject changed.

'How did you find Her Majesty, then?' said the professor. 'I hear you were called to attend her for the birth of Prince Leopold last year? You are privileged to have gained her patronage, I must say. Pain relief in childbirth; will it catch on, do you think?'

'All I will say is that Her Majesty was impressed with the new anaesthesia,' said John.

'But what was she like, in person, I mean?' cajoled Parsons.

'I will say no more about it, even for you, Joshua,' said John, a hint of a smile playing on his lips.

'Most unusual idea, anaesthesia for childbirth, if you ask me, but one must move with the times, I suppose,' replied the professor, pushing his spectacles back up his nose.

When we had at last escaped the crush of congratulation and questions, we stepped outside into the warm evening and I looked at my pocket watch. A carriage passed a little too close for comfort, spattering our breeches with the fetid soup of the gutter, and I frowned down at the murky spots. 'Come, we must hurry, or we'll miss the overture,' I said, as we set off on foot in the direction of the Opera House. At seven in the evening the streets were alive with people. Carriages ferried the well-to-do to their evening entertainment, while their horses scattered the less fortunate, who weaved and wended their way through the crush. Everywhere was a jumble of revellers, traders, entertainers, children, vehicles and animals. The air was ripe with the mixed scents of cigar smoke, ale, cheap perfume, gas lights and the rotting debris and excrement of the street. It was a heady mixture which lent a pungent aroma to the scene that was London.

As we scurried along, two women fell into step with us.

'Orf anywhere nice, are you, gents?' the first one slurred, the smell of cheap gin on her breath. She wore a flouncy red dress, which was low cut, revealing the swell of her bosom. She stank of common perfume and wore so much rouge and make-up it covered her pocked face quite well until you looked closely.

'Need a bit of company, do ya?' joined in her companion, similarly attired, and even more the worse for drink.

'No, no thank you, ladies,' I said firmly.

'Oh you is engaged is ya? Engaged to each other are ya? There's laws against that ya know, find ya'self in the Newgate, love…' the first one leered, dropping her wrist at me as the second one hooted raucous laughter at their wit. 'Wanna good time then, sirs? Go on, only a shillin' to you, sir, 'cause I like ya.' She fluttered her thickly caked eyelashes, walking backwards in front of me.

'No, no thank you,' I said, groping for the words as a distant memory flashed into my mind unbidden. 'Goodnight.' I stepped around her to continue and as a police constable appeared around the corner, they gave up their sport and slunk back into the shadows. John raised his bushy eyebrows at me.

'Not tempted then, Frank, young fellow like yourself?' he joked when they'd gone.

'I hope I can do better for myself than that.' We were even later now.

We arrived in Covent Garden, the whole of the market place a throng of colour, noise and lights, musicians, jugglers, tricksters, revellers and pickpockets. A man had rolled a barrel to the square and was selling porter from a solitary tankard. An old woman was selling walnuts, a girl with a muffin tray hawked her wares and a fellow was sizzling early chestnuts at a brazier in one corner, but we had no time to linger. I loved the new Opera House. Huge yellowy gas lamps illuminated the front, and inside the atrium and the auditorium itself were well proportioned and graceful, timeless structures that added to the wonder of the music performed there.

I was always a lover of music, a trait I inherited from the father I never knew, and I was forever trying to interest John in the beauty of it. Sometimes it filled my brain with light, bright explosions; sometimes it was a soothing balm which smoothed the vicissitudes of life. It lifted my soul when my dark days came. John and I arrived out of breath, but just in time to slip into our seats, before the curtain went up.

'Well, John, what do you think? Did you enjoy it?' I asked, leaning across, as the auditorium rose as one to applaud the final aria.

'I did, I did, Frank; although I confess it was not quite what I expected. I very much enjoyed the music, but the experiences of Don Giovanni are, shall we say, rather beyond my own,' John replied. As often, I wasn't sure whether he was in earnest. I looked sideways at him, quizzical.

'You may be older than me but I ever aspire to broaden your horizons, John, musically and otherwise. Your diligent application to medicine over the years has deprived you of other pleasures,' I said, amused, as the cast returned for a second bow and I roared my approval once more.

'Well, I thank you for your consideration Frank but, at my time of life, I believe my horizons are quite broad enough,' said John with his customary wry smile, still clapping. 'Leave leisure for the young, I say. But my horizons do extend to a visit to a coffee house, or how about some oysters?'

'The coffee house is a fine idea, once we can make our way out.' Eventually, the audience calmed and we fought our way through the bustling, energised crowds out into the warm London night. The sky was a dark inky blue, not quite black yet, and the light of the distant stars sparkled like tiny diamonds.

'Which do you prefer: Wilkins or Brewers?'

'It is good to be in the fresh air again. Let's go to Wilkins, it is less smoke ridden,' said John. 'I do believe that it will one day be proven that tobacco is not good for the constitution.'

'Tell that to the masses and they will laugh you out of the room, John. I confess I enjoy a pipe myself from time to time,' I said as we strolled along Long Acre, heading towards Leicester Square and Wardour Street on our way home to Soho. The dusk settled over the city in a warm haze. The yellow gas lights of the shops blazed a welcome, enticing the late evening shoppers. The streets thronged with the great mix of Londoners; theatre patrons, street vendors, and entertainers jostling along side by side with the beggars and street children. Everywhere was noise and lights, laughter and merriment. A juggler threw hats with skill, rotating one after the other via his own head and then up in the air, as a gaggle of children cheered him on. A busker played his ukulele and sang a love song in French. *'Mon amour, mon amour, oui c'est toi que moi j'adore…'* The sounds of everyday life rang out in the sultry evening, humming with the anticipation of a summer Saturday night. After a few moments soaking in the atmosphere, I turned to John as we walked. 'So, your practice keeps you occupied?'

'Yes, yes, thank you, I am happily employed. Indeed, I am often asked to travel across London these days. But there is always more to learn.' Now thirty, I had first come to London eleven years ago to complete my training. Since then, I had watched as John had experimented first with ether and then with chloroform. He had described and published the five degrees of etherisation and he had worked to develop a succession of different methods of administration of anaesthetic gases. He was thorough and methodical, honing the techniques and dosing, the safety of his patients paramount. He had even experimented on himself, saying he believed he should administer to others only that which he had sufficient faith in to administer to himself. His star had risen. He was renowned for transforming surgery for both patients and surgeons, providing anaesthetics for the first time. But I knew he had another passionate interest: the cholera.

'You have done our patients a great service with your work.' With a lurch in my stomach, I broached Professor Clutterbuck's remark earlier in the evening. 'What of the cholera, though?' I said, with a lightness I did not feel.

'I have been continuing with my work on cholera these past months. You know William's death has always been with me and I hope one day to be able to further our understanding of the disease.'

John was, at first, a friend of my brother William, who was ten years older than me. When I was nine, my life changed. William died of the cholera in the epidemic of '32. John was learning to be an apothecary by then, in Newcastle, and he came home to see William when he was sick. He'd seen cholera in the mines in the north and he knew how deadly it could be. I'll never forget his face as he crossed the garden to tell me William was dead. I buried my face in his side as he held me tight. Mother died of the cholera too, the next day, and my life had spiralled rapidly downwards as the soft pinks and whites and blues of my childhood were replaced by the harsh greys of life with my aunt. I had harboured a dread of the cholera ever since, which I had struggled to battle in my professional life.

'The cholera isn't back in London, is it?' I said, my throat tight.

'There have been cases south of the river again this summer, yes.' We were approaching the welcoming sight of Wilkins coffee house, the windows bright and warm, the rich aroma of coffee wafting tantalisingly out onto the street. However, before we could enter, John was interrupted by a boy running up to us.

'Doctor, Doctor Roberts, your housekeeper said I might find you 'ere,' he gasped, bending over, his hands on his knees to catch his breath. It was Jack Jones, from the coroner's office. 'Sir, you're wanted down at Middleton's, for an examination. Mr Cornwell says could you come, please, sir?' he panted, breathlessly.

'*Now*, Jack?' I asked, surprised, for it was past eleven. Middleton's was the undertaker on Dean Street in Soho, not far from the rooms on Edward Street where I saw my patients. I had offered my services to the coroner and I was sometimes called upon to do post-mortem examinations, especially on a Saturday night, when the regular doctor was often not available.

'Yes, Doctor, this one's in an awful state, won't wait 'til morning 'pparently. Found dead in a cesspit, Mr Cornwell says.'

'Very well, I'll get my things from home and come straight away.' I turned to John. 'I'm afraid, my friend, our discussion must wait. I am sorry to leave you in this manner.'

John patted me on the shoulder. 'Do not worry, duty calls. I shall see you at the Westminster?'

'Indeed you will, and you must tell me more about the cholera. Goodnight.' As I set off for home to get my bag, I could not help my gut clenching in fear at the prospect of the cholera returning to our shores.

TWO

I perform an examination

I hurried towards my home in Great Pulteney Street, trying to put the cholera out of my mind. I had mixed feelings about the post-mortem. It had been a long day and I would have liked a quiet drink with John and then to retire to bed, but I always felt a certain excitement at the chance to examine the dead. The opportunity didn't come along that often, and I always liked the chance to practise my surgical skills, to see if I could remember from my days apprenticed at the Westminster, where sometimes, I'd been allowed to wield the knife.

Mrs Hook, my housekeeper, had left my bag in the hall and with mounting anticipation I left for Middleton's, walking up to Broad Street, along Edward Street and cutting through St Ann's Court. Familiar as it was by day, at night I took care to avoid the shadows. Harold Middleton was a respected undertaker and I liked working there. He and his son, Gregory, who was old beyond his fifteen years, were courteous and respectful, even to their charges. As a man who looked after the living, I liked those who treated the dead with equal care.

I knocked at the black door, studying the bow window in which stood a plain gravestone topped by a small white marble angel. It was surrounded by mourning bands, hat ribbons and black gloves, white sashes for children: the trappings of death, black and white. The angel's wings were spread and her simple face looked down lovingly upon the space where the deceased's name would be inscribed. It was a tasteful tribute, but surely beyond the means of most of the clientele. Many of the parish in Soho would end in a pauper's grave and would count themselves lucky they were interred at all.

Gregory ushered me through the sombre funeral parlour with its display of coffin woods, metal handles and inscription plates which ranged from the simple to the ostentatious, into the back of the premises, where the real business was carried out. Mr Cornwell, the coroner, was there surveying the corpse laid out on a metal table. Two large oil lamps reflected off the white tiled walls of the small room to afford just enough light to view the body. The syrupy-sweet air of the oil burning could not mask the smell and I struggled not to gag as my nose acclimatised to the scent of death and decay. Mr Cornwell was a rotund, balding man, who seemed to think himself very grand to be coroner for St James's district in his early middle age.

'Evening, Roberts,' he said imperiously. 'Got a funny one here; fellow found in a cesspit on Broad Street. Don't know who he is, or how he got there. It's taken a couple of hours to get him presentable for you, I can tell you.' The stench was noisome and foul. Gregory Middleton had done his best, but it was impossible to rid the body of the filth in which it had lain submerged. 'Need to know if he was dead when he went in or if the poor sod drowned in the stuff,' said Cornwell, dispassionately, 'and anything else you can tell us about him.'

'Right, I'll get prepared.'

'The night soil men found him; with this heat, everyone's desperate for the cesspits to be emptied, the bad airs are everywhere. Folks are getting nervous the sickness will return.' I felt a stab of fear at the thought of the cholera. 'I want to know how long he's been there, what he died of and anything that could identify him. Who knows, he might have a wife somewhere?' He wrinkled his nose in disdain.

'I'll bring you my report in the morning, sir,' I said, dismissing the coroner. I took a bloodstained apron from a hook on the wall and tied a cloth around my mouth and nose, trying to ignore the man's look of disgruntlement.

'Yes, well… thank you, Roberts. I'll see you first thing tomorrow at my office?' He left and Gregory grimaced after him, displaying his rotten front tooth, peg-like and black.

'Caring soul ain't he, Doctor?' he smirked. 'Sorry about the stink, sir. I've washed him three times but it don't make no difference.'

'No matter, Gregory. We'll all smell the same in the end.'

'You are right there, Doctor,' chuckled Gregory as he left me to it.

In the peace of the evening, I set about my task. The evening was cooler than the heat of the day and I relished the challenge of the questions posed and the solitude of working alone. I had always felt a strange privilege in making incisions in the living or the dead, the wonder of being privy to the marvellous inner structures and workings of the human body, a privilege which so few could experience first-hand. The pinks of the tissues, the yellows of the fat and sinew, the tulip purple of stagnant blood. I unrolled my knives and tools with care and laid them out on a small trolley adjacent to the corpse. Now, where to start?

I scanned the exterior of the body and noted the broad shoulders and torso, the flabby fat around the stomach, visible despite the post-mortem bloating. I estimated that the man was in late middle age: perhaps late forties or early fifties. His limbs were muscular but when I lifted them, they moved awkwardly. A splinter of bone poked through the skin of the left leg at mid-shin level. There was a tattoo on the left forearm and wrist, a snake: thin wavy lines enlarging to a reptilian head with a forked tongue over the dorsum of the wrist. The body was missing the left thumb and half of the left index finger, which looked to have been severed at the proximal interphalangeal joint, but these were old injuries as the stumps were well healed.

When I had examined the front of the body, I called to Gregory to help turn it over. The whole of the back of the head was swollen and bruised, the skin and soft tissue ragged and decaying. Over the occipital region at the base of the back of the skull was an open wound; the edges were soft and pappy. It appeared that there had been a specific injury to the occiput and a more widespread blow to the back of the head. I called Gregory to help turn the body face upwards once more.

I started with the chest and, imagining myself a great

surgeon, made an incision in the grey skin from sternum to navel. Carefully, as if I were operating on a live patient, I opened the ribcage to examine the contents. The heart showed signs of age, yellow fat surrounding the coronary arteries; the lungs were surprisingly pink. Often, the lungs of Londoners revealed black-specked lung tissue from years of living with the coal smuts.

When I made an incision into the lungs, though, a foul brown-green substance oozed from the cut surfaces and I drew a sharp breath. The man had drowned in the cesspit. I imagined him sinking under the surface and taking a breath, his mouth, nose and lungs filling with the stinking semi-liquid excrement. I shuddered, and felt a stab of pity for the man; I could not think of a worse way to die.

I completed the rest of the examination, the only other findings of note being broken bones in both legs and the right arm. The man had probably been hit on the head, sustained blunt trauma resulting in the other injuries, and was placed in the cesspit alive where he had drowned. In view of the extent of the injuries, he could well have been unconscious: unconscious, but breathing. Perhaps he could have hit his head and fallen in, but that would not explain the other injuries. If he had been placed in the pit, it must be murder.

When had he died? A difficult one. Usually, one could tell from the state of decomposition of the corpse, but what effect would submersion have? Would the body decompose more quickly? Or would it, in the absence of air, decompose more slowly than normal? I didn't know. In addition, the weather had been so hot that decomposition would occur more quickly. In any case, it couldn't have been there long; I would say a week at most. But it was a guess.

'Gregory, I have finished, he's all yours,' I called and the lad came through to prepare the body for the cold room. I cleaned myself and my instruments at the cracked sink in the corner, looking at the green oblong tiles there, the only colour in the room. I softly whistled "The Queen of the Night" from *The Magic Flute* as I struggled to cleanse myself of the terrible smell. Then I sat in the office to write my report, while it was fresh in my mind. When I had finished, I bade Gregory goodnight and left.

The angel in the window, eerily illuminated in the moonlight, seemed to bid me farewell. The rounded nose cast a moon shadow on the stone cheek, which looked soft and plump, and the childlike eyes seemed to look back at me. I shook myself. I strolled home, keeping to the lighted streets and walking in the middle of the road once more, as the bells of St Luke's tolled three. Apart from a couple of drunks and a few whores half-heartedly selling their wares, I saw no one, and I relished the cool fresh air of the summer night. John Snow's lecture and Don Giovanni seemed a very long time ago.

THREE

Reflections, I visit the coroner and I receive some assistance

I woke, unrefreshed, from a turbulent sleep. I had been overcome by a sense of melancholia last night on my return from Middleton's and, foolishly, I had tried to ease my mind with a glass of wine; always a mistake, for I knew from experience that wine and the dark dog made for fitful rest. From time to time, I suffered with my black moods and the events of the day had sat heavily with me. I thought of the dead man from the cesspit and how he had met his end, of the whores by the Opera House, just girls some of them, and of just how hard it was for so many to survive in the city. More than anything though, the mention of cholera had haunted, unsettled me. The combination of factors had given me uneasy rest.

I had always felt alone in the world, ever since my mother and brother died. My Aunt Maria who took me in cared little for children. I was a religious obligation, a duty which must be fulfilled. She had rescued me from starving in solitude as the cholera raged in York and I had no means to survive. My aunt had given me a home, but it was not the loving home I had known. There were the trappings of wealth, good food and a warm bed but no humanity, no colour, little human contact with any living soul. I had a tutor at home and we lived away from my native York, so all contact with my former life was severed. My formative years, nine to fourteen, where I should have learned how to forge my way in the world, were spent with books in a library. I knew my classics, knew my French, I knew my literature, yes. But I didn't know how to earn her love, how to be happy in my own skin; how to be me.

After Mother and William died and my life disintegrated around me, John visited sometimes. He was apprenticed to an apothecary by then, through a well-connected uncle. When I was fourteen, he arranged my apprenticeship with the same master and I left my aunt and her grey stone house forever, vowing never to think of her again. However, I must be grateful that she left me her estate when she died, which has enabled me to live and work in London. I have been able to try to do some good with my life. But I was a fragile child and those early years took their toll on me, although I have striven to rise above it.

But today was a new day and I felt better in the daylight, wondering where the melancholy had sprung from. I got up and set off for the coroner's office bright and early. As I walked up Great Pulteney Street towards Wardour Street, the sun on my face was already hot. I couldn't remember a summer like it. The heat had sat over London like a thick blanket for weeks and while it was welcome at first, it had become dispiriting. There was no relief for indoors was as warm as outside and there was little breeze to shift the heat which enveloped everything. My patients lived in cramped quarters, several to a room, the young and the old all living on top of one another. The smells of the open gullies, the cesspits, the animals and the waste were always full and malodorous, but this summer it was even worse. Flies were everywhere. In the warmth of the morning, I shivered at John's words about the cholera returning to London.

I reached the coroner's office, above a cobbler. Small as it was, Cornwell had done his best to impress upon visitors his importance and the room was expensively decorated with dark red hues, an ornate mirror over the black iron fireplace. On the mantelpiece two stuffed, brightly coloured birds sat in glass cases, one either side of a carriage clock. The timepiece ticked loudly to remind people of the value of the coroner's time. The room was otherwise dominated by a walnut desk, before which sat two high-backed chairs. Cornwell himself was seated in his own burgundy leather chair behind the desk, lord of his opulent domain. Burgundy, red: rich colours, colours of success.

Cornwell had mistrusted general practitioners ever since the death of his wife from a grand mal fit many years ago and since he had attained his position, he took pleasure in lauding it over the doctors he dealt with. I had developed a thick skin in my dealings with him and I enjoyed doing post-mortem examinations, so I was always courteous. He didn't get up as I entered, but peered over his glasses, territorially, as if determined to re-establish his importance. Not to be outdone, I stood before him, looking down at his porcine face, already damp with sweat.

21

'Well, Roberts?'

'Almost certainly murder, sir,' I said, placing my report on the desk before him.

'I remind you, your job is to ascertain the cause of death, Doctor.'

'Drowning in the cesspit. There was a blow to the back of the head and other injuries consistent with blunt trauma. He was put in the pit while still alive and he drowned there. He may well have been unconscious, of course, in the light of his injuries. It's all in there,' I said pointing to my papers.

'Any other explanation possible?' asked Cornwell, mopping his forehead.

'Well, I suppose he could have banged his head by accident and fallen in. But that wouldn't explain the extent of his injuries and I'd say it's unlikely.'

'That's for me to decide, Roberts. Thank you,' said Cornwell pompously. 'You can go now.'

'Can Middleton's release the body, if it is claimed?'

'No, not until this is concluded. It's certainly one for the bobbies; someone'll swing for this, mark my words. I'll hurry the formalities along.'

'I'll let them know,' I said, and I left the oppressive office and stepped out into the sunshine again, thinking no corpse would last long in this weather. I bought some bread at a coffee seller and headed back to my bed.

In the early evening, I headed to my favourite public house, The Newcastle, for a drink. The building on the corner of Broad Street was full of people and I had to push my way through the crush to the bar, avoiding tankards and cigars at every turn. The brass taps were sparkling, the dark wood of the bar highly polished and the bottles of spirits multiplied in the mirrored backdrop. 'Pint of porter please, Daisy,' I greeted the landlord's wife, as I stood sideways, squashed between two men.

'Nice to see you, Doctor, 'aven't seen you in 'ere for a while?' she said.

'No, I've been busy, Daisy, but with this heat, I am in need of refreshment, thank you.' I paid and pushed my way to a seat in the corner as I carried my drink clear of the heads. I didn't go there often, but I felt in need of a change.

There was always a wide cross section of people at the public house. Through the whirls of tobacco smoke, I studied what I could see of the clientele. At the bar stood five men, looking hot and tired as they took big gulps of beer from their tankards. At the table nearest the door there was an old man and another man, who looked like his son. They were deep in conversation, and the old man patted the younger man's shoulder from time to time, as if comforting him. The rest of the floor space was filled with groups of men in various stages of inebriation, even on a Sunday. Customers spilled out onto the pavement and the street noise wafted in to create a comforting hubbub of activity and life. A fiddler came in, plying his music; Bruch's concerto it was. I enjoyed the notes which he played better than I could ever hope to, but the bar was too crowded and he soon gave up. Daisy was laughing with the customers, good cheer flowing from her wide smile, but looks were deceptive. Once, I saw her with a grown man on the floor in an arm lock, pinning him there, her sheet of auburn hair covering his face. She was sharp as nails beneath her smile and she kept good order when her husband, Jimmy, wasn't there.

As I looked around, I saw a face I recognised near the window. It was Stanley Parker, whose daughter, Jo, had been attacked a couple of weeks ago; it was a bad business. Mr Parker, his shirt sweat–stained, stared glumly into his pot of porter, his chin on his chest, the weight of the world seemingly on his shoulders. I thought, not for the first time, that life was hard for the poor in the big city. I drained the dark ale from my tankard and rolled my head on my shoulders, easing the tension. I'd best get home, but I'd have one more drink before I went. I pushed my way back to the bar.

'Another half, please, Daisy,' I said and as I waited, I caught a snippet of conversation between the man next to me and Pip, the pot man.

'Jimmy says you saw a man with a funny 'and, Pip? Can you remember 'im? Big fellow missing 'is left thumb and 'alf 'is finger?' said the man. Out of the corner of my eye, I could see Pip considering.

'Yes, I do remember a fellow like that. I 'adn't seen 'im before but 'e stuck in me mind as 'e 'eld 'is tankard with three fingers. 'E was quite nifty with it.'

'That's 'im; d'you know where 'e was staying?' urged the man.

'There you are Doctor,' said Daisy and I didn't hear Pip's reply.

'Thank you,' I said and I returned to my seat trying not to spill my drink, the man's words in my ears. The man I'd examined had such a hand; I wondered why this man wanted him. I finished my drink and stood up, just as old Pip limped past.

'Sorry, Pip,' I said, 'I just heard you mention a man missing a thumb? Do you know who he is? I have a colleague who was after information about him.'

'Sorry, Doctor, like I told Mr Bates, I don't know who 'e was, never seen 'im before.'

'Mr Bates?' I said as Pip picked up the pots.

'Yes sir, James Bates, 'e lives just opposite,' said Pip as he went on his way. "Bates": where had I heard that name before? I sighed to myself. It was time to go home; I dropped a penny on the table for Pip and left.

Outside The Newcastle, people spilled out onto the pavement and I pushed my way through. A troupe of jugglers was entertaining the crowd, lifting hats, handkerchiefs and even a bunch of flowers from the audience and throwing them high in the air to each other, never dropping an object once. The crowd was laughing at their antics and the entertainers passed around a cap from time to time to collect pennies. A horse went by depositing a forceful spray of urine onto the filthy cobbles and the outermost ones yelled after the horseman as they were splashed. I set off down Cambridge Street, the whole road crowded with people on the warm summer evening. I strolled along thinking how the constant bustle of London never ceased to stimulate my senses. Although the people were poor, they were, for the most part, resourceful and resilient. Even the children on the streets knew how to eke a living, cadging scraps from the stallholders and coffee sellers, the bakers and greengrocers.

Also, London was a haven for lovers of music. From time to time I got out the violin I'd inherited from the father I never knew and I rubbed the rosin on the white horsehairs of his bow. I enjoyed every opportunity I could to listen to classical music all over the city. Every week, I revelled in the choice of performances, ranging from intimate quartets or ensembles to full orchestral concertos. Compared to my native York, it was a different world.

But in the years I'd lived here, I'd seen many changes. The number of people seemed to be forever on the increase. People came from all over, seeking work, seeing opportunity in the inexorable rise of the city. There was new building everywhere, red brick and pink plaster dust filling the courts and alleys, as more and more dwellings were needed. The streets were ever more crowded with people, carts, horses and omnibuses and the river was a constant hive of activity, as ships set sail and people criss-crossed the brown muddied water at their business. The prisons were bursting and the great hulks in the estuary housed the excess. London was booming.

As I passed the end of Pulteney Court, I was roused from my reverie.

'Oy, Mister, 'elp!'

I peered into the relative quiet of the court, a narrow street with tall buildings on either side, making it dark. A fetid smell of rotting garbage assailed my nose and a mangy tomcat slunk out, hissing at me. I could just make out a figure on the ground in a doorway, another figure straddled on top and a third rifling through the clothing of the victim.

''Elp!' I heard again, a girl's voice. I hesitated and stepped into the court.

'What's going on?' I demanded. 'Stand away!' But before I had an answer, the trio were on their feet, surrounding me, light-fingered hands everywhere, in my back pocket, my inside pocket, under my jacket. They were cutpurses, pickpockets; children of about nine or ten, two boys and the girl. They wore rags and no shoes and they were dirty and unkempt, as they pawed at me, trying to steal whatever they could.

'Stop, stop!' I cried, furious that I was foolish to have been tricked.

'Go on, Mister, just a bit of change, we's 'ungry we are,' said the girl in a wheedling tone, looking up at me. She had big dark eyes, with a grubby brown face and dark, straggling ringlets of unwashed hair falling around her shoulders. She wore a dirty old dress which might once have been blue; her feet were bare and she looked thin and undernourished. Meanwhile her companions were dancing around me, running in and retreating out of reach of my fist. Suddenly, I was aware of another man at my side, hauling the boys off and dangling them by the scruffs of their necks.

'What 'ave we 'ere?' the man demanded.

'You let 'em go, Mister,' pleaded the girl. 'They're not doing no 'arm. We was just 'ungry, that's all,' she said, looking down at her filthy toes as she spoke. 'You let 'em go, sir.'

''Ave they taken anything, sir?' asked the man, and I recognised him as the man in the public house who'd been asking Pip about the dead man.

'Just my watch, I think,' I said, as I checked my pockets.

''And it over,' said the man, 'or I'll take you to the bobbies, and don't think I can't manage you two all right,' he threatened.

'Best give it to 'im, 'Arry,' said the girl, resignedly.

'Where is it?' asked the man, his grip tight on the boys.

'In me britches,' replied the boy called Harry, squirming in the man's hold, legs flailing. 'You let us go, Mister. We're not doing no 'arm, we're not.'

'I'm not sure about that, lad,' I said. I retrieved my silver chain pocket watch from the boy's trousers, while the man held both boys firmly.

'Sure that's all, sir?' asked the man.

'Yes, thank you, it is. Let them go, they're only kids.' I remembered what it was like to be hungry; who could blame them? 'Get away, you three, and if I see you here again, I won't be so forgiving.' The man dropped the boys and all three children ran off, fast as the wind, laughing and whooping.

'We nearly had 'im!' said Harry with glee. 'Nah, there's plenty more folk about…'

'Kids, little thieves, they're everywhere,' said the man.

'Thank you. That was my father's watch; he passed away before I was even born and I would have been sorely upset to lose it. I am Dr Frank Roberts. Thank you.'

'Pleased to 'elp, sir,' said the man. 'James Bates.' He was a strapping young lad of eighteen or so, brown-haired and clean shaven, with deep nut-brown eyes. He reminded me very much of the girl, Emily, who'd been there when I'd seen young Jo Parker after her attack, and I knew straight away that they must be brother and sister. "Bates": that was why the name was familiar. His face had a pleasantly open look and he was well-mannered, despite his shabby clothes and open-necked shirt.

'Well, thank you, James Bates, I am much indebted to you.' I rubbed my temple, shocked by the encounter. I hesitated. 'You were in The Newcastle just now, if I'm not mistaken? Forgive me, but I couldn't help but hear you making some enquiries at the bar.'

'Yes, but Pip couldn't tell me much,' he said dejectedly. I hesitated again. Really it was a professional confidence, but I didn't see what harm it could do.

'It is a coincidence for I was involved in the examination of the body of the man.'

'Were you? What did ya find?' said Mr Bates, his brown eyes staring at me.

'I'm afraid I'm not at liberty to divulge the details. Why do you seek him?'

"E was found in the cesspit for our privy yesterday and today me father's been taken to the magistrate for questioning about 'is murder,' said Mr Bates, anxiety in his voice. 'Me mother's out of 'er mind with worry.' He looked down at his tattered shoes.

'The man was found in *your* cesspit?'

'The cesspit at the building where we live, yes.'

'And you presume your father innocent?'

'I swear God's truth 'e could never murder a man,' he said fiercely.

'Then I am sorry, my friend.' I bit my lip. 'Between ourselves, he died of drowning in the pit, with a blow to the head. I know nothing of his story before he came to meet with that grim death. You could ask at the workhouse on Poland Street; if he had fallen on hard times, he might have gone there?'

'You're right. But now I'm off to Bow Street to see whether the magistrate's gonna let Father go,' he sighed.

'And I must head for home. If I can ever be of assistance, you can find me in Great Pulteney Street. Farewell James Bates and thank you.' I felt him staring after me as I hurried out of the dark court and back into the evening sun. I walked down the road bound for home, thinking how it was the second time I had come upon the Bates family.

FOUR

Monday 28th August

I visit my early master

The next morning I set off for the Westminster Hospital. Every Monday, I returned there, a change from the rest of my week when I held surgeries in rooms above the apothecary in Edward Street or visited patients at home. The Westminster was where I had been apprenticed to George Williamson more than a decade ago. John Snow had arranged it for me. I'd completed my surgical training in London with Williamson, and now worked as an apothecary-surgeon, or general practitioner, in Soho. John had been good to me over the years and we met from time to time to discuss cases or new developments. He sometimes worked at the Westminster and I often saw him there.

I looked up at the hospital, beside the great abbey of Westminster, close to the Houses of Parliament. Patients with all manner of ailments were treated there and many surgical procedures were undertaken. I always enjoyed returning once a week, to see interesting cases and to update my knowledge and skills, for medical men must keep abreast of developments. I also enjoyed lunching with my colleagues and peers for, aside from my housekeeper, I lived and usually dined alone.

I went onto Cavendish Ward and joined Mr Williamson. The ward was white: white sheets, white tiles, wooden floor bleached white by cleaning. The twenty beds did not afford much privacy, but men and women were on separate wards. Matron Elsworth, a small shrew-like woman, accompanied us on the round.

'Good morning Matron.' I found her a difficult woman as she always behaved with a brusque manner towards me and I had witnessed that she was often equally curt and humourless with her patients. I tried to forgive her as John had once told me that her four children had been crushed and killed by an overturned coach many years ago and she had never recovered from her grief.

'How is Mr Charles today, Matron?' asked Mr Williamson, at the bedside of the first patient, an amputee from two days ago.

'Well, Doctor…' Mr Charles began.

'The wound is improving but he is a little breathless, Doctor,' said Matron cutting in. 'He's had an inhalation this morning, without much relief, I'm afraid.'

'No, Doctor, not much better…'

'Listen to Doctor, Mr Charles,' said Matron, silencing him.

'Let's listen to your chest there, Mr Charles.' Mr Williamson bent over the man, who fell quiet, grey and unwell. He took out his stethoscope. 'Big breaths,' he ordered. I watched as the man tried to take breaths, the very effort seeming to cause him distress, but he obeyed.

'Have a listen Dr Roberts, and tell me what you

think,' said Mr Williamson as he stood up straight. I took out my stethoscope and stepped forward. The patient was out of breath, perspiring and grey, slumped on his pillow with his rheumy eyes looking up at me. I felt a stab of irritation at Williamson ordering him around.

'Sorry, old chap, do you mind if I just have a listen too?' I said, my hand on the fellow's shoulder. I caught a stern look pass from Matron to Mr Charles.

'Go on, then, Doctor, if it helps,' he gasped. I listened, and could barely hear any breath sounds at all. The man's chest was full of crackles and wheezes and over the left side all sounds were muffled as if encased in fluid. It was a wonder he was alive at all.

'There, easy now Mr Charles,' I said gently, signalling he could stop taking the breaths which were causing him distress. 'Let's pull you up the bed a bit; you might breathe a little better if you're more upright.'

'Yes, thank you, Doctor, we can manage that,' said Matron.

'Well?' asked Mr Williamson, looking at me.

'There are added breath sounds indicative of inflammation, and quietened sounds on the left, suggesting an effusion of the pleural cavity,' I replied, not wishing to alarm the patient.

'And your recommendation, Doctor?'

'I would advise attempted drainage of the fluid in the first instance.'

'Quite so, Dr Roberts. Matron, prepare the tray. I will return at the end of the round to perform the procedure.'

'Very good, Doctor,' said Matron and, as they moved

on to the next patient, I looked back apologetically at Mr Charles.

We went around the rest of the patients, seeing a mixture of cases with heart failure, respiratory problems or problems of the digestive system, and various surgical cases, awaiting or recovering from operations. Although patients were attended primarily by one doctor, we saw all the patients on the round with Matron. Often there was little to be done and I sometimes wondered if admission to the ward did more harm than good.

At the end of a long morning, I returned with Mr Williamson to assist with the drainage of fluid from Mr Charles' chest. Matron had prepared a trolley with a wide-bore, hollow, metal needle, a length of rubber tubing, and a bell jar to collect the fluid. The needle needed to be inserted over the top of a rib, as underneath each rib lay the blood vessels. Most importantly, the needle must not penetrate too far and enter the lung tissue itself, or even worse, the heart. Every procedure was fraught with danger.

Mr Williamson rolled up his sleeves and took the needle in his hand. Feeling Mr Charles' ribs, he counted down until he reached the tenth, and then with the conviction necessary to make any assault on a living person, he thrust the needle over the rib midway between the line of the armpit and the spine on the left side of the back of the chest. The needle stopped and Mr Williamson faltered, appearing unsure of whether he had hit bone. He pushed a little harder and under the added pressure, the needle shot forward. Mr Charles gave a gasp of surprise before he clutched his chest, as bright red blood spurted rhythmically from the hollow bore of the needle. Williamson was paralysed into inactivity by this catastrophe.

'Withdraw the needle, sir,' I urged under my breath. 'It's pierced the heart, sir.' I grabbed the needle and withdrew it a little, but it was too late. The patient had collapsed backwards, his hand at his chest, bright red like a sea of poppies extending vividly over the white sheet, his eyes wide and staring at the ceiling. He was dead. Mr Williamson, white-faced, composed himself and withdrew the needle.

'Must have an enlarged heart, jolly unlucky, wouldn't normally extend down that far,' he murmured, his bloody fingers struggling to loosen his necktie. I noticed beads of sweat on his upper lip. I doubted that he would acknowledge what he had done; I had seen him make mistakes before. I was annoyed at his arrogance but it was not my place to comment; my sense of my own lowly beginnings in the world and my teaching had imbued in me a traditionalist view that one's elders should be respected for their greater experience. Who was I to question?

'Clear the trolley, please, Matron,' he ordered and head held high, without a backward glance, he left the ward taking me with him. As we left, I heard Matron ordering two nurses to stop staring and clear up the blood.

After a long day, I stepped out into the bustle of the evening street. Often I took a cab home, but today I felt in need of some air. I looked around and gazed up at the ornate majesty of Westminster Abbey, the stained glass windows glinting blues and greens, yellows and reds in the early evening sun. The street below was full of people going about their business, returning from or going to work, street sellers and street children all a seething mass of humanity on a hot evening. I set off towards home, thinking about Williamson. I knew I shouldn't think it, but he had behaved like an ass today. Some doctors thought themselves invincible, treating their patients as pawns to experiment on. I had always thought it a privilege that other people entrusted their bodies and their lives to me. I had always felt it my duty to do the best I could or, as the Hippocratic Oath stated, at least to "do no harm". The trouble was my "best" was rarely enough. I'd not seen John today, so I hadn't been able to ask more about the cholera. A shadow crossed my mind: if it returned, there would be little anyone could do.

FIVE

I attend the inquest and I pay a visit to Harley Street

It was another bright sunny day as I set off early to attend the inquest. I had been summoned by Coroner Cornwell to present my evidence but I hoped it wouldn't take long, as I was due at the Institute for Gentlewomen in Harley Street that morning. One of my well-to-do patients, Frances Hobson, a distant acquaintance of my aunt, had sent word asking me to visit. I had never been to the hospital before and I was curious to see it. I had heard that a new superintendent, a woman no less, had taken over and was bringing in some new ideas.

I hurried up Great Pulteney Street, along Broad Street and into Wardour Street. The sun already adorned the sky, but the streets still felt cool in the shade of the tall buildings. I approached the coroner's court which stood next to The Castle, a public house of dubious reputation. A couple of whores emerged, bleary-eyed, their lip-rouge smeared, their night's work over.

I entered the court and took my place on the witness bench. Unlike Cornwell's office, the court was simple and functional. The coroner sat at the raised wooden table at the front, looking very much as if he fancied himself a proper judge. The clerk who recorded proceedings was ready with his ledgers at a small desk below. The rest of the room was filled with narrow benches on which were seated a few people including, I noticed, James Bates and the girl who looked so like him, his sister Emily. A sergeant I didn't recognise was there, with the bobby from Broad Street, Constable Lewis. Proceedings got underway.

'Silence,' announced Cornwell, and the mutterings ceased. 'I call Robert Bolder to the stand.' A man stepped forward.

'Robert Bolder, can you tell the court your occupation?'

'Night soil man, sir,' said Mr Bolder, looking nervous. The clerk made rapid notes.

'Tell the court how you came to find the deceased.'

'Last Saturday, sir, me and me assistant were emptying the cesspit, and we'd not long opened up the drainage channel and got started when me shovel 'it something, and it was a boot.' There were further murmurs around the room.

'Silence,' ordered Cornwell. 'What did you do?'

'Pulled it out, sir, 'ard work it was too; the boot was on a foot, attached to a body and the body was all swollen up and wedged in.'

'Where was this cesspit?'

'Yard of 19 Broad Street, sir.'

'Thank you, Mr Bolder. That will be all for now. I understand Mr Albert Bates is not available, so I call Mrs Elizabeth Bates, of 19 Broad Street,' Cornwell announced. I saw James Bates stand up, clutching his cap, his knuckles white.

'I am James Bates, sir. Me mother is sick, so I've brought me sister, Emily, who was there, to speak for 'er,' declared Mr Bates. Emily stood and walked to the stand.

'Very well. Miss Bates, tell the court of the discovery of the body.' Emily Bates bit her lip.

'Mr Bolder found the body, and as Mother and Father weren't in, I came down and sent for Father and the bobbies,' she said, levelly.

'Did you or any of your family recognise the man? Was he known to you?'

'No, sir, none of us 'ad ever seen 'im before.' She spoke confidently for one so young in such a place.

'Thank you Miss Bates. I call Gregory Middleton.' Emily Bates flushed as she returned to her seat and the undertaker's boy took the stand. 'Tell the court your job, Mr Middleton.'

'I clean down the bodies for me father, sir: Harold Middleton, the undertaker.'

'And you cleaned the body in question for the examination? What did you find?'

'I did, sir. Didn't find much, sir. The body was covered in shit, pardon me language, and I took off the clothes and cleaned 'im up ready for the doctor, sir.'

'Did you find anything else, Mr Middleton?'

'Only a pipe, sir.'

'A pipe. In a pocket?'

'No, sir, under his jacket: must've come out of 'is pocket.'

'Thank you Mr Middleton. I call Dr Frank Roberts.' I stood and passed Gregory as I walked to the stand.

'Tell the court your role in this affair, Dr Roberts,' ordered Cornwell.

'I am Dr Frank Roberts. I conducted the post-mortem examination on the deceased late last Saturday evening, the 26th.'

'Summarise your findings, Doctor.'

'The deceased was male, in late middle age. He had a laceration and contusion to the occipital area over the base of the skull and a wider contusion over the back of the head and torso. He had two broken legs, a broken arm and two broken ribs. The other obvious external finding was that he was missing his left thumb and half of his left index finger, but these were old injuries. On dissection, the body showed the normal changes associated with a man of that age. In addition, and significantly, the lungs contained feculent material.'

'In your opinion, what was the cause of death, Doctor?'

'I conclude the cause of death was drowning in the pit, following a blow to the head or an assault which resulted in the injuries I have described.'

'You are certain the cause of death was drowning?'

'Yes. The presence of faecal material in the lungs indicates that some breaths were taken once he was in the pit. He was alive when he went in, although he may have been unconscious, of course,' I explained. There were more murmurings from the audience.

'Anything else of note?'

'His lungs didn't show the usual black inclusions which are often seen to result from breathing in the smuts of London, so perhaps he was new to the city.

Nor were they of the gravelly consistency often seen in the lungs of smokers.'

'And yet he had a pipe?'

'So Mr Middleton says.'

'Thank you, Doctor. I call Constable Lewis.' Thomas Lewis took the stand. His baby daughter of five months had suffered repeatedly from diarrhoea all her life and I was often asked by Thomas' wife, Sarah, to call. They lived on Broad Street, like the Bates family. The young constable tugged nervously at the collar of his dark blue uniform. Dark blue: a colour of solidity; reassuring, safe. He shot an uncomfortable glance at James Bates.

'Constable Lewis, did you attend 19 Broad Street last Saturday afternoon?'

'I did, sir.'

'And what did you find there?'

'I arrived to find that a body 'ad been found in the cesspit. I interviewed those present and arranged for the body to be removed.'

'Were there any features of note in the yard?'

'There was waste spreading from the cesspit and the channel was open; the body lay to one side, covered in a sack.'

'The channel?'

'Yes, sir, like many, the cesspits on Broad Street 'ave a brick-lined channel with an opening for emptying the pit. It's about two foot by a foot and an 'alf and covered with ironworks. It leads into the pit itself, sir, so the night soil men don't fall in.'

'I see. Have your enquiries since established the identity of the deceased, Constable?'

'No, sir.'

'Has any progress been made towards finding the person or persons responsible?'

The constable shot a worried look towards James and Emily Bates, and then directed his gaze to his sergeant, on the benches. 'Sergeant Granger said for me to go back and question the residents of 19 Broad Street about the pipe, sir, and when Albert Bates said it was 'is, the sergeant told me to take 'im to the magistrate.' He said this in a quiet voice, his face troubled. I looked at James and Emily who were staring forwards, heads unbowed; Emily's lips were set in a thin line, her jaw clenched.

'What did the magistrate decide?'

''E thought there was a case to answer, with the pipe and the body found where it was,' said Lewis. 'Mr Bates is in the Newgate.' The young man fiddled with a button on his uniform, looking desperately as if he wished he were no part of it.

'Thank you, Constable.' Lewis returned to the bench and I saw Cornwell draw himself up in his chair, ready to announce his verdict. 'I have considered the findings here presented and it is my opinion that the deceased received a blow or blows to the head and body and was then placed in the pit, where he drowned. In view of the circumstances, I record the cause of death as murder. It is for the police and a court of law to determine which person or persons are responsible. If the identity is not established and the body is unclaimed, it may be released for burial fourteen days from now. Good morning to you all.' With that, he stood and swept out of court, as all present stared after him.

When the coroner had left, the room relaxed and there was a low drone of chatter as people dispersed. I passed near to James and Emily Bates on my way out of the courtroom.

'Mr Bates, we meet again.'

'Yes, Doctor. This is me sister, Emily. Mother is sick and Father's in the Newgate, as you've just 'eard,' he said, his jaw tight.

'I have met Miss Bates before.' I nodded at Emily at his side, her long brown hair tumbling about her shoulders. She looked back at me with the same nut-brown eyes as her brother, her steadfast look giving her a spirited air, despite her faded old dress. 'I am sorry for your trouble. I hope this business is cleared up soon.'

''Ave you met Em before?' said James.

'Yes, I met her at the home of Miss Parker. How is she now, Miss Bates?'

'I'm 'fraid she's in a poor way, Doctor. If they ever catch them brutes, I swear they'll 'ave me to answer to. It was lucky me mother saw 'em off or they could've killed 'er,' she said fiercely, 'and poor Mother's dreadful upset 'cause Jo's mother is her oldest friend. And now Father's been taken…'

'I'm sorry to hear Miss Parker is not recovered and to hear of your other troubles.' I looked at Emily's flushed face and once again, I caught a glint of steel in those hazel eyes. 'Well, I must get on. Good day to you,' I said, and I went on my way.

I hailed a hansom cab for the journey to Harley Street, avoiding the crush of people walking to work, and the multitude of tradesmen and street sellers ever ready to serve them. I had acquired a few well-to-do ladies from the relationship with my aunt, which was fortuitous as most of my patients were too poor to pay for my services and I never charged those who could not afford it. I had been helped on my way in the world and I wanted to repay the debt.

As the cab drew up, a street sweeper was clearing the road in front of the hospital and compared to Soho, the air felt clean and fresh. I alighted, stepped onto the pavement of the wide street and I looked up at the grand building, with a white facade at ground level, and red brick storeys above. Each floor had tall, elegant sash windows fronting onto the street and as I looked, I noticed all the windows were open. A nurse reached her hand up to close one of the first-floor windows and I could hear her calming her patient within.

'It's all right, Mrs Welcombe, we'll explain to Miss Nightingale that the birdsong rattles your nerves, and we thought we'd close it a little. She will allow it, I'm sure...'

I went up the wide steps and knocked on the door, which was opened by a nurse in uniform. Her long, plain dress was covered by a white apron, and she had her hair covered by a white headdress. I thought how hot it must be wearing drapery on your head in this weather, but the large hallway inside felt cooler.

'Good morning. Dr Roberts to see Mrs Hobson,' I announced.

'Very good, Doctor, wait here a moment, please,' the nurse replied. I sat on a wooden bench and I looked around. There were two closed doors to left and right and a wide staircase ahead, with a fernlike potted plant beside each newel post. It was all painted white and it felt pleasantly cool after the heat of the street outside. A bowl of yellow dahlias on a table just inside the door exuded a pleasant fragrance. I thought fleetingly that if I were a gentlewoman, I would certainly prefer this to the Westminster. At the top of the stairs, I could just make out a large painting of Queen Victoria as a young woman. After a few minutes the nurse returned.

'If you'll follow me, Doctor, I'll take you up.'

'Thank you. Tell me, how many beds do you have?' I said, as we climbed the stairs.

'We've three wards of twelve beds each, Doctor, but we're half full at the moment,' she replied. 'Just as well, in this heat. Although Miss Nightingale does like all the windows open, which helps a bit of a breeze, I suppose.'

'Miss Nightingale is the new superintendent?'

'Yes, Doctor. She took over last year and she believes in the benefits of ventilation.'

'I see,' I said, as we arrived at the doors to one of the wards.

'Here we are, Doctor, I'll leave you with Nurse Irvine,' she said, and she retreated back down the stairs to her position by the front door.

A young nurse of about twenty came over from her desk and smiled lopsidedly. She had a harelip, which had not been repaired very well: a pity for a young woman, I thought. Apart from the deep red scar, I was struck by her porcelain skin: a combination of pinks, whites and peaches, which seemed almost lit from within. Brown wisps of hair escaped her cap but she looked smart and professional in her blue striped uniform and long white apron. I recognised her as the nurse I'd seen closing the window a moment ago.

'Dr Roberts to see Mrs Hobson I understand? She's just over here,' she said pleasantly. I looked down the ward which had six beds on each side, each with a crisp white counterpane. Seven of the beds were currently occupied.

'Nurse, a pan please,' called out one elderly woman as we passed.

'Excuse me one moment, Doctor,' the nurse said; 'Mrs Richardson, do you really need another? You had one just a few minutes ago, didn't you?' she soothed.

'Ah yes, got to get ready to go out.'

'I'll help you when I've finished with the doctor.'

'Doctor? Is that Doctor Dickson, then? Is he here to let me go home?'

'No, no, it's not Dr Dickson. Rest easy, Mrs Richardson, I'll be over in a moment,' she said firmly. 'Quite lost her mind, poor thing,' she murmured to me as we continued down the ward. 'Thinks she's back in Islington; she keeps thinking she's going to the theatre with her husband, who has long since passed.'

I studied Nurse Irvine as we walked down the ward. She was small and slight in stature, with eyes the colour of cornflowers. She was not pretty in a conventional way, in fact some might say she was rather plain, but I thought she had a pleasingly open countenance and, aside from her lip, fine features which gave her a self-contained air of quiet confidence. She was not at all

46

like the other nurses I'd met at the Westminster and elsewhere. Many women turned to nursing after being on the streets and in consequence, the profession didn't command the respect it deserved. But this nurse looked as if she was cut from finer cloth, and her frank and confident manner intrigued me.

We walked down the middle of the ward, which was painted white like the entrance hall and looked much cleaner and smarter than the wards at the Westminster. White: the colour of purity. Along one wall between the beds were five large sash windows which looked out onto the street, and all except one of these were wide open, their blue flowered curtains riffling in the breeze. Nurse Irvine must have seen me looking at the windows.

'Miss Nightingale's orders,' she said, 'all windows to remain open unless there's a rainstorm or if the fog is too thick. Only the weather can override Miss Nightingale's wishes!' She checked herself, looking momentarily at her shoes. 'I am sorry, Doctor, I did not mean to be disrespectful. Here's Mrs Hobson.'

I looked at Mrs Hobson who was sitting up in bed looking as fit as ever. Her fine grey wispy curls framed her face as usual, and she had even applied a little rouge to her cheeks. She had a fruit bowl full of apples and two books at her bedside, and she wore an immaculate bed jacket of cream wool.

'What can I do for you, Mrs Hobson?'

'Well Dr Roberts, I'm not at all well.' She looked up at me. 'The superintendent says I should go home, that there's nothing the matter with me, and I am most put out. Dr Berners admitted me, but you were so good to my poor husband in his final illness, I would value your opinion before I do anything too rash.'

'Can I see Mrs Hobson's charts, please, Nurse?' I said, and as she turned to get them, I was sure I caught her expression as she raised her eyes in amused exasperation, but she said nothing. She returned a moment later.

'Here you are, Doctor. All observations correct, these past three days.'

'Thank you, Nurse.' I studied the charts of temperature, pulse and evacuations, which were all perfectly normal. I put the charts down and sat next to Mrs Hobson.

'Why don't you tell me how this all started, Mrs Hobson?' She took a breath and launched into her story.

'Well, Doctor, this last week, I just haven't felt right. I've aches in my arms and my legs, and if I try to walk, I am all wobbly, and I want to know what's the matter with me,' she finished lamely.

'Have you any pain anywhere?'

'Not *pain*, Doctor, just aches.'

'Any breathlessness?'

'No.'

'Any stomach trouble, sickness, purging, that sort of thing?'

'No.'

'Any trouble with your limbs, headache or trouble with your eyes?'

'No, just a little wobble sometimes, as I said.'

'Well, that's a good sign. Let me examine you, Mrs Hobson. Nurse, the screens please.' I conducted a thorough examination, and asked her to dress.

'Mrs Hobson, I have to say I can find nothing untoward. I think perhaps the superintendent is right on this occasion? Is your son at home; would he come to collect you? As you are no doubt aware, Nurse, Mrs Hobson's husband sadly passed away two years ago,' I murmured. 'Perhaps the nurse could send for your son?' I suggested, but Mrs Hobson burst into tears.

'Oh Doctor, his regiment has been sent to the Crimea, along with all those poor boys out there. It sounds dreadful and I fear very much that he will be killed and then I'll have no one left,' she sobbed. I placed my hand on her arm and as Mrs Hobson cried into her lace handkerchief, I looked up at Nurse Irvine, quietly begging for her help. I had other patients to see, patients with physical ailments who were more in need of my ministrations than this sad, lonely old woman. Nurse Irvine looked me squarely in the face, gave a slight nod, and sat on the bed, squeezing Mrs Hobson's hand.

'There, there, Mrs Hobson. It must be a terrible worry for you. But I am sure the commanders out there will take care of our men.' She leaned in, conspiratorially. 'Shall I tell you a secret? My very own brother is also to be sent there soon, to Sevastopol. My poor mother is as worried as you are. But I have faith that they will be well looked after,' she said, exuding quiet confidence. Mrs Hobson stopped her crying, twisted her handkerchief in her fingers and looked up.

'Which regiment is he, Nurse?' she asked.

'Edmund is in the 30th Regiment, in the infantry. He is to be stationed near Sevastopol: Inkerman, I think it is. He loves the army, he thinks it's all terribly exciting,' she recounted, with a sparkle in her eyes. 'Mama says it will be good for him to see a bit of the world before he settles to life in London.'

'Yes, my John loves it too, says it's turned him into a man. He's in the Light Brigade; the 17th Lancers, in the cavalry,' Mrs Hobson smiled. I took my chance and made my escape.

'I'll leave you with Nurse Irvine, Mrs Hobson; I'm sure she can help arrange for you to go home. Then if your son sends any correspondence, you'll be there to receive his news. Thank you, Nurse.' I took one last look back at the eminently capable Nurse Irvine, and then I left the ward and the hospital, stepping once more into the warm street. I hailed a cab to take me back to Soho and I sat back and watched as the wide leafy streets became narrower and dirtier as the driver directed the horse through the traffic homewards.

As I alighted in Silver Street to walk the rest of the way home, the streets thronged with people and the sounds and smells of Soho hit me, a contrast to the peace and tranquillity of Harley Street. This was where I felt at home, these were the people of my childhood. I paused to buy some apples from the fruit barrow at the bottom of Carnaby Street and I threw a coin to an amusing fellow who sung a sea shanty with a model boat perched upon his head. Then, loosening my collar, I strolled towards home. Hopefully, the draining heat would lift as autumn came and cooler days arrived. As I took a bite of crisp apple, I thought of Mrs Hobson and I wondered if Nurse Irvine had escaped her yet, and I smiled to myself.

SIX

A terrible scene and I witness a death

The next day, I returned from my morning surgery in
Edward Street to find Mrs Hook hovering in my hallway
awaiting my return with six messages from people
asking me to call. My housekeeper was a widow of
middle age, a slight woman, greying about the temples.
I rented a small set of rooms on Great Pulteney Street,
and although simple, they were comfortable. She was a
capable housekeeper, but a little prone to worry about
sickness, which did not sit well with working for a
general practitioner. But she had been with me for ten
years and I had grown quite fond of her as we rubbed
along well enough.

'That is unusual, so many,' I frowned. 'Could you get
me a little bread and cheese, and some of your chutney
please, and then I'll be off?' She hovered, uncertainly.

'The airs are bad aren't they, Doctor?' she said,
fiddling with her cuff. 'It's this heat; I've never known a
summer like it.'

'Hopefully all will be well; some cheese, if you
please?' I reminded her.

'Very good, Doctor,' she said and she scuttled away.

I called first at the bakers on Marshall Street. Mrs Hook often called there as their bread was of good quality and unadulterated. Outside, four dirty-faced urchins, homeless children, squatted on the cobbles sharing an unexpected windfall of a loaf. I smiled, remembering how as a child a pilfered apple, an unforeseen morsel, tasted all the better. It was stifling in the shop, the heat of the ovens penetrating through to the front where the counter was stacked with rows of penny loaves and some sweet buns. The delicious smell made my mouth water. Mrs Ruby, the baker's wife, was serving and she motioned me behind the counter leaving her assistant in charge. We went up the narrow stairs to the small, single room above, where the family of eight lived.

'Terrible purging, Doctor, can't keep nothin' in 'er, she can't,' Mrs Ruby explained, taking me over to her daughter. I examined the girl of nine or so, pale and quiet.

'When did it start?' I asked.

'Middle of the night, Doctor, she was all right yesterday…'

'Get her to drink some water and rest, Mrs Ruby. Hopefully it will pass,' I reassured her. I looked around the stifling room. A white dusting of flour coated every surface and impregnated every corner. A baby was crying in its simple crib as a half-naked toddler burbled to itself, banging a wooden spoon on a pan. Two other young children sat at a table with a mug of milk between them, and an older boy played jacks underneath the open window. It was uncomfortably hot and the air was laden with dust and sickness. I didn't say so, but I knew it was highly likely the other children would all come down with it too. Mrs Ruby showed me out.

'Thank you, Doctor,' she said, pressing a small cob loaf into my hands.

'Thank you, Mrs Ruby. Send word if she doesn't improve.' I left, forgetting my thought to buy some buns, preoccupied as I was with the dismal scene. The bakery was on the corner of Marshall Street and Broad Street; there were several requests to visit there too.

I turned the corner to visit Constable Lewis' lodging again, at number 40 Broad Street. The street comprised tall, dark brick buildings with faded curtains at the grimy windows on the upper floors. At street level, many of the buildings housed small businesses: a carpenter, a sign maker, a hat maker, a tallow works, a tinker. Many more sellers plied their trade up and down the streets from barrows, handcarts or trays. At night, I knew the whores and the rent boys lurked in the doorways. I looked at number 19, opposite, where James and Emily Bates lived and I wondered whether any progress had been made on the dead man.

I called on Sarah Lewis to see her baby; they were a respectable working-class family and I liked Thomas and his wife. I pulled the bell at the front door of the building where they lodged and Sarah came to the door.

'Good afternoon, Sarah. How is Martha today?' I asked as we ascended the stairs to their two small rooms on the top floor, familiar to me now after my many visits there. It was sparsely furnished but clean and tidy, and the curtains were tied back with scraps that matched the old rag rug before the small fireplace.

'Much the same, Doctor. She's had an upset stomach again for a few days now.'

'I'm sorry to hear that, Sarah; she's hardly thrown off the last bout, has she?' I crossed to the wooden crib, to see the baby within. She looked pale and still, ghostlike. When I placed my hand on her chest, I could feel her little heart pulsing against my fingers through her thin body.

'Is she managing to feed?'

'She won't take the milk, but I've got 'er to take a little water. But so much is coming out of 'er, I'm sure it can't be enough,' said Sarah, stroking the baby's forehead.

'You are doing the right thing, Sarah. Encourage her to drink and pray that she will recover.' The truth was, so many babies died before they reached one and there often didn't seem to be much rhyme or reason about who survived and who didn't. I had no idea whether she would recover or not. Worse, there was nothing I could do apart from offer words of advice. As I looked at her drawn face, I was consumed with guilt at how people like Sarah looked to me with such hope, as if I could perform miracles. I wished fervently, and not for the first time, that I practised medicine in an age when more was known. There were advances all the time, but it never seemed enough.

'She is a fighter, Sarah. Keep trying with the liquids and I will call again if she is not better in a day or two.'

As I left, I saw familiar faces at the water pump outside: James and Emily Bates were talking with a short man with a trim beard who I recognised as the younger Mr Eley who, with his brothers, ran the percussion cap factory on Broad Street, making gun parts. I went over.

'Good morning Mr Bates, Miss Bates, Mr Eley. Is there any news of your father?' I said to Mr Bates.

''Fraid not, sir, the bobbies don't know who the feller was and...' he glanced at Mr Eley and checked himself. 'Mr Eley 'ere was just askin' as Father works at the factory.'

'They'll find the culprit I am sure, Mr Bates. I like your flask, Miss Bates,' I said, as Emily was holding an elegant glass bottle with an ornate metal and cork stopper.

'Oh sir, it isn't mine, I was 'elping Mr Eley 'ere fill it,' she said, looking me straight in the eye with the spirited confidence I had noticed before.

'Yes, my dear mother has moved to Hampstead but she prefers the taste of our Broad Street water, so we send a flask to her each day. It ensures she doesn't feel we have forgotten her,' Mr Eley smiled, stroking his beard.

'You are a dutiful son, sir. But I must get on; good day to you all.'

I called next at number 28, a few doors up. Here, in a second-floor room, resided the Barrett family. Alfred Barrett worked as a tailor, making suits for an outfitter on Savile Row. His wife, Ann, supplemented the family income by selling trinkets and fancies made from the scraps Alfred was allowed to take as part of his meagre wage. She went out with her wares, when it was too dark for Alfred to sew, to catch the workers returning home. Her lavender bags, pomanders, aprons and rag dolls brought in a few more shillings a week, if she was lucky. I rang the bell and eventually the door was opened, not by Mrs Barrett, but by another resident of the building, who pointed the way to their lodging on the second floor. When I reached the Barretts' room, I knocked on the bare door.

'Good afternoon, Mrs Barrett, Dr Roberts here,' I called. 'May I come in?' I listened at the door, hearing no sound. 'Mrs Barrett?' I repeated. I waited, and after a minute, I turned away to leave. But as I did so, I heard a faint moan from within. 'Mrs Barrett? Mrs Barrett?' As I listened, my ear to the door, I heard another moan. I tried the door handle, and the door opened. A terrible stench of death assailed me as a swarm of black flies, disturbed, rose as one and hovered cloudlike in mid-air.

'Ugh, what the …?' I mumbled, covering my nose and mouth with my handkerchief, choking and gripping the door jamb to steady myself. I stepped into the dingy, fetid-smelling room, to a terrible scene. On the bed in the small, poor room lay Alfred, Ann, and little Maggie Barrett, and the three other children lay prostrate and lifeless on the floor beside them. Between the adults and the children were two metal buckets. Both were filled with a watery substance. On the floorboards lay pools of watery vomit and effluent and over the whole tableau hundreds of flies darted furiously.

Struggling to maintain my composure with my hand firmly clamped over my nose and mouth, squinting through almost closed eyes, I made myself walk to each person, checking for signs of life. Three of the children were dead. A girl of six or so was cold and lifeless, her lips tinged blue and her eyes sunken in her little face. Her dark hair was matted with vomit and indefinable liquid, and her little doll lay soiled in her hand. I'd hardly ever seen the family and I felt ashamed now that I couldn't even remember her name. Next to her lay a boy of about eight; he, too, was dead. He lay on his side, and the lower part of his body was soaked with slimy fluid. Beside him lay an older girl; a deathly pale to her lifeless face, her cheeks hollowed.

Next to her mother on the bed lay the youngest child, Maggie, who was four; that much I could recall. Although pale, I perceived a slight rise and fall of her chest and at her wrist, I could discern a faint, thready pulse. She was not dead, but what hope was there for her? Beside her, her mother moaned imperceptibly.

'Mrs Barrett, can you hear me?' There was no reply. 'Mrs Barrett, it is Dr Roberts. How long have you been sick?' She struggled to speak and I put my ear as near to her mouth as I dared, batting away the flies.

'Sick… Diarrhoea…' she mouthed faintly.

'When did it start?'

'Last night… Alfred. Today us all…' she whispered.

I looked across to Mr Barrett whose legs were twitching, and watched as he doubled up in pain, gripping his stomach. I had a sudden vision of my mother in her bed. Was this the cholera? The sickness had struck this family so swiftly that they had died before I had even had a chance to see them. Even for cholera, it was frighteningly rapid; usually the cholera took a couple of days to kill, and some recovered. If it was cholera, it must be a most terrible type. I was filled with dread. The immediate problem was what to do for this poor family: I could send for the undertaker, but what of the three who were still alive?

'Mrs Barrett, do you have anyone who could help you?' There was silence and I wasn't sure that she had even heard me. After a minute, there was a faint whisper.

'Sister… 23…'

'I will ask her to come,' I said, wondering whether anyone could be prevailed upon to come into this room of death. 'I must go now, but I will call upon your sister.' With that I departed the nightmarish scene and fled down the stairs, only gulping in lungfuls of air on my return to the street. I steadied myself and tried to think. Calm; think. I could not rid myself of the nagging fear that it was the cholera, and my stomach felt twisted in knots; but I was not yet aware of other cases, and apart from John mentioning a few cases south of the river, I hadn't heard of it returning to London. Perhaps it was not the cholera and the Barrett family had some dreadful misfortune in all coming down with the same terrible symptoms at the same time. I had to break the news to Mrs Barrett's sister, and get on with my other calls.

I went on my rounds and only two of the other calls were cases of vomiting or diarrhoea, and they were not so badly affected as the Barrett family. Joan Wilson, Ann Barrett's sister and a spinster, had bravely agreed to tend to the family and make arrangements. I admired her strength of character, taking on such a daunting and upsetting task which, if it was cholera, was highly likely to result in her own demise. My remaining calls were for sundry other ailments and as the afternoon went on,

I felt a little easier in trying to dismiss the prospect of the cholera from my mind. But I couldn't wholly dislodge it and the spectre kept appearing, unbidden.

The memory of William and my mother dying of cholera would be with me forever. I still dreamed about it; their hollowed, sunken faces, skeletal in their last hours. Their soaked and fetid bed linen, the agonising cramps, limbs twitching uncontrollably, the blue pallor of their lips, their cold hands. John Snow and the local apothecary had come, but it was too quick; there was nothing to be done. John had tried to get them to drink, but they could not. I was left alone, aged nine. I shuddered; my mind still ran cold at the thought of the cholera. Please God, it would not return again.

As I passed The Newcastle on my way home, people were spilling out onto the street, as often happened on a warm day. Although I felt anxious that the cholera may indeed be among us, the people went about their business, happily oblivious. Men were drinking and laughing, gossiping and arguing, and the mood was ripe for humouring any passing entertainer. A dapper old conjuror had set his case outside the pub and the patrons, befuddled and dim-witted through drink, made willing targets. In his case, he carried a range of props, including a large black hat, a deck of cards and three brightly coloured silk scarves. I paused to watch.

'Now then, now then, ladies and gents, who will be next?' He wore a trim beard and a moustache in the continental style, finely waxed into two curling points. At his neck, he sported a jaunty cravat of deep purple, and a monocle of what looked to me like plain glass completed the look. His hands weaved the deck of cards skilfully, spreading and stacking the pack, shuffling them through the air temptingly and stopping to catch one in mid-air.

'A farthing, just a farthing there. Name your card, tie the blindfold, I will shuffle this deck and produce your card. If I fail, your money back! No risk, no tricks! Come along now gents, who's gonna be the first to try me?'

Despite myself, I was tempted to watch to see if he could accomplish this stunt which defied the laws of probability. A man stepped forwards proffering a farthing.

'Four of clubs,' he said.

'Blindfold me yourself, my good sir,' the trickster offered, taking a black band from his pocket. 'Make it good and tight, mind!' The participant tied the blindfold and stood back.

'Right, here we go, gents,' the conjuror announced, with a sweep of his arms through the air. He expertly shuffled the deck, each card falling from his raised right hand to his left hand at waist height, a splayed rainbow of card backs arcing between his hands. He passed the whole deck from one hand to the other in this way, and then reversed the positions of his hands and repeated the manoeuvre. This time, though, before the deck had run fully through his hands he stopped, catching a card in mid-air and showing it to the crowd, who gasped.

'Four of clubs, it's the four of clubs!' called those nearest. 'Bravo, bravo!' The magician unveiled his eyes to confirm his success and gave a modest bow to the gambler, who gave a slow clap in return, his expression a mixture of admiration and annoyance.

'Who's next? Can I do it again? Was it luck or skill? Or, dare I say, was it magic?' Another taker stepped forward as the crowd jostled close, keen to witness any sleight of hand.

'Jack of spades,' the second participant said clearly, rummaging in his pocket for a coin. He was a muscular man, with sandy hair and as he took the blindfold and stepped behind the conjuror to tie the blindfold, I could see he had tattoos down both arms. Others in the crowd surged forward to advise on the tying of the knot, the positioning of the fabric and so forth. I noticed among them a shorter figure, perhaps a woman, hooded by a black shawl, so the face was obscured from where I stood.

The tying of the band took an age, the conjuror milking the crowd. 'Aye, be sure to tie it well, I would not like to be taken for a cheat or a charlatan! Affix it well, my friend.' Above the general hubbub, the Jack of spades fellow gave a startled cry and staggered backwards, a look of mild surprise on his large face. He tottered unsteadily for a moment before falling heavily to one side.

'Oy, take care, mate,' cried the man upon whom he had fallen. This man stepped back, whereupon the first fellow collapsed into the dirt of the gutter. A woman screamed and the crowd melted back to study the man on the ground. A dark red wetness was rapidly spreading from his side, pooling in the roadside gulley before starting to drain away. A pair of scissors protruded from his left loin, pushed to the hilt into his flesh.

The magician remained unaware of what had

happened, and only removed his blindfold at the rising screams of a few women who could see the spectacle. On seeing what had happened, he quickly packed up his case and hurried away.

I came to my senses and pushed my way through. 'Doctor, I am a doctor, let me through.' The crowd parted and I knelt beside the man, his face already pale and lifeless. I felt for the pulse at his neck, which was absent. 'He's dead,' I said, sitting back on my heels.

'Police, get the constable, murder!' a man shouted. 'Get the bobbies!' A boy ran off up the street and a woman screamed as the crowd dissipated.

I looked up to see the shawl-clad hooded figure across the street, on the corner of Dufours Place. The figure gave a fleeting half glance back and scurried away into the warren of alleys and courts beyond, and I could see it no more.

PART II

PART II

SEVEN

Friday 1st September

The cholera is unleashed upon us

It was still dark outside but as I turned in bed shaking off my dreams, I heard three rings at the door downstairs. I had an immediate sense of foreboding; there were never calls before dawn, unless someone was dying. I heard Mrs Hook answer the door and a murmur of voices, and then she came up and knocked at my door tentatively.

'Come,' I called sleepily, reaching for my robe. She came in, her nightgown covered by a white shawl, her face and loose grey hair lit eerily from below by her small oil lamp. In the semi-darkness, she looked almost like a ghost.

'Oh, Doctor, I'm sorry to wake you,' she said, 'but there's been three calls already: Mrs Jarvis's boy from Little Windmill Street, Mr Featherstone and young Jack Collins. They're all saying the same thing – their families have got a terrible sickness.'

'I see; I'll come, Mrs Hook. This is grave news, indeed,' I said, wide awake now and reaching to light my own lamp.

'Oh, Doctor, is it the cholera back?' she asked, her normally placid face wide-eyed. She had lost her husband and only son in the first epidemic in '32, and she had worked as a housekeeper ever since.

'Let us hope not, Mrs Hook, but it is some kind of stomach ailment. I saw a couple of cases yesterday too,' I said, trying not to alarm her, as I turned up the wick and got up.

As I dressed, I heard the bell ring twice more and, with increasing apprehension, I went downstairs, gulped down the tea which Mrs Hook had prepared for me, and stepped out into the relative cool of the very early morning. I stopped for a hunk of bread from Paolo, the coffee vendor, who was just setting up in the dark, and before the first of the sun's rays rose above the spires of London, I was on my way to my first patient.

I called first at the Jarvis family. Mr Jarvis was a tailor but, like most, even with a respectable job, the family could only afford to rent two small rooms at a house on Little Windmill Street. It was a tight squeeze for the seven of them. Little George Jarvis opened the door, a stub of candle in his hand, and he showed me up the dark staircase.

'They've all taken sick,' he said. 'Mother told me to get you.'

'Let's see then, lad,' I said, gripping the bannister in the near blackness, following the tiny circle of candlelight. As I entered the lodging, my stomach churned at the now familiar scene. In the first sparsely furnished room, Mr and Mrs Jarvis were lying on the bed, their pot and buckets next to them. A small lamp burned low on a table, giving the scene a shadowy, illusory quality. Again I had a momentary searing vision of my mother, similar on her own bed, and my heart lurched; I shook myself back to the present. Mr Jarvis was ashen grey in the shadows and was barely moving. Flies hummed and harried over the scene as George stood mute beside me.

'Doctor, the children...' Mrs Jarvis mouthed, as I hovered over her.

George was roused from his reverie as his candle burnt out and he pointed me towards the other room. I picked up the lamp to light my way, plunging the first room into blackness. In the second room, which was tiny and windowless, a terrible sight awaited me. The other four Jarvis children, who ranged from two to ten, lay on the bed. Each had the same sunken cheeks and the unnatural bluish tinge to the lips which I had seen before: the blue-grey of death. There was one bucket, filled with watery effluent, and there was vomit on the floor. A cloud of flies hummed over the children, insistent, but as I entered they were attracted by the light. I swatted them away, keeping my mouth tightly shut as I passed to each child in turn. Two of the four were dead, their thin little bodies cold and lifeless, their eyes glassy and staring. Little Joe, five, and Millie, eight, were barely alive between their two dead siblings. I returned to the first room and turned my attention back to the adults.

'Mrs Jarvis, when did this come on?' Her eyes fluttered at the sound of my voice, but there was no reply. 'Mrs Jarvis, how long have you all been ill?'

This time she whispered her response. 'Mary, last night, rest of us a few hours...'

'I will try to get help,' I said, although in my heart I knew that any help would be too late. George, who had been silent, looked up at me, his little face white with terror. He reminded me so much of my childhood self, my heart wrenched to look at him.

'Will they get better, sir?' he whispered, his eyes wide.

'I hope so lad, but I can't promise anything.' I put my hand on his shoulder. 'Have you any other family who could help you?'

'Me aunt, Doctor, next door,' he replied.

'Go to her, you cannot stay here,' I said and I ushered him out. The tiny skylight in the ceiling above the stairwell admitted the first light of the grey dawn as we retraced our steps down the stairs. I left the boy knocking at the neighbouring door and walked away.

I felt helpless. There was nothing I could do for this family. It *was* the cholera; it had to be. I had other calls to make, and if the story was the same all over Soho, it didn't bear thinking about. With a heavy heart, I hurried to my next visit, the Featherstones. The story there was similar with three of the six Featherstones ill, albeit not as severely as the Jarvis family. The Collins family were the same, with all but one child struck down. Even as I walked between visits, I was regaled with people coming up to me and begging me to call. I felt overwhelmed. Did the whole of Soho have this terrible disease?

At two o'clock, after fifteen more calls, I stepped out into the street, light-headed. Everything seemed normal outside; it was another swelteringly hot day and the road thronged with the usual mass of humanity, oblivious to the horrors lurking just yards away. I'd lost track of time. It was past lunchtime, and I remembered that I had planned to meet John Snow for lunch. I could not afford to stop but I was so thirsty, I needed a break and a brief respite from the sickness. Also, John had a keen interest in cholera and he had done a lot of work in London during the last epidemic in 1849. I set off for Mrs Bootle's coffee house, in the shadow of the big Lion's Brewery on New Street.

The comfortable salon was always welcoming. Wooden booths furnished the walls, their leather seats burgundy, the colour of warmth and comfort. Small round standing tables of dark wood stood in the centre. As I opened the door, the familiar smell of coffee and cigar smoke wafted out to greet me and the babble of talk and laughter was a welcome distraction after my morning. I looked around for John, hoping he hadn't already left. I spotted the familiar receding hairline and bushy sideburns and saw that he was still there, seated in a booth in the corner, reading *The Times*. I passed the counter and went over to join my friend, slumping down opposite him in the booth.

'Mrs Bootle, two coffees please, and some bread and ham,' I called as she walked past, before leaning forward and continuing in a low voice. 'John, I am sorry I am late. I have been sorely taxed this morning.'

'It sounds terrible out in the Crimea,' he said, putting down his paper. 'What ails the good people of Soho then, Frank?' he said. 'I spent several happy years living among them; I shall always hold them in regard.'

'The district is stricken with a terrible diarrhoeal disease. I have seen many cases this morning. I do not want to be alarmist, but I tell you, I am worried at the extent and rapidity of it.' I rubbed my forehead. 'And to top it all, I witnessed a murder in front of my very eyes yesterday.'

'The diarrhoeal disease: is it the cholera back again?' he said, ignoring my latter comment and studying my face with a keen interest in his sharp grey eyes. I leaned in closer to ensure we were not overheard.

'Yes, I fear it is. I've seen cases of normal summer gastroenteritis these past months, as it has been like a furnace in Soho. But the cases this morning are completely different: the disease is devastatingly quick, and it is deadly.'

'Are the patients showing the classic signs? Do they have the rice-water diarrhoea?'

'Yes, I have seen the watery effluent in many houses. But the course of the disease is so swift; most of the people were well last night, and by this morning, many are dead. I have seen whole families struck down, it is terrifying.' I held my head in my hands. 'There is little I can offer them; I feel a fraud as they look to me with such hope…it… it brings it all back.' My heart clenched with fear and futility.

'There were three cases of diarrhoea admitted to the Middlesex this morning, but I thought little of it,' said John, rubbing his chin, as he often did when he was thinking. 'Perhaps I can help you? We can give advice and comfort, even if there is little treatment,' he offered. 'I have no engagements this afternoon.'

'I confess that would be a great help, if you can spare the time…' I said, looking at him and feeling a little less alone. 'I don't know what to say to them. Is there anything new in the way of treatment since '49?' John thought a moment longer.

'There are many ideas talked of, but as to whether any of them actually work, I am doubtful. I am not aware of any effective treatments.'

'How are the cases that make it to hospital treated?'

'In the premonitory stage of mild diarrhoea, they are given external warmth and stimulants, with hot poultices, blankets and brandy. But these have little effect in the second, classical, rice-water stool stage. Many agents have been tried to treat the profuse watery diarrhoea, vomiting and spasms, but without success. Some recommend calomel, to increase diarrhoea and vomiting to rid the body of it, others recommend opium which has the opposite effect of binding the stools. Charcoal, lime water, sulphur, sulphuric acid, silver nitrate, whey and many other concoctions have been tried. By the third phase of profound collapse, when the pulse is barely palpable and the extremities dusky blue, nothing is of use.'

'I recommend replacing the fluids which are lost by drinking, which does not seem like much.'

'From what I know of the pathology, I reason that simply drinking water is likely to be of most help, to replace the losses. Some recommend saline treatment, drinking water containing natural salts, as back in '32 saline injections were in vogue for a time, but that has fallen from favour. On a practical level, drinking copious fluids is most likely to be of benefit, in my opinion. The problem is that often the victims are unable to take much in and they suffer from the effects of collapse too rapidly.' He paused. 'Shall I assist you?'

'That would be a help; I have twelve more visits to make and no doubt there will be more as people see me on the streets. I met Dr Rogers of Berners Street and he has been as busy as I have. Half of Soho seems to have the disease.' John leaned back in the booth, looking thoughtful. Mrs Bootle brought the drinks and the lunch, and she had brought two small sweet pastries for us, as I was a regular customer. She was a short woman but she always staggered under the large tray, preferring to make one journey, instead of two.

'There you are, Doctor,' she said, lowering the tray and sliding it safely onto the table, her round, pockmarked face smiling as ever. 'All well with you, sir, is it?' she asked, conversationally, as she unloaded the plates and cups. 'How is my good friend, Dorothy Hook? I haven't seen 'er for a while. I keep meaning to call round your house, Doctor, to bring 'er some of my pastries.'

'You would be very welcome and I'm sure she would like that,' I smiled. Little did she know that if the cholera took hold, soon it was likely that no one would be paying visits. 'Thank you, Mrs Bootle,' I said, handing her some coins. When she had gone, John continued.

'Where are the cases so far?'

'Marshall Street, Silver Street, Broad Street, Little Windmill Street, Cross Street; all over Soho, it seems. Why?' I ate my lunch hungrily, speaking with my mouth full.

'I am just wondering. I have been studying cases south of the river again of late.'

'Yes, you said; what are you doing?'

'Farr passes me the details of cholera deaths in the districts each week and I visit the houses of the victims and gather information about the cases, the dwelling, the water supply and sanitation. You remember I undertook similar work in the '48-'49 epidemic and I developed a theory that the cholera was transmitted in the water? I published my findings but they fell on deaf ears. I am trying to test the theory again now. My work in south London is not finished, but it has only strengthened my view of the idea.'

'Farr?' I said blankly.

'William Farr, the chief statistician at the General Register Office. Each week he prepares a bill of mortality outlining the numbers and causes of deaths in different parts of London for the week. It's all new since the work on the labouring poor a decade ago and the Public Health Act; the government collects all manner of statistics these days, although I'm not sure it does much good. They're in the papers each week.'

'I have little time for reading the papers; but what of the water? It is the miasma which causes cholera; the bad airs in the atmosphere. What makes you think it is the water?'

'I do not believe in the miasma,' replied John, dismissively. 'Let us see your remaining cases this afternoon and confirm it is the cholera. If there are more cases, it may help confirm my theory; or refute it, I suppose.' He paused. 'Do the houses have piped water?'

'Some do, but even where there is piped water, the supply is erratic. Most rely on the street pumps. The people collect their water and generally they have a tank to store it. Why?'

'Where are the pumps located?' John ignored my question.

'There are many: there's one on the corner of Broad and Cambridge Streets, one at the top of Carnaby Street, one on Rupert Street, one on Little Marlborough Street, and others.'

'Let's go to the pumps on our way to the visits,' said John standing up, draining his cup. I did likewise and picked at the last crumb of pastry on my plate as we left the coffee house. I felt better for some sustenance and the support of my more experienced friend. We walked together the short distance up New Street and along Broad Street until we reached the pump at the corner of Broad and Cambridge Streets. The streets were full of people and you wouldn't know anything was amiss. John reached into his bag and brought out a small glass bottle. He went to the pump handle and filled the bottle and held it up to the light.

'It looks normal,' I said.

'It does; it looks clear,' said John, who held the bottle to his nose. 'There is no unusual odour,' he said, replacing the stopper and putting the bottle in his bag. 'I'll get Hassall to look at it with his microscope. Now, let's go and see the next patient.'

'Let us go to Poland Street, I have a call to make there.'

'Not the workhouse, I hope? The cholera would spread like wildfire there.' John raised an eyebrow in alarm. We turned into Poland Street, a narrow street off

Broad Street, distinguished mainly by the presence of the St James's Workhouse on the left at the far end. The great walls dominated the whole street and at all times of day there was a straggling line of people waiting, hoping to be admitted through the large studded door which was opened in the evening. I had seen young mothers with babes suckling, old men, disfigured by war or disease, and every section of humanity in between, all slumped against the wall in the past, their faces blank with resignation and hopelessness. Today, however, the street was quiet.

'Number 17,' I said, walking up the street, 'here we are.' I knocked and, after a minute, the door opened to reveal a pale sandy-haired boy, whose eyes scanned the street behind us. 'Hello there, what's your name? I'm Dr Roberts. This is my colleague, Dr Snow.'

'Jonny, sir,' mumbled the boy, standing back to let us pass.

'Who is ill, Jonny?'

'Me brother, sir.'

'And your mother?'

'Ain't got no mother, sir. Died when I was born, sir,' he replied.

'Your father?'

He looked stricken. 'Killed in the street yesterday, sir. Murdered not an 'undred yards from 'ere,' he whispered, in a tight voice. I felt an ice-cold stab of pity for the boy.

'I am sorry, Jonny. I was passing and I saw him, but I'm afraid there was nothing I could do. Have they caught the assailant?'

'No, sir. The bobbies 'aven't got no idea who it was. All they found was the tailoring scissors in 'im, but there's plenty of tailors in Soho.'

'You are right there,' I said, thinking of the many patients I had who were tailors of one sort or another. The lucky ones supplied the shops of Bond Street and Savile Row with their smart mannequins in immaculate window displays, while those less fortunate barely survived on piece work, sewing for middlemen who supplied the slop shops.

'How long has your brother been ill?' said John.

'Since last night, sir; got the sickness, 'e 'as. Mrs Perkins upstairs says it's back, and I should get you, sir, but I don't know where Father kept the money,' he said, looking uncertainly at me again, his tear-streaked, freckled face serious and earnest.

'Don't worry about that for now, Jonny. Let's see your brother then.' We followed Jonny up the stairs to the second floor, to a room at the back of the building. It was the same story as I'd seen all over Soho that morning. In the dingy, poor room, the patient lay on soaked bedding, moaning.

'Since last night, it's flowin' out of 'im. I can't get 'im to the privy or the pot.' By the wall stood a pot and a bucket filled to the brim with fluid. While I looked at the boy, John went to look in the receptacles. He motioned to come and I went over. Each held a watery liquid, clear and odourless. In it floated many small white filaments.

'The classical sign: rice-water diarrhoea. There's no doubt,' whispered John.

'Try to get him to drink, if you can, Jonny,' I said. 'I'm afraid he has the cholera; perhaps Mrs Perkins could help you?' Jonny nodded as we made for the door.

'Doctor…will I get it too?' he asked.

'We'll have to wait and see. I pray you will not,' I said.

'Maybe 'e caught it from the fellow that was staying with us?' said Jonny.

'Which fellow was that?'

'Friend of Father's, Wilty; 'ad a funny hand, didn't have no thumb, sir.'

'When was that, Jonny?' I asked, my mind leaping to James and Emily Bates.

'A week or two ago, I should say. 'E knew me father in the army years ago; they were mates, them and a couple of others. 'E stayed with us a few days,' said Jonny.

'What was his proper name, Jonny? Was "Wilty" short for something?'

'Wiltshire, Father sometimes called 'im, sir.'

'Had he come here to see your father?'

'No, 'e was 'round 'ere lookin' for someone, 'Lijah I think it was, and 'e stayed for a day or two and then I never saw 'im again. 'Ope 'e didn't bring the sickness.' I would have to pass on the information to Constable Lewis. A "Wiltshire" in the army; it might help.

'I don't think so, lad. What was your father's name?'

'Samuel Harrison, sir.'

'Thank you, Jonny. Let us go to Mrs Perkins, to see if she can help.' After leaving a message, we left for the next visit. As we walked down the road, the workhouse queue was forming and three whores, babes in arms, sat disconsolately in the gutter at the foot of the great door.

'Show ya a good time, kind sirs? Just a penny, loves,' one of them called out softly to us. As she spoke, her baby bawled furiously and she cuffed its filthy face with the back of her hand. 'Shuddup, you,' she said roughly, her exhausted face old beyond her years. I said nothing but drew a shilling from my pocket and handed it to her. 'Thanking you, sir,' she said, not even raising the energy to look at me. John and I walked on; he was grim faced.

'We must brace ourselves, Frank: a terrible cholera is back in London, for certain.'

EIGHT

Saturday 2nd September

Death comes to Soho

I struggled to sleep and spent much of the night staring at the patterns from the yellowy-orange gas lamps outside reflected on the ceiling. The slivers of light which escaped the curtains seared across the ceiling and formed sharp angles as they hit the far wall. They reminded me of the terrible last night with my mother, when the lights of York had thrown similar patterns which illuminated her last hours. I had struggled then to stay awake so she would not be alone, but my nine-year-old self couldn't bear it and I had slipped into a deep, protective sleep, waking to find she was dead.

Eventually, back in the present, I gave up trying to sleep and got up in a grey dawn to prepare for the day. I prayed I would be wrong, but all my instincts told me today would be as busy as yesterday. Sure enough, as I walked down Broad Street on the way to my first visit, I heard a woman calling my name from a window.

'Doctor, Doctor, please come,' the woman called in desperation. It was Sarah Lewis.

'I'll come, Sarah,' I called up, as I steeled myself for what I would find. I crossed the street and the door was open, so I went up. The room was as I remembered, but this time there was a deathly, deadly quiet.

'Doctor, is there anything you can do? Please?' Sarah pleaded, grief etched on her tired face as she stood, the lifeless form of her baby in her arms. I knew she knew the child was dead. I had tended her previous baby who died and there was a calm desperation about her, as if she knew it was too late, but she had to go through the motions of seeking help.

I looked at the baby. Her little face was pale and drawn, a grey pallor to her skin, and her little rosebud lips emitted no breath. She smelled not of soft baby smell, but of death. She had struggled on for a few days and I'd thought she might pull through, but I was wrong. Diarrhoea killed so many babies and infants; their little bodies could not withstand it. I picked up her limp wrist to feel for the pulse I knew would be absent, and opened an eyelid to look at one vacant eye, the life gone from it. She had gone the way of so many little ones. I raised my eyes to Sarah, knowing my words would break her heart.

'I am sorry, Sarah, she is gone.' A tear rolled down her face.

'I was knitting 'er a new blanket; just finished it a couple of days ago,' she said, looking down at the little corpse. 'How is a mother to cope, Doctor? We labour to give our littl'uns life, and they don't stand a chance in this cruel world,' she said, her face red and angry now, biting back her fury.

'The loss of a child is a terrible thing, Sarah. But you are young, you could have more children. I am afraid it has always been this way, that the world is a treacherous place for those least able to withstand it.'

'I could not bear to have more, for this to happen again and again,' she raged bitterly, her livid eyes staring me in the face, 'but it is our lot, us women, is it not, to die in the effort of bringing 'em into the world, or to live and bury our own children? You are lucky you are a man.' Her eyes shone with tears.

'Indeed it must seem like that sometimes, Sarah. But do not lose all hope. God must have a reason for calling Martha to Him so soon. I will ask Reverend Whitehead to call.'

As I left Sarah Lewis, I steeled myself to return to the cholera cases. In the doorway opposite, I saw James Bates. He looked tired and distracted. 'Good morning, Mr Bates,' I called, but he didn't seem to have heard me. 'Mr Bates, I have some news,' I called again, going over. He looked up, his tousled hair a mess and a stale smell about him.

'Oh, Doctor, I was lost there a minute; me mother and sister 'ave passed away in the night from a terrible sickness.' His eyes were red, his expression stunned, disbelieving.

'Not Emily?' my stomach lurched at the thought of the spirited girl.

'No, not Em, but me younger sister, Mary.' He looked close to tears and I didn't know what to say. 'I'm off to Middleton's on me way to work, though we 'aven't got the money,' he said, pulling himself up tall. 'I've got to be strong for the others; but I wish me father was 'ere…' he tailed off. I felt desperately sorry for the poor lad, struggling with so much, and I felt almost glad that I was alone, with no one close to lose.

'I am very sorry for your loss. There is a terrible sickness on the streets at the moment. I am afraid the cholera is back in London; I wonder if that is what took them? Could I go up?' He looked at me with an air of irritated defiance.

'Don't see what good it'd do, but go if ya like, second floor; Em's layin' 'em out.'

'I'll just be a minute,' I said, going in and climbing the stairs. When I reached the door on the second floor I knocked and Emily opened it.

'Doctor,' she said, surprised, her face tear stained and her hand fiddling with something around her neck.

'Emily, I have just seen James. He tells me your mother and your sister have passed away; I am very sorry. Can I come in?'

'If ya like,' she said, disconsolately. 'How can they 'ave gone so quick? I'm layin' 'em out, I am, ready for Middleton's, though 'ow we'll pay 'em I don't know. Have to do the work of three I s'pose.' She glanced over towards the table where heaps of fabric and bobbins of thread rested; like many, it seemed the women of the family took in piecemeal sewing. She went back to the small room where the victims lay and picked up her cloth to resume wiping her sister's body. I followed her, ignoring the pervasive poverty and the smell of death.

'I wanted to see if they had the cholera, for there are many cases on the streets at the moment,' I said lamely, feeling an intrusion on her grief. I looked at the girl,

Mary Bates, whose face was sunken and blue tinged, her abdomen hollowed, her fingers a dark bluish purple. Mrs Bates was the same, her round face lifeless.

'They couldn't keep nothin' in 'em,' said Emily. 'I tried to get 'em to drink but it weren't no good.' A tear rolled down her cheek, which she brushed away angrily, standing straight and surveying the bodies. She brushed a straggling hair behind her ear and then she took the locket around her neck and brought it up to her lips, kissing it.

'That is a fine necklace,' I said. She enclosed it protectively in her hand.

''Twas me mother's,' she said, gazing at her mother's face. 'It was her most treasured thing. She'd 'ad it since she was a child; the only nice thing she ever 'ad. It makes 'er feel closer to me now,' she said, kissing it again.

'Listen, Emily, I'm afraid they died of the cholera, and I have seen many cases these past couple of days. You must wash your hands after tending to them and try to keep yourself well, and if there's anything I can do, I would be pleased to help.' She nodded mutely and I left.

As I stepped into the street again, James Bates was returning.

'I'm afraid there's no doubt, it was the cholera,' I said to him.

'The cholera? Then there ain't nothin' to be done, is there? Just have to 'ope me and Em aren't next. There won't be no one 'ere for Father when 'e gets out; *if* 'e gets out.'

'Perhaps he will escape the sickness by being away,' I said. 'But it is very hard on you and your sister. That

83

was what I was going to tell you; I have learned from a patient that the man found in your pit was called Wiltshire. He'd stayed in Poland Street with a friend of his from army days, a man called Samuel Harrison, but I'm afraid now *he* has been killed too. I'm going to tell the constable. Is there any progress in the investigation?'

'No, sir. I visited Father and it was terrible in there. They've charged 'im, just 'cause 'is pipe was with the body, but it weren't 'im, 'e *swears* it.'

'I am sorry. Wiltshire had been asking about someone at the workhouse, "Elijah", the boy said. Try to keep the faith; something will turn up.' My words sounded hollow.

As I set off down Silver Street, a horse-drawn hearse passed, laden with three coffins and I had to step back into a doorway to allow it to pass. I was still thinking of James and Emily Bates and their troubles and as I stepped, I trod on something. I looked down and my heart wrenched. Huddled in the doorway were two little street children. They were nine or ten, and they lay with their arms around each other, in a last embrace. Both had the telltale deathly bluish pallor to their little faces; the sunken cheeks, the purple lips. I reached down to them. They were dead. The girl's straggling dark ringlets were matted with the dirt of the street, her dirty blue dress stiff with dried evacuations. The boy was bare-chested, and his breeches were torn and filthy. I studied their little faces; the girl looked familiar. Then it came to me: they were two of the trio who had tried to steal my watch that evening. What a life these children had suffered: a life on the streets, a death on the streets. I turned away, fighting the urge to run from this nightmare of sickness and death. I stopped and steadied myself, for I could feel the distant threat of my own black clouds looming; I must fight them for God knows I was sorely needed now.

I took a deep breath and continued. The next six calls presented six more families struck by the cholera overnight and yielded ten more deaths. It was the same everywhere: the disease was terrifyingly quick and the death rate was much higher than I remembered in the last epidemic. I offered simple advice and meaningless words of comfort.

As I passed down Berwick Street on my way to more calls, I saw Reverend Whitehead emerging from St Luke's Church, his long white beard belying the fact that he was no older than me. He often seemed it though, with a wisdom and compassion rare in one so young. The church was small and nestled between the other buildings which crowded the busy street. The tall, pale brickwork and small grassy graveyard uneven with the graves of decades made a welcome oasis from the grimy brick of London. On a Sunday, the bells rang out, clear and true. St Luke's stood in the heart of Soho and in his three years as assistant curate, Reverend Henry Whitehead had spent many hours getting to know his flock, sharing their joys and their miseries, going out of his way to provide help and comfort. I remembered him taking in two children, orphaned by an explosion at the gun factory a couple of years ago. He cared for them for three weeks until their aunt travelled from Scotland.

'Reverend, I bring news that little Martha Lewis has lost her fight with this world. Perhaps you could pay her mother a visit? Sarah is distraught at the loss of another child and is quite desolate. I am sure you could bring her some words of comfort, and she will need to make the burial arrangements.'

'Ah, Doctor, that is indeed sad news. I was there yesterday, praying for the little soul,' he said. 'She did look in a poor way, I must say. I will go and see Sarah.'

'Thank you. But I must warn you that our streets are beset by a terrible cholera; little Martha had a simple diarrhoea, which she has suffered from all her short life, but I have seen many cases and many deaths this morning from a new and deadly form of the cholera.' A vision of the two street children filled my mind and I pushed it away.

'That is grave news, Doctor. The miasma is bad, then?'

'If miasma is the cause,' I sighed, thinking of John. 'It looks like it will be a busy few days for us all. I must leave you and get on with my rounds.'

'If there is anything I can do, Doctor, I am at your disposal. God be with you.'

'Thank you, but you will have work enough yourself, Reverend, in the coming days.'

I stopped to buy a roll for lunch at the bakery; there were no street children outside today. Mrs Ruby was not there and I learned from the woman serving that Molly Ruby had passed away and now two of the other children had the same sickness. I thought of my last visit there and how my fears had proved correct. With a heavy heart, I went to my next visit: the Parkers, next door.

The splintering black paint on the door reminded me of the last time I had been called there, to tend young Jo Parker after her attack three weeks ago. I climbed the rickety stairs to their room once more. It was small and airless as I remembered, and it offered barely enough floor space for the seven Parkers and the old deaf couple who shared the room with them. Stanley Parker had worked for the slop shops since he lost his job last year, and they could barely make ends meet. I wondered what I would find this time. I knocked and a voice bade me come.

The room was festooned with tattered washing drying on lines across the room, and I had to duck under two old sheets and assorted undergarments to enter.

'Sorry, Doctor, couldn't wait 'til Monday for the washin',' a young woman said, greeting me with bloodshot, tired eyes. She would have been pretty but her blonde hair hung limply down her back in a rough plait, her apron was filthy and her young face was pale and worried. 'It's me mother and me brothers,' she said, pointing.

'I am Dr Roberts,' I said, going over to the four patients, lying on the floor.

'It was you saw our Jo, wasn't it? I'm Becky, her big sister.' She looked down at her charges. 'What's the matter with 'em, Doctor? They was all right when I got 'ome yesterday and they all got sick so quick I didn't know what to do for 'em,' she said, despair in her eyes.

'Let's see then, Becky.' I felt the pulse of the girl's

mother, which was barely palpable in her cool wrist. 'Has she had much diarrhoea?'

"Fraid so, sir, I can't keep up with it. Ain't got enough buckets, but now they can't get up anyway. Every scrap of clothes is covered, I keep washin' it but it don't dry quick enough.' I moved to look at the boys. The youngest lay curled in a ball, his grey face turned to the wall. He moaned and whimpered as I approached, but did not stir. Next to him his two older brothers lay pale and lifeless, a bluish tinge to their lips. They were the boys who had been playing in the bucket of water when I'd visited Jo that day. I remembered the eldest, laughing joyously; there would be no more laughter from him now.

'I'm sorry, Becky, I'm afraid these two have passed away. The littlest lad here needs to drink and your mother, too. They have the cholera; I've seen a lot of cases of it these past couple of days.' She looked close to tears as she threw a glance at her brothers before staring resolutely at her mother, as if by not looking at them, they would go away. I felt desperately sorry for her, as she looked so exhausted. 'Is there anyone who can help you look after them?' I said gently.

'No, there ain't. Father took Jo to our aunt in the country yesterday. Thought it'd do 'er good; she's taken to wandering about in a dream, she 'as. She's not right in the 'ead. Be good to get out of London for a bit, after what 'appened to 'er. Father'll be back tomorrow.'

'Well it may do her good to leave Soho for a bit while the sickness is here. It would be good for you to leave too.' She looked at me as if I was soft in the head.

'I can't leave, Doctor; who'd look after me mother and little 'Arry? Unless I get sick too. 'Sides, I 'aven't got no money to go travellin'.'

'No.' I felt foolish. 'Get them to drink and wash your hands well after tending them.' I turned and the boy doubled up in pain as his bowels released a large quantity of fluid. I should have stayed and helped, but I couldn't afford to get sick myself. I had more cases to see; I could not nurse them all. She, like all the others, would just have to manage.

I left and went back out into the street. As the door closed behind me, another hearse rumbled past, carrying two more coffins: the deaths had started in earnest. I rubbed my hands with vinegar and rinsed them at the pump on Carnaby Street, ate the roll from the bakery and allowed myself some coffee from Paolo, and then steeled myself for the afternoon's work.

On the way to my next call on Silver Street, I remembered that I had been hoping to attend a recital at the Royal Academy that night. I thought longingly of the shiny browns and blacks of the polished violins, violas and violoncellos. I could do with some rest and music always chased my black thoughts away. I sighed and put the thought to one side; I would doubtless be needed in the course of the evening. Besides, I had lost heart for going out. I sincerely hoped there would be no more cases but I knew it was unlikely. I set about my afternoon's work, thinking how I would have to tell John tomorrow. What would he make of it?

NINE

I discuss the cholera and I feel sorry for James Bates

I was up and dressed early and as the bells of St Luke's rang out for the Lord's Day, I opened the door to John Snow and ushered him into the room I called my parlour. It was simply appointed, with a couple of red armchairs in front of the fireplace, a small mahogany table and a wooden settle. My bureau was the only handsome piece of furniture, gifted to me upon her death by the aunt who had cared little for me when I was a child. I had inherited her entire estate, but I had disposed of most of the furniture for it held only bad memories for me. I had kept the bureau; I still sometimes felt, as I went to open it, that I must heed her order to my childhood self never to touch it.

'I sent Mrs Hook away yesterday. She was so terrified she's gone to stay with her sister until the epidemic has died down so I'm fending for myself for a bit. I don't need one more death on my conscience. Would you like some tea?'

'Thank you. How many cases of cholera are there now?' said John, direct as ever.

'I have seen probably one hundred or more; I saw Dr Rogers this morning and he says the same. We've never seen anything like it. There must have been upwards of 250 cases just in these last three days and they're just the ones we know of.'

'Gracious; that is terrible, even for the cholera. I have never known it spread so rapidly. How many deaths do you estimate so far?' said John, following me as I went to set the pan to boil.

'One hundred and fifty, maybe? Middleton's can't cope. They've had to draft in help and the carpenter on Dean Street has died, so there are not enough coffins; they are being brought in from all over London. The hearses are carrying several coffins piled atop one another. There was even a farmer's cart in Marshall Street yesterday, carrying several. Whole families have been wiped out. People go to sleep well and by morning, they are dead. It is hard to believe the extent and speed of it.'

'The streets are very quiet today.'

'It's still early and Sunday's usually quiet, until people get going to finish their chores before church. The people are leaving if they can; they're all terrified. Not everyone has somewhere to go, though, and now many aren't well enough to travel.'

'What are the authorities doing?' asked John.

'Not much. The outbreak has erupted over the weekend; perhaps tomorrow they will start to act, but that will be too late for many poor souls.'

'Where are cases that you have seen?'

'Well, I've seen deaths at houses on Marshall Street, Broad Street, a few in Pulteney Court, a few on Poland Street, several on Cross Street, New Street and Husband Street, and cases in various other streets. Those are just the ones I am aware of; from the number of coffins, there must be many more. Whole families are dying at once.'

'This is grave, indeed,' frowned John. 'It is imperative that we find the source of the outbreak, then perhaps we can help stop it spreading further.'

'What can *we* do? We can do nothing to change the miasma.' I poured the water into the pot and gave him the cups to carry.

'I do not believe in the idea of miasma, and I do not believe cholera is spread in the miasma,' said John firmly. '"Miasma" is the atmospheric change arising from decomposition of vegetable matter, although colloquially it includes effluvia arising from animal matter as well. The anti-contagionist view states the atmospheric change, through inhalation, produces fever in susceptible individuals, which results in symptoms,' the cups clinked as he walked, 'but I think the cholera agent is transmitted in the water. If we can work out the *water* source where it is coming from, we can act to prevent it spreading further.'

'But whether it is in the water or the miasma or however the terrible disease is spreading, what on earth can *we* do to stop it?' My treacherous stomach rumbled, protesting the lack of breakfast, as I struggled to follow what John was saying.

'I will visit the houses where there have been deaths, and make enquiries as to the water supply and the sanitation arrangements, as I have done in my work south of the river,' said John. 'We need to find a factor that is common to all the affected cases.'

'But in many buildings, there's no one left; many are dead or flown or too sick to tell you. Anyway, even if you are right, John, what can *we* do? The parish has jurisdiction over the water supplies and sanitation. I doubt they'll listen to you.'

'We can gather evidence to test my theory. Now Edwin Chadwick has been replaced at the Board of Health by Sir Benjamin Hall, he may be more open to alternative theories,' said John, raising his bushy eyebrows. I knew John was no follower of Chadwick, who was a confirmed miasmatist; he had crossed with him on several occasions in the past.

'I know you don't like Chadwick…'

'It matters not whether I *like* him, but I disagree with his views,' John snapped. 'His belief in the miasma underpins all his ideas and the work of his sanitarian colleagues. To remove the atmospheric odours from the cesspits and open gullies by draining waste to the new sewer systems is the lynchpin of their work. They care not that the sewers discharge into the Thames, so people drink the contagion rather than inhale it.'

'Well, I am not so sure and it will be hard to convince them.' Surely the whole medical establishment couldn't be wrong? I bit my tongue.

'I know,' sighed John. 'I have not convinced them in the past. But let us examine what we know: let us list the deaths and see if that provides any clues.'

'As you wish.' As I spelled out the addresses of cases, John noted them down. Each one represented an impending tragedy for the family concerned; each death, so easy to list, the tragedy realised and the potential undoing of a family. As we finished, John sat staring at the addresses. Eventually, he spoke.

'There *must* be a common factor linking the addresses where the disease has struck.'

'The miasma?' I suggested mildly, but John ignored me and continued.

'What proportion of the dwellings in Soho have piped water?'

'I don't know. Perhaps half the houses have a piped supply, maybe fewer. But even for those with piped water, it is unreliable. Often the supply is off altogether, or it's intermittent. Even here in my house, for example, Mrs Hook often as not has to go to the pump. Most of the buildings are the same, I think.'

'The addresses where there have been cases are spread over many streets. If even buildings with piped water often use the pumps, that could be the common factor,' said John slowly, sitting back and rubbing his chin.

'How could you prove it?' I said, not quite sure how he had reached this conclusion.

'The pumps are well used and the outbreak is quite localised; the cause must lie in something common to those afflicted,' said John.

'But why the pumps? Why not the miasma, or something else about the dwellings visited by the disease? Many of them are in a terrible state, very low and poor. Could the miasma not be particularly noxious in the area and worsened by the heat of the summer? There is much overcrowding and poverty. All these factors tend to a predisposition to affliction by disease, I think?'

'Have you not heard a word I have said, Frank?' said

John, his lips pursed. 'I know the miasma theory is the popular view. But I believe the contagionist view makes much more sense. I think diseases must be caught by the transmission of discrete poisonous agents: there must be a specific agent to cause a specific disease, not just a vague atmospheric change. These agents in the bodies of the sick are spread from person to person by touch, soiled articles, clothing, bedding and the like. If there is a specific agent responsible for causing a disease, why should it be carried only in the air, and not in the water, or the food, or the ground we walk on? Besides, the cholera produces symptoms showing a disturbance of the *gut*, a fluid disturbance. It makes much more sense that it is ingested by mouth.'

'I only say that medical teaching has long been that bad airs carry diseases, which susceptible individuals contract, and the poor are more morally susceptible to disease.'

'I do not believe that the poor have any inherent or moral predisposition to disease,' said John, preacher-like. 'It is rather the conditions in which they live and work that means they are exposed more often to the agents causing disease. You *know* what the dwelling houses here are like: they are in a terrible state, with little light, ventilation or sanitation. It stands to reason that if the poor have unclean water and poor sanitation, they will be more exposed to any poisonous agents which are carried in water. If they live in dwellings which are damp or poorly ventilated, they will be more exposed to any poisonous agents borne in the air,' said John with a passion and intensity which I had not heard before.

'My work to date indicates that the cholera is carried in the water. I merely say that the common factor for the affected dwellings in Soho could be the street pumps.'

'But there are many pumps; how would they all carry the cholera at the same time?' I said. 'Even if it was in the pumps, what has changed? What has happened? Why are they contaminated with cholera *now*?' I had great respect for John, but I was struggling with the notion that all I had ever learned was wrong.

'I don't know,' he conceded after a moment, 'but something has happened; somehow the water of the wells below one or more of the pumps has been contaminated. I am sure of it. Anyway, it matters not, for now, *how* the water has become contaminated: if it *is* contaminated, the important thing is to stop the people using it.'

I was silent for a moment, flummoxed. 'But how can we find out? And what can we do? Even if you are right, we can't stop the pumps being used, we cannot provide water for the people, or alter the water supplies, or improve the sanitation. We can only try to help with our limited efforts and console people in their grief,' I said. 'We are powerless to act.'

'No. I believe if we could persuade the guardians of the parish that a pump or pumps are the cause, then if they remove the handles of the pumps, it would halt the spread.'

'But they won't listen to *us*; the guardians of St James's will take their lead from the Board of Health, just like everyone else.'

'You're right; we will need to build a compelling

case. Chadwick's efforts have turned the Thames into one huge open sewer. Many sewers empty in the very stretches that the piped water for drinking is drawn from,' said John with disgust. 'But Hall has taken his place and the new Board of Health came into being not two months ago; this could be the opportunity to persuade them of my theory.'

'I understand you feel strongly about it, John,' I said, quietly sceptical. 'But what should we *do*?'

'We can start by drawing water from all the Soho pumps, to see if there is anything unusual,' said John. 'A couple of days ago, the Broad Street pump water looked innocuous, but perhaps that has changed? And I will visit the dwellings where people have died and make my enquiries.'

'Well, I must get some breakfast,' I said, suddenly irritable with hunger. 'Let's go.'

Out in the streets, there was a subdued quiet. Normally, on Sundays, the Soho streets were full of people. Women carried their meat to the cookshops, children fetched vegetables and porter from the pubs and those who worked all week scoured the shops and stalls in the brief opening hours before the closure for church services. But today, the streets were quiet and deserted and the church bells of London echoed around the buildings.

'You are right, it is very quiet.'

'If people have left that should prevent more deaths,' said John. I did not reply.

We reached the nearest pump, on Broad Street, near the corner with Cambridge Street. It was a similar design to the many public water pumps all over London: it had a large handle which, when pumped up and down by hand, drew water from the well below. How deep or wide the well was, I didn't know. John again took a vial from his bag and held it under the flow while I pumped the handle, the surplus splashing into the drain below, the droplets wetting my breeches. The little vial filled with water and after smelling it, John replaced the stopper. He held it up to the light.

'It looks clear to me,' I said.

'Indeed it does.'

'Is there any odour today?'

'No,' said John raising the vial, and opening it under my nose. 'But the cholera agent may be too small to be visible. Also, I have noticed that if the water is left to stand for a while, sometimes at the base of the flask there is a residue of detritus. I will ask Hassall to look at it under his microscope again,' said John. 'I thought there might be a more obvious change, but we'll see,' said John, putting the vial in his bag. 'Now for the other pumps.'

'I'll leave you to it, for I must get to my patients; I have many calls to make again today,' I said, shaking him by the hand, eying up the coffee stall setting up behind him. 'Will you have some breakfast?'

'I have eaten. I will start making enquiries and I'll call tomorrow and see how many new cases there are.' John looked me squarely in the eye. 'And Frank, even if you doubt my theory, as my friend, please practise perfect cleanliness in your dealings with your afflicted patients, and do not drink the water from the local pumps. I would hate you, too, to succumb,' said John. I looked into his serious face and I could see how he truly believed he was right.

'Very well,' I agreed, trying to hide my scepticism. 'I promise. Farewell.'

I watched him leave and then I bought a meat roll and coffee to sustain me through the morning. As I stood there, I saw James Bates opposite.

'James Bates!' I called to him, for he looked distracted.

'Ah, Dr Roberts,' he said, visibly pushing his worries to one side.

'Did you ask at the workhouse about the dead man?'

'Yes, the master said 'e 'ad been there asking about a child from years ago. The master now wasn't there then, so 'e couldn't 'elp , but 'e sent 'im off to the old master on Peter Street. When was 'e in Poland Street, sir?'

'A couple of weeks ago; as I said, he was looking for someone called "Elijah", the lad said. Number 17 Poland Street; second floor, at the back, but I must warn you, his brother had the cholera when I saw him. He may have succumbed too. But I am sorry, how are your own family?'

'In a bad way: now it's Em and me brother and I don't know 'ow to 'elp 'em.' He looked down and kicked out angrily at the wall, sending a cloud of dust over his shoe.

'Emily?' I said, feeling a pang of regret.

'Yes, and George, who's fourteen.'

'Can I help?' I offered.

'I'm afraid we 'aven't got no money for doctors,' he said, his face colouring.

'Don't worry, I will see them if you would like?'

'Well thank you, sir. I couldn't bear to lose Em, too,' he said, his jaw clenched.

'Let's go.' I downed the rest of my coffee as he opened the door and showed the way upstairs to where I'd seen Emily before. Today I noticed the larger room that looked over Broad Street as we passed through it. There was a small stove in the corner, two wooden chairs and an old table with a faded cloth over it, the sewing materials untouched. Some dead violets in a jar were placed in the middle of the table. The only comfort was a shabby armchair, threadbare and dirty, by the window with an old rug in front of it. Some chipped enamel cups and plates and two pans sat on a shelf next to the stove and a metal tank held water brought up from the pump outside. A pile of worn blankets and three thin pillows lay in a pile.

In the second room, Emily lay on the bed where her mother had lain before. The tiny room had a window overlooking the yard at the back. As I glanced out, I could just see the walls of the workhouse on Poland Street. Next to Emily was her brother, on the floor. I turned my attention to Emily first. I remembered her as a pretty girl, but today she was a grey shadow, all the spirit gone. Her striking eyes were sunken in their sockets and her lips had a bluish tinge to them. Her pretty hair was matted and damp, snaking across her thin pillow. Like my mother's hair had done. She was still but her thin chest moved up and down with each breath. I saw she wore the locket I had seen before. It was small and silver coloured, with an oak tree and five acorns on the front.

A bucket was at her side, and a cup of water was on a tea case by her head. I bent to look at her.

'Emily?' I said, my hand on her arm. She opened her eyes a little to look at me. 'Emily, its Dr Roberts. You are unwell, but you must try to drink.' She closed her eyes again and I turned back to James, but she spoke, her voice soft but determined.

'I ain't gonna die, Doctor; can't leave James now, can I?' she murmured.

'You must drink, Emily,' I said, but as I spoke she doubled up, gripping her stomach, moaning. 'I am afraid she has the cholera, too, James,' I said. I looked on, feeling helpless. 'You must try to get her to drink. And I would take her necklace off, save it getting spoiled; it's a nice one,' I said, gently.

'You're not taking that off me,' she whispered, grit in her voice.

'No, Em, I won't. I promised I wouldn't,' said James to me. 'That's Mother's locket; Em's been wearing it and she made me promise not to take it off, but it's daft 'cause it's the only thing we 'ave's worth anythin',' said James, looking down at her. 'Me other sister went so quick. Is George the same?' he asked looking towards his brother, his voice cracking. I looked at the lad on the floor, who was barely conscious. His breathing was rapid and his sunken eyes rolled, as spasms shook his body. His lips, too, had a blue tinge, and he was oblivious to my presence.

'I am afraid that your brother is in a poor state, James; but your sister looks a little better,' I said.

'Is there anything I can do, sir?' he whispered.

'I'll leave you some laudanum for George,' I said,

101

the obvious unspoken. 'Emily needs to replace the fluid she is losing, so if you can get her to drink, that will help.' I thought of John Snow's words and continued. 'I have a colleague who believes there may be a problem with one of the pumps in the area at the moment, so I would advise fetching water from further afield until this outbreak clears up, just in case.'

'Something wrong with the pumps, sir? But we all get our water from the pumps.'

'I'm not saying it *is* one of the pumps. But if you want to do something for your sister, it could not hurt to go further afield for water. There are other pumps: across towards Regent Street, there's one on Warwick Street, for example. There is no cholera in that district. And take care to wash your hands well after tending to her.'

'All right,' said James. 'Thank you, sir.'

'Is there any more news of your father?'

'No. I visited 'im in the Newgate again. They don't feed 'em nothin' in there and 'e's in a dark old cell with three others. One's gonna be executed tomorrow, 'e thinks. 'E's dead scared. Now I'll 'ave to go and tell 'im Em and George are sick too.'

'At least he is well in there, compared to the people of Soho.'

'Yes, I s'pose. Goodbye, sir.'

I left James Bates looking gloomy and stepped back into the street, to continue with my visits. Poor lad, I thought to myself; he's got a lot on his young shoulders, for sure.

TEN

Monday 4th September

Deaths, deliberations and a welcome distraction

I got up after another sleepless night. The bell at the Newgate gaol had been ringing all night for an execution this morning and in my dreams I saw James Bates calling out to his father. The sound of the bell carried on the night air, a warning to sinners. Eight o'clock on Monday morning was the appointed hour when some poor soul would fall through the trapdoor, from this world into oblivion. I had seen one execution, and it had sickened me: the baying crowds, the festival atmosphere. People paid handsomely for the best vantage points, and street vendors and entertainers plied their trades; all to watch some poor fellow hang by his neck until he was dead. Sometimes, a woman was executed, and that drew even bigger crowds. It was said that the executioner positioned the knot to ensure a quicker death for a woman, but it still took an age for the poor soul to depart this world. Why were people so keen to witness the agony and death of others? It had always been so, and it seemed a flaw of humankind. I imagined James Bates' father hearing the bell toll and his cell mate being taken away.

I turned my thoughts to the day. I had sent word to the Westminster that I would not be there today as my work lay closer to home. How many more cases would there be today? Yesterday I'd seen twenty-six, but there were more deaths than that; I'd seen Middleton's hearse and Holley's, drafted in to help from Marylebone. How many more deaths would there be? It was an unprecedented mortality rate in such a short space of time.

John Snow was coming around later. I didn't know what to make of his theory: I admired and respected John, but his was an unusual idea. I had taken his advice though, and I'd been scrupulous in my hand-washing after seeing each patient. Would my luck hold? The doorbell rang, and I took a deep breath; the day had begun.

'Doctor, can you come and see our Daniel, please?' said Thomas Lewis. He looked tired and anxious.

'Of course, Thomas, let me get my bag. Does he have the sickness?'

'Yes, Doctor, since yesterday. I've heard the cholera's back? He's not like the baby; it came on 'im so sudden. I don't 'spect there's much you can do, but Sarah said we had to try,' he said, resignation in his face.

'How is Sarah?' A cloud passed across his face and his lips thinned.

'She's coping, Doctor, just about; she can't think of the baby now Daniel is sick.'

'It is very difficult to be a mother.'

'And a father, too, I'd say,' he snapped.

'Indeed. Let's go.' As we stepped into the street, the gutters were stained with a white milky substance with a sharp odour, which I recognised as lime. 'The authorities have limed the streets, at least,' I said, to break the silence. 'They do that with all spreading diseases, to purify the air.' Thomas Lewis did not reply. As we walked down Great Pulteney Street, we passed two horse-drawn hearses, with a total of five coffins, and I noticed Thomas crossing himself and turning even paler. I changed the subject as meeting him reminded me of something that had been niggling at me since my visit to Poland Street.

'Forgive me, but I wanted to speak with you about the fellow in the cesspit again. You remember I told you his name was Wiltshire and that he had stayed with a friend in Poland Street not long before he met his death? Well, the man stabbed outside The Newcastle last Thursday was the friend Wiltshire had stayed with: Samuel Harrison was his name. I spoke to Harrison's son and he told me they were in the army together years ago. I wondered if you knew of the link?'

Thomas Lewis looked at me. 'That's odd: two men closely acquainted, each meeting an untimely end at around the same time.' He took out his pocketbook and made a note.

'Has there been any progress in the investigation into Wiltshire's death?'

'No, Doctor. Albert Bates 'as been charged as it was 'is pipe found on Wiltshire in the pit, 'e said so 'imself; and with the fellow found in 'is backyard, it doesn't look good for 'im. You oftentimes find the culprit close to the scene.' I thought of James and Emily with regret.

'I am acquainted with the Bates children, and I must say I find it hard to believe their father would do such a thing. They seem a good family.'

'I 'ave to say I agree with you, but me sergeant says you never can tell. I'll make some enquiries about 'Arrison.' He raised his eyebrows at me and I nodded.

We reached 40 Broad Street and, unlike little Martha, Daniel had become sick very suddenly, with copious diarrhoea. He lay on the bed, pale and ill, gripping his stomach. Sarah Lewis, in black mourning for her baby, hovered as I examined him.

'Try to get him to drink, Sarah. You know there is cholera on our streets.'

'Not the cholera, Doctor?' she whispered, her exhausted eyes full of fear.

'I am afraid so. I have a colleague who has suggested it may be worth trying water from a pump in another area, over towards Regent Street for example, and you must take care to wash your hands well after tending to him. Shall I ask Reverend Whitehead to call again?'

'I won't trouble 'im, Doctor; save 'im for the living,' she said with a grimace. 'I've never known a time like it; what 'ave we done to 'ave this sickness unleashed on us all? We need a miracle if any of us are to survive.' She paused. 'But what about the pump?'

'I have a colleague who believes it may be worth getting water from a different pump as there are a lot of cases of the cholera near this pump at the moment. It can't hurt, can it? I must go now, for I have other patients to see. Goodbye,' I nodded and left. The cholera was threatening tragedy once more.

By lunchtime, I had seen another twenty cases and upwards of thirty coffins. The windows which normally spilled chatter were empty; no children were playing outside and a deathly quiet hung in the streets. The only people about were the undertakers' men and frightened people leaving their homes, carrying what they could on their backs. Whole families were heading out, in a desperate bid to escape the cholera. One woman carried her three young children and dragged a fourth by the hand; there was fear in her eyes as she hurried past, as if she expected the cholera to jump out from a doorway.

At intervals, yellow quarantine flags hung limply on poles at the roadside, to warn anyone unaware that the district was harbouring disease. The rubbish and detritus was piled high, as the sweepers had abandoned the area for safer pickings. Horse dung littered the road, and rats scurried about, even in the daytime. Every street stank of decay and death. Soho was turning into a scene from hell; terrified souls scuttled through hot streets which were gradually sinking beneath rubbish, filth and vermin. I wished *I* could leave. The more tired I became, the more the threat of the melancholia loomed. I had to keep well; I couldn't desert my patients at this terrible time.

As I passed The Newcastle, I wondered if Samuel Harrison's murderer had been caught. Probably not. He'd doubtless slipped away through the crowds and was long since gone; an argument about a debt or unfinished business of some kind or a woman wronged. Death on the streets was a feature of city life, but murder in broad daylight was unsettling even for me, accustomed as I was to death.

I stopped at the pump on Broad Street, and drew

some water to give to John. I held the vial up to the light and swirled it around. It looked clear, although there was a tiny whitish filament of detritus visible today. Could John be right? Was this life-giving liquid I held in my hand killing the people? It was a terrifying thought: if the people of Soho, the sick and those caring for them, were even at this very minute quenching their thirst with lethal fluid.

It was a brave man who defied the popular view of disease theory. It didn't surprise me that John could be that man. Ever since I had known him, John's way had been to search methodically for the truth; it was what drove him on. His success as an anaesthetist meant he could now live comfortably off his practice if he wished. But he cared more about furthering knowledge of medicine and disease to improve the lives of many. I admired him very much; he wasn't loud and charismatic, he was quiet and serious. However, respect John as I did, I wasn't sure I believed him this time.

At lunchtime, John called at my house again.

'Good day, Frank, is the epidemic abating yet?'

'No, I have seen another twenty or so cases this morning.' Over some bread and cheese, I relayed the details of the new cases to John. They were clustered on Marshall Street and South Row, with a couple in Cross Street, and a few others. John sat back and thought.

'From memory, Marshall Street and South Row are equidistant from the Broad Street pump and the one on the corner of Carnaby Street and Little Marlborough Street.'

'But there are also cases on Berwick Street and to the east of the Broad Street pump; they would not use the Carnaby Street pump?'

'I have an idea. Let us mark the cases on a map,' said John. 'That will demonstrate the geographic distribution of the outbreak. Do you have one?'

'Somewhere I do; I had one when I first moved to practise here. But without Mrs Hook, I am not sure whether I can lay my hands on it. Oh how I wish she would return; but I cannot send for her until the epidemic is over,' I sighed, going to my bureau. After a few minutes of cursing my paperwork, stuffed unceremoniously into my desk since my housekeeper's departure, I straightened up with a flourish, waving a folded paper. 'I have it!'

'I will mark the buildings where there have been deaths on the map, and see where that leads us,' said John, taking it from me.

'I'll make some tea and don't worry, I sent a boy to Warwick Street for the water.' I retired as John started to mark the cases on the map. When I returned, John had drawn black bars, a bar for each death at an address. He looked up as I came in.

'Look, Frank. Already there is a pattern. See how many of the cases are on Broad Street?' We bent over the faint map, spread on my table.

'There are cases on Broad Street, but see here, there are quite a few on Cross Street, and another group around Pulteney Court and Husband Street. The cases are all over Soho.'

'Yes, but so far the disease has affected Broad Street

and Marshall Street the most. Residents there would predominantly use the pump on Broad Street, wouldn't they?'

'Yes, or the one on Carnaby Street. I drew some more water from the Broad Street pump for you this morning. Look, today there is a tiny filament visible,' I said, getting it out of my bag. 'Has Hassall studied the other samples yet?'

'No. He has other priorities. He is my friend, but even he thinks I am wrong,' said John. 'And you are not sure whether to believe me. If I cannot convince my friends, it will be hard to convince others.'

I felt myself blushing at his insight. 'John, I only say your theory is a large step away from the accepted view,' I said. 'But God knows, I long to find the answer. I would be delighted for you to be proved right. All I say is that you will need proof, for it will be hard to convince others without it.'

'You are right, Frank, and I do not take offence. Proof requires a thorough and systematic study of what we know. I have requested a list at the General Register Office of the deaths from cholera registered last week, so we are aware of *all* the deaths, even the ones you have not seen. I plan to visit *every* dwelling where a death has occurred and gather information about the water supply, use of the pumps and the sanitation arrangements. That is what I have done in the past and in south London this year.'

'So, what have you worked on this summer?'

'I've been repeating my work of six years ago; the cholera is back in the same districts as it was in '48. The areas are supplied by two water companies: the Lambeth Water Company and the Southwark and Vauxhall Water Company. Last time, there was no difference between death rates in the houses supplied by each company. But two years ago the Lambeth Company moved its works. Now it draws water from much further up the Thames, well above the reach of the tide, where it is no longer polluted by the city's sewers.'

'What difference has that made?'

'*This* year, people in houses where the supply is from the Lambeth Company have been much *less* likely to get cholera than those who get water from the Southwark and Vauxhall Company. I've got the mortality figures from Farr and I've visited the houses in Southwark, Bermondsey, Stockwell, parts of Brixton, and some areas in between where people have died of the cholera.'

'So?'

'So the *only* thing which has changed since the '48-'49 epidemic is that some people now have cleaner, unpolluted water and *those* people have experienced much lower levels of cholera. The houses, the occupants, the miasma are all the same as before. It is a natural experiment, which confirms the waterborne theory. I am calling it my "grand experiment"!'

'But how do you know which houses have which supplier?'

'Ah yes, that was the difficult part as adjacent houses often differed in their supplier. Most of the tenants had no idea and I approached the water companies, but they couldn't or wouldn't tell me. But, fortuitously, I discovered that the water of the Southwark and Vauxhall

Company contains much higher levels of salt, and so by adding silver nitrate to the water and seeing how much silver chloride was formed, I was able to tell with certainty which company supplied each dwelling or pump,' said John modestly. I stared at him and marvelled at how ingenious and dedicated he was in his research. He was so thorough, so determined; I felt a fresh wave of admiration for him.

'How large is the difference in cholera rates between houses supplied by the two companies?'

'The difference is great. This year, the mortality rate for people living in houses supplied by the Lambeth Company is more than *eight times* lower than those supplied by the Southwark and Vauxhall Company.' I stopped and stared at him.

'*Eight* times lower? That is a very great difference.'

'We'll see whether it is enough for the miasmatists,' said John mildly, a hint of a wry smile on his lips. 'I have yet to pull all the figures into a suitable form for publication. But it does convince me; it *is* waterborne.'

'But what about in Soho? What has happened to bring this deadly new outbreak of cholera to Soho *now*? How does your work help us *now*?'

'I am not sure yet. But don't you see, Frank? If cholera is waterborne, if we can deduce the water source that is carrying it, we can act to prevent further spread. We need to *act* to help the people of Soho now, before it is too late for them all.'

That afternoon, as I walked along Silver Street, the stench seemed even worse in the heat of the sun. I pondered

John's words: it did sound as if he had some evidence, at last, that he could be right. However, I had no doubt it would be very difficult to convince anyone. As I walked along turning over in my mind what John had said, on the other side of the street I was surprised to see a young woman I recognised alight from a carriage. But no; what would she be doing in Soho?

'Nurse Irvine?' I called out uncertainly.

The woman stopped and looked across at me, faltering for a moment as she struggled to place me. Then her face brightened.

'Dr Roberts,' she smiled and, even from a distance, I was struck by the soft, gentle expression on her face. I crossed the road to her.

'What brings you here, Nurse? Surely the institute does not have a patient here?'

'No, I come on a private matter.' She looked down at her white gloves and hesitated. 'I am on an errand for my mother.' She looked at me, her blue eyes striking in her pale face.

'Can I be of any assistance?' I offered.

'Thank you, Doctor, but I am sure you are busy. Miss Nightingale says the cholera is back in London?'

'It is. I have seen many cases in these streets in the past few days. You would do well to avoid them at present, Nurse.'

'I cannot delay in my task; it is of the utmost importance to my dear Mama.'

'You are sure I cannot help? It would provide me with a little relief from the cholera,' I said. She hesitated for a moment.

'Do you know of a young woman, Emily Bates, Doctor?'

'Yes, I do, but I fear she has the cholera.'

'You know her?' said Nurse Irvine, her cheeks flushing. 'That is good fortune.'

'Yes, but she was unwell when I saw her. She may not have survived,' I cautioned.

'When did you see her?' she said, undeterred.

'Yesterday; I saw her yesterday morning.'

'Then she must be recovered, for I saw her yesterday late afternoon.'

'How; where did you see her?' I said, confused.

'She was delirious, in Regent Street.'

'*Regent* Street? What was she doing there?'

'I don't know. She was crossing the road and she just stepped out in front of Mama's carriage. I'm afraid she was knocked down and hit her head quite badly on the street as she fell. She was dazed for some minutes and then she kept raving about her father and how she couldn't die or there'd be no one left; she said she had to find someone called James. I was worried about her, she didn't look well at all. I insisted that Mama stop and I tended her wound, and I waited until she was well enough to get up, for I wasn't sure she'd be able to find her way home. But then a friend of hers, Becky I think her name was, came along and when I asked she told me the girl's name was Emily Bates and I saw they headed off into Soho,' said Nurse Irvine. 'Do you know where I might find Emily?'

'Her lodgings are at 19 Broad Street, but I cannot allow you to go there alone. She may still be ill; I saw her brother who was close to death from the cholera there yesterday morning. It may not be safe for you to visit,' I warned.

'Doctor, I am well used to sick patients, as you know. I am not afraid. My mother is most desperate for me to speak with her.'

'Can it not wait?'

'No, it cannot,' she insisted.

'Well, you must allow me to accompany you, Nurse. These streets are no place for a young lady.'

'Very well, Doctor, if you can spare the time, I would be grateful,' she assented.

'It is this way, then,' I said, and we turned and walked together down Silver Street in the direction of Broad Street. We talked as we walked, and I caught myself stealing glances at her and thinking how attractive her clear blue eyes and steadfast, open face were. Although self-assured and capable, I thought I caught a hint of sorrow about her, a hint that perhaps things had been hard for her. Of course, her lip disfigurement must have singled her out ever since childhood. Life could be cruel, even for well-to-do young ladies. And yet I sensed that the imperfection had made her stronger, she had risen above the difficulties to become a confident and independent woman. Nonetheless, I felt protective towards her; I didn't like to think of her walking through Soho alone. As we approached the address, I hesitated.

'It is a lowly sort of a place. And if there is more sickness… '

'I am not afraid, Doctor, I must do as my mother bids,' she said, looking me straight in the eye. I felt my neck hot under my collar as she stared at me, but I held her gaze and paused for a moment before speaking.

'Very well, then.' I knocked on the door. After a few moments, there was the muffled sound of footsteps on the stairs and the door opened. It was Emily, looking pale and dishevelled, her head bandaged with a handkerchief.

'Miss Bates, I am glad to see you are better from your sickness, but I see you have hurt your head?' I said. Emily looked uncertain, as if she was unsure who I was.

'Sir?' she said.

'I am Dr Roberts. I know your brother, James, and we have met two or three times, if you remember. He asked me to call yesterday to see you and your brother, for you were unwell. I am glad to see you look much better today,' I said, 'although I am sorry your younger brother was very sick.'

'Oh yes, I am better today, but George 'as gone,' said Emily, confused. Then she caught sight of Nurse Irvine, standing behind me and she gasped, as if in recognition. 'Miss, what brings you 'ere?'

'I have come to see if you are recovered from your accident yesterday, Miss Bates; for I am a nurse, as I told you. Also, I have something I wish to speak to you about. May I come in?' she asked gently.Emily looked around uncertainly, embarrassed, putting her hand to her head, which was still bloodied and dirty.

'Well, Miss, 'tis a poor place we live in, I'm sure...'

'I have been in many types of lodging, Miss Bates. Please do not worry on my account. I would very much like to speak with you,' said Nurse Irvine.

'Well...' flustered Emily.

116

'*Please* can I come in, Miss Bates? I assure you I mean you no harm.' After a moment more, Emily stood to one side and allowed her in. 'Thank you,' Nurse Irvine said, and she turned to me. 'Thank you, Doctor, but I have private business with Miss Bates and I am sure you have your work to attend to. Thank you for your help.' I looked at her. In truth I wanted to stay; I was reluctant to leave her company. But I did have many patients waiting, and I knew I ought to get on.

'Very well, Nurse, if you are sure?' I said, my eyes lingering on her face.

'Thank you, I am; and Doctor, please do call me *Miss* Irvine. I am not under Miss Nightingale's eye now,' she said, with a hint of a lopsided smile.

'Good day, then, Miss Irvine; Miss Bates,' I bowed and left the two women. Emily was of strong character and constitution to be up and about already; she must have taken my advice and had luck on her side but now the poor girl had a head injury as well. I walked down the road to my next patient, wondering what it could be that Miss Irvine wanted to discuss with Emily Bates: the two women came from very different worlds. I could not make Miss Irvine out; she was unlike any other nurse I had ever met. Quietly confident in her position in the world, she carried herself as an upper-class lady would do. She was not beautiful in a classical sense, but I felt drawn to her. I shook myself for there was work to be done.

ELEVEN

The Board of Health inspectors arrive and I visit the workhouse

As I left my house on Great Pulteney Street I saw three men I didn't recognise. They were well dressed and their polished black shoes looked rather out of place in Soho. Each carried a large leather case and one had a sheaf of papers in his hand. With the streets so quiet, it was unusual to see strangers, particularly when the district was displaying quarantine flags. They were consulting the pile of papers as they studied a map and I couldn't help but overhear them.

'I'll take this street and Little Windmill Street; you, Hughes, start on Silver Street and Pulteney Court and you, Ludlow, make a start on Cambridge Street and New Street,' said the leader of the trio, a tall man with a fine beard and elegant moustache. 'Then we'll meet at two o'clock and tackle Broad Street together.' He replaced his chain watch in his pocket.

'Do we have to ask all these questions at every house, Mr Fraser? What if they don't want to answer? What if they're too sick to answer?' asked the man called Hughes.

'Do your best, and keep good records. If no one answers, we'll have to go back another day. This is Sir Benjamin Hall's plan to sort it out once and for all. It relies on thoroughness and accuracy,' replied the leader. 'Remember to cover your mouth and nose if you enter a house where there is a case.'

'Why did old Chadwick never get us to do this sort of thing, Mr Fraser? We've never been sent out on the streets like this before,' said Ludlow.

'He's not "Old Chadwick" to you, Ludlow, and maybe that's why the cause of the cholera has never been found,' said the leader, poking his forefinger in the man's face. 'Now Sir Hall is president of the Board of Health, he's got new ideas. Anyway, we are not paid to question; right then, we'll meet at two.' The men studied the map once again. I was interested by the snippet of conversation, and I walked over.

'Can I be of any assistance, gentlemen?' I offered. 'I am Dr Frank Roberts, and I know these streets well.'

'Thank you, Doctor. I think we have oriented ourselves now,' replied Mr Fraser.

'I could not help but catch that you are working on the cholera. May I enquire as to the nature of your work? I have been much engaged with the dreadful disease these past few days.'

'We have been asked to collect information from all the houses afflicted by cholera in the present epidemic, Doctor. Sir Benjamin Hall at the Board of Health has set up a scientific enquiry and we are collecting information.'

'May I ask what information you have been asked to collect? Any knowledge of factors suspected of contributing to the cholera would be welcomed by my patients, even if it is unproven. They are desperate to escape the terrible scourge that has befallen them.'

'We are to enquire about the number of cases, the occupations thereof, the living conditions and number of occupants, and the physical characteristics of the area.'

'The physical characteristics of the area?'

'The atmosphere, ventilation, smells, layout of the streets, overcrowding, the privies and the drains, the water supply; that sort of thing,' replied Fraser.

'It is a long list, indeed, and the people can do little to change the physical characteristics of where they live. I have a colleague engaged on a similar task, but his enquiry is more limited; Dr John Snow, perhaps you know of him?'

'I am not aware of such a gentleman, Doctor, he is not involved in the official enquiry to my knowledge,' replied Fraser.

'Perhaps you will meet him on your travels? If I can be of any assistance, you can find me here at home in Great Pulteney Street,' I said, indicating my house. 'Good day, gentlemen,' I said, bowing and walking down the street. At least the government was taking the epidemic seriously. The trouble was that so much power was held at local level, in the hands of the parishes and each parish could do as it liked. There was no overall strategy, and no requirement for any parish to implement measures that were not approved locally. It would be so much better if all parishes were obliged to implement the same regime of measures in times of epidemic. Perhaps Sir Hall was the man to change things.

I knew John Snow did not have much time for the Board of Health. The last president, Edwin Chadwick, had become unpopular. John fundamentally disagreed with him over his measures to clear the miasma. Although Chadwick was known as a sanitarian and champion of public health, John believed that his miasmatist views dictated and clouded his actions. Something had to be done; England and London could not go on with epidemics of cholera and disease wiping out thousands every few years.

I turned my attentions to the day. I had to visit Poland Street this morning, and call at the St James's Workhouse. There was a case of sickness there; if the cholera took hold within its walls, hundreds would surely succumb. As I walked up Poland Street, past where the boy Jonny Harrison lived, I eyed the high walls surrounding the building, twelve-feet tall or more, and I felt a sense of dread. A couple of drunks lay snoring loudly near the door, their feet bare and completely black with the filth of the street. The stench of urine filled my nose as I passed them. A small child of only three or four was asleep on the doorstep of the workhouse, a tag around his neck which read "Plees elp". My heart wrenched at the sight of his little face, sleeping peacefully, oblivious to the hardships and desperate choices of the adult world. I stepped over him to knock on the great wooden door and as I looked down at the child I wondered what it would be like to spend your whole childhood in such a place. The door was opened by a young, disinterested woman servant, in a lanky skirt and grey apron.

'Yes?' she said, with dead eyes.

'Dr Roberts to see the master,' I said.

'Come in,' she droned dully, opening the door for me to enter. 'Wait 'ere, sir, I'll get Mr Brimblecombe.'

She shuffled off, her hands twitching, and a minute later the master appeared from his office. He was a large, rotund man, with round glasses perched on his large red nose, the latter of which I ascribed to the partaking of too much strong drink. I had met him a couple of times before, and I did not like him, believing him to be self-serving and lacking compassion for the paupers in his care. I had patients who told how he took bribes for better conditions and he was reputed to sate his sexual appetite with the young women unable to escape his clutches.

'Dr Roberts,' he greeted me jovially, and I was sure I detected a whiff of ale on his breath, even at this time of day. 'Come in. I have an inmate I fear may have cholera.'

'An inmate?' I said coldly. 'Is this a gaol, Mr Brimblecombe?' The master gave an ingratiating laugh. 'Are you aware there is a child asleep on the doorstep?' I said, but he nodded dismissively and gave me a conspiratorial smile as we walked along.

'Later; we open the doors later, if we have room,' he said waving his hand over his shoulder. 'But Doctor, my charges are akin to inmates. Most will never leave, you know,' he said smoothly, making light of his indiscretion, but I was not to be won over.

'That may be so, but I believe they are free to leave at any time if they are able and willing?' I said, disgusted by this fat, arrogant man, and feeling a pang of pity for the poor souls who had no choice but to fall under his jurisdiction. The shift towards "indoor relief" for paupers, after the Poor Law Act twenty years ago, was supposed to be a deterrent against sloth and idleness, as conditions inside the newly created workhouses were harsh and strict. But, in my experience, it seemed that most paupers were not poor through idleness, but through illness, disability or obligation to care for others. The enforced move into the workhouse made their ruin complete and offered little chance of rehabilitation or self-improvement. Many lived within the walls until they died, or were rescued by some turn of fortune. They had no choice but to fall under Mr Brimblecombe and his colleagues. 'I will see the patient, now, if you will?'

'I will escort you to Matron, Doctor.' Mr Brimblecombe turned and led me down a dark corridor. Even in the heat of the summer, there was a pervading musty smell of damp, and I could see the shadows of the mould at the foot of the walls. There were feeble oil lamps at intervals, but they were insufficient to light the way and I stubbed my toe on an uneven section of floor. From the depths of the building I could hear a keening cry, audible above the muffled mixture of shouting and raised voices which penetrated the gloomy space. At the end of the corridor, we turned right and stopped at the first door we came to, which stood open. The room had one small window, too high to admit much light, and within I could see the bird-like matron, her nurse's cap perched on her head, seated at a small desk with a candle illuminating her papers. She stood as we entered.

'This way, Master; Doctor,' she said, and we set off again, further into the maze of corridors, until we reached a room with no window. Mr Brimblecombe remained at the door, reluctant to cross the threshold.

By the wall, illuminated by the light of a low candle, a man lay on a bed. The candle threw shadows of the man's unkempt hair onto the uneven wall, a wild-haired giant, his body heaving up and down with each racking breath. Beside the pillow there was a bucket, but it was empty. The man turned over as we watched, and moaned.

'Joseph Standley, Doctor,' said the matron.

'Has he been in the workhouse long?'

'Two days. He started sickening yesterday. Is it the cholera?'

'I will take a look at him. Has he had watery evacuations from his bowels?'

'No, Doctor,' replied Matron. I went over to look at the man.

'Mr Standley? Mr Standley, can you hear me?' I asked. The man stirred, but did not wake. I could not conduct a proper examination in the feeble orange glow of the candlelight, but from what I could see, he did not have the telltale sunken features and bluish complexion characteristic of cholera. I took his thin, warm wrist, and the pulse felt strong, if a little rapid. I stood up. 'How many times has he vomited?'

'Three times,' said the matron. 'I've had Agnes keep an eye on him, but she doesn't want to get too close, if it's the cholera.'

'But no diarrhoea?' I repeated.

'No.'

'I can't be sure, but it is unlike the other cases I have seen. Many of them have perished within hours of becoming ill. Most have suffered terrible diarrhoea and agonising stomach cramps. He may have a simple summer gastroenteritis; in any case, the treatment is the same. He needs to drink to replace the fluid he has lost. Time will tell; hopefully he will recover,' I said. 'Have you had other cases of sickness these past few days?'

'No, sir, Mr Standley is the first. I pray it will stay that way,' she crossed herself. 'I remember the epidemic of '48; some workhouses lost scores back then.'

'I am hopeful he does not have the cholera,' I said. I felt cautiously relieved. Cholera within these walls would be a catastrophe: more than five hundred souls lived under this roof. It was overcrowded, the sustenance meagre and the work hard.

'Not the cholera then? That is good news, indeed,' said Mr Brimblecombe, taking a cautious step into the room, his shoulders relaxing.

'I am hopeful that it is not,' I repeated. 'Give him some water every hour, and I hope he will improve. Keep him away from the others for now,' I directed the matron. 'Send for me tomorrow if he is no better, Mr Brimblecombe.'

'Very well, thank you, Doctor.' He turned and called a girl who came running. 'Agnes, Agnes, go to the well and fetch some water, will you?'

'You have your own water?' I asked, mindful of John's theory.

'Yes, Doctor, we have a well in the courtyard, to supplement our piped supply. We could not manage if the inmates had to traipse around London for water; imagine the disorder that would cause. The residents, I

125

mean, yes, yes, the residents,' he corrected himself, as I felt another wave of revulsion towards him.

'Thank you, Matron; Mr Brimblecombe. I will leave you now. I can see myself out,' I said and I retraced my steps out of the gloom back into the sunny September day.

As I emerged back into the rest of the world on Poland Street, I breathed a sigh of relief to be out of the oppressive atmosphere in the building and the unpleasant company of Mr Brimblecombe. The child was still sleeping on the doorstep. I looked down at him and wondered who his mother was, and what had driven her to leave him there. In all likelihood, she was no more and someone else had seen no other option. What would the future hold for him? Little good, I thought. The workhouse was a grim place and whenever I visited, I felt eternally grateful that I was able to leave.

As I walked back past number 17, on impulse, I knocked to see how Jonny and his brother were. After a moment the door was opened by a woman. She looked worn out, hair escaping from a low bun and a streaked, dirty apron covering her old grey dress.

'Yes?' she said, blankly.

'I am Dr Roberts, I was wondering how Jonny and his brother are?'

'Ah, yes Doctor,' she replied, the furrows in her brow relaxing a little. 'Jonny 'as the cholera now, and little Mikey has passed away. I'm Mrs Perkins from upstairs.'

'Would you like me to see him?'

'I won't trouble you, Doctor. 'E's not so bad as Mikey was, and I'm gettin' 'im to drink.'

'Well, if you're sure.' I turned to leave.

'Only thing is, 'e keeps mumblin' somethin' 'bout "Elijah" and "Christmas"? I'm not sure what 'e's talkin' about.'

'I see. Tell him thank you, and let me know if you want me to see him.' I left and strode down the road away from this lowly street and all its human misery. I would tell James Bates what Jonny had said about Christmas, although it did not sound like much to go on.

Later, I sat in my parlour with John, discussing the epidemic once more. Even he was starting to look tired from his door-to-door enquiries, which he was fitting around his other work, but he was not to be deterred.

'I have marked the new cases from yesterday on the map, and the outbreak is quite localised, look. The cases are still mainly on Broad Street, Marshall Street and on the streets off Carnaby Street. Broad Street is the worst affected. I think the pump on Broad Street is most likely to be the source,' he said, taking the folded map from his pocket to show me.

'*If* it's from one of the pumps at all,' I reminded him.

'You must agree; look how localised the cases are around the Broad Street pump. They are clustered around it and spread in all directions from it. But yes, yes, I know, it is far from proven,' John conceded. 'We must continue to be thorough and methodical in our work. I have started to visit each house where there has been a death to question them. We will see if that will help build the case.'

'I met some of Hall's men this morning,' I said. 'They are out to collect a wealth of information about the cases: their occupation, living conditions, the street layout, sewage arrangements, atmosphere, water supply; everything you can think of.'

'It is good that the government is taking some action, but *more* should be done. So far, there are only the signs, the flags and the lime washing. What's the Board of Health for? They could be sending more doctors, advising people about the need for fluids and hand-washing. They should have an *army* of men on the streets trying to work out the cause; it is scandalous.' He punched his palm with his balled fist. 'And Hall's men, collecting so much information: what do they hope to prove? It will take an age to analyse the information, and the people of Soho will all be dead by then,' said John, passionately.

'I agree; we could do with some help with the cases. But at least Hall seems to be trying to understand the problem more than Chadwick ever did.'

'Pah, he made the problem worse. That is why it is so important to find the truth,' said John, his voice resolute and serious. 'With my work on anaesthesia, I have been able to help a few; but my work on cholera, Frank, could help save hundreds and *thousands*.' He looked at me with frustration in his grey eyes, willing me to understand.

'Well, if anyone can do it, you can,' I said, feeling a surge of affection for him, but still not quite sure what to make of it. 'Let me tell you of the deaths and the new cases I have heard of today. I saw Dr Rogers, who was at the Middlesex this morning, and he gave me the details of twenty-three more deaths.'

John drew bars on his map at the addresses which corresponded to the latest deaths. I had to agree that there did seem to be a clustering of dwellings on Broad Street. Could John be right? Was the cholera coming from the Broad Street pump? But I knew as well as John that a clustering on a map would not constitute proof in the minds of the parish authorities. The people with the power to act locally needed hard evidence.

'I have the figures from Farr,' said John. 'There are eighty-nine deaths recorded so far from cholera for the week ending 2nd September, in the Golden Square, Berwick Street and St Ann's districts. Some deaths may not have been recorded yet; there will be more. I've marked them on the map and I have started my visits.'

'You were always methodical, John; let me know what you find.' He left and I sat back in my favourite armchair and stared at the empty hearth. It was still so hot I couldn't imagine ever lighting the fire again, and I fanned my sweating forehead with my unread *Morning Chronicle*. Was John right? Did he have the answer? It seemed a strange idea and it went against everything I thought I knew. Maybe medicine was not as black and white as I thought; perhaps there were grey uncertainties. Grey, everywhere grey. At least it was not black; not yet, anyway.

Later that day I was called back to the Institute for Gentlewomen in Harley Street to see a patient. I found myself desperately hoping Miss Irvine might be there again; I was surprised to find that my heart beat quicker at the thought and I felt my cheeks flush. I had to quell my feelings for there was work to be done.

As I walked up the wide steps and entered the cool, light hallway, the door to my left opened and Miss Irvine herself came out. She didn't see me as she lingered on the threshold, her hand on the brass door handle, as a voice within the room spoke to her. I glimpsed past her and saw a formidable looking young woman in a well-cut dark grey gown, buttoned to the neck, standing behind a smart mahogany desk. She had fine features and a small nursing cap pinned to her black hair, which was drawn back rather severely into a tight chignon. She stood firmly straight-backed and although slight of stature, even in that brief glimpse, I could see that she commanded authority. After a moment, Miss Irvine closed the door and as she turned to leave, she saw me.

'Miss Irvine, I hope you are well?'

'Dr Roberts,' she said, looking up into my face, her cheeks blushing slightly and her eyes momentarily confused. 'What are you doing here?'

'I have a patient to see.'

'Of course, of course you do.' She recovered her composure.

'Will you be able to escort me to the ward?'

She looked flustered again. 'No, I am sorry; I have just been telling the superintendent that Mama has forbidden me from nursing while the cholera is in London.'

'The lady you were speaking with was the superintendent?'

'Yes; that is Miss Nightingale. She expressed her disappointment in me, but at least she has said she will take me back when, or should I say *if*, Mama allows me to return. She says I show promise as a nurse, but there we are. I must obey my mother.' She looked down at her polished, laced boots, peeping out beneath her skirts, and I stole a glance at her crooked scar.

'Indeed. We must hope the cholera will pass and you can return, if that is what you wish,' I said. 'How do you find Miss Nightingale? A woman superintendent is quite the talk of some of my colleagues.' Miss Irvine glanced back at her door and then looked me in the eye.

'She is strict but fair. She works us hard but I think it is because she wants us to know our work and to be *useful* women. She is from a very well-to-do family, you know, but she has made her own way in the world. Her parents are perhaps more liberal than mine,' she smiled ruefully. 'But there we are and Mama is right, I would not like to catch the cholera.'

'Was your business concluded successfully with Miss Bates?' I said, changing the subject. I confess I was intrigued to know what she wanted with a lowly poor girl in Soho. She looked distractedly away.

'Partly. When she was injured by Mama's carriage and I tended her wounds, I noticed she wore a locket about her neck and for reasons I am not at liberty to tell you, I was interested to see it again.'

'Yes, a silver one, I saw it when she was sick. It was her mother's.' Miss Irvine looked uncomfortable, as if she had said too much, so I let it drop. 'Well, I must see my patient. Will you travel home safely?'

'Yes, Hopkins, Mama's driver, is waiting outside for me.' She looked contemplatively around the big hallway and up the stairs to the wards. 'I wonder if I shall ever work here again? I truly hope so.' Then she roused herself and bade me farewell.

'Good day, Miss Irvine.' I gave a little bow and she left. I allowed myself a moment and then I turned to a nurse coming down the stairs, who escorted me back up to the ward.

TWELVE

Wednesday 6th September

I feel unsettled and John gathers evidence

I spent another unsettled night. I had strange dreams in which Miss Irvine was present in every cholera-ridden dwelling I visited. Her twisted lip, the wispy curls which framed her face, everywhere I went she seemed to be there. I kept warning her of the danger but she smiled and nodded, never uttering a word as I grew frantic for her to leave me, the risk of disease too great. The truth was I had never formed any romantic attachment and my only experience of women was long ago, a few months after I had come to London, an inexperienced young man of twenty. The memory resurfaced, intruding on my dream and I woke feeling anxious and flustered.

One Saturday evening, all those years ago, it had hit me how alone I was. I had craved real company, not the transient acquaintance and professional distance of my patients. My shabby lodging had echoed with darkness and desolation. My life was all work and little escape. I went out to The Newcastle; the public house was a beacon in the night. The gas lamps exuded a warm glow which spilled through the windows onto the pavement, lighting it like gold. Inside, all was merriment; people laughing, carousing, forgetting their troubles for a few hours. They wore faded shirts and holed jackets, but I remember how they had radiated warmth; shared experiences, shared confidences. I had felt very alone.

I had sat at the bar, where I studied my reflection in the mirrored wall. The drinks kept coming. Someone banged out tunes on the old piano in the corner and there was singing; singing for the sake of it, singing to be alive. The clientele got more rowdy and I was swept into their revelry. The ale and cigar smoke, the noise and the clamour were intoxicating; I had felt part of it, I had felt alive.

As they had closed up shop in the early hours, the last of us stragglers spilled onto the street. My new friends drifted off. In the freezing night I had staggered towards home, stopping to vomit in the gutter. The melancholy had started to hit me; nausea, pounding in my head, the realisation it was all falsehood and transience. A woman fell into step with me and her skirts swished against my legs as she put her arm around me, and she had smelled of honeysuckle. My aunt had honeysuckle in the garden and the scent always evoked a strong memory of my childhood. I found myself leaning on the woman. In the cold night, she was warm and I had been overcome with the simple pleasure of a human touch. We reached my lodgings, less salubrious then than my current home.

'Let's just get you to bed, shall we, Frankie,' she had said, as she pulled me in. She peeled off my clothes, whispering loving words. I had no experience of such matters but I lay there that night, as she did her work, coaxing, cajoling my body. I couldn't take in what was happening and it had all seemed hopelessly unreal, as if I was watching myself from a distance, a swirling fantasy.

I had opened my eyes. Despite her soft tones, she had been rifling through the pockets of my trousers, while she looked around the room in a bored, disinterested fashion, taking in my possessions as she murmured her practised feigned moans of pleasure. I had felt sick as I came to my senses. This woman was just a common whore who had taken advantage of my drunkenness to rob me. How could I have been so stupid? Lonely, I was, desperate, I was not. I sat up and threw her off me and grabbed my wallet. In her gaudy eyes, I saw a flicker of surprise that I had it in me and then she had merely cackled a hollow, mocking laugh.

'Can't quite finish the job, can ya?' she had said. 'A pint or two and you fellows ain't fit for nuthin'. Well, that'll be a crown for me trouble if ya please or I'll send me pimp round.' She had put on her clothes with lightning speed, and I sat nauseous and ashamed. I pulled the money from my wallet and handed it to her, but she stood her ground. 'And another for the 'elpin' 'and,' she said, winking and sticking out her tongue, with its metal stud. I fumbled for a coin and shoved it at her.

'Now get out,' I'd said. She had slammed the door behind her and gone on her way into the night. I had lain on my bed, flaccid and shivering, humiliated beyond measure. I had never been with a prostitute since; I had never been with a woman since. Now I was dreaming of Miss Irvine: a sign she had unsettled me for sure.

However, once I was up and about, I felt better and after another busy morning, John came around once more at lunchtime. I told him the news. 'Did you know Sir Benjamin Hall himself visited Soho yesterday? I was in Harley Street, so I didn't hear what he had to say, but he was here for a while, apparently.'

'No, I didn't know he was coming. I would like to have seen and challenged him directly about my theory,' said John absent-mindedly, as he studied Farr's list of deaths from the General Register Office in my parlour.

'I met with Reverend Whitehead today; the curate at St Luke's. Do you know him?'

'No, is he a good sort of fellow?'

'He is a fine man of the church; he's only young but he has compassion and wisdom.'

'What took you to him?' asked John, not looking up from his papers.

'I had to ask him to visit a few patients and their families. What a grim business, picking up the pieces of lives destroyed by sickness and death. He told me about Hall's visit and he was asking me what could be done to help halt the epidemic and I mentioned your theory to him. I hope you don't mind? He was talking about the miasma and what could be done to alleviate it. He'd seen Hall's men and said he wasn't sure why they were asking about the sewerage and water, as he believed Chadwick had helped matters on that score and the answer must lie in improving the atmosphere. It just slipped out; you know, that you think the water might be the cause of it all.'

'What did he think? I plan to present our preliminary

findings at the Board of Guardians meeting tomorrow evening and I believe he will be there. It would be useful to have one supporter on the board,' said John. I frowned.

'He was sceptical. He looked doubtful when I said you had concerns about the pumps, and particularly the pump on Broad Street. He asked why people were unaffected here in the last cholera epidemic if it was the water. Why don't people succumb to cholera all the time if they use the pump every day? I have to say, he didn't believe in the idea.' John sighed.

'What has happened is that the pump well has become contaminated with cholera *now*. There must have been a first case, an index case, from whom the cholera passed into the well water. Somehow, the vomitus or bowel evacuations from that case found their way into the well and from then on, others who drank from it became infected,' said John.

'So who was the index case? How can we tell which case was first when there have been hundreds over such a short space of time? And besides, how did the index case get it?'

'The index case must have come into contact with infected water from elsewhere, from south of the river perhaps. I don't know, maybe the cholera agent lies dormant, or changes so it is not so infectious, only to resurface later. To stop this epidemic now, it matters not how the index case caught the cholera. If a case has contaminated the water, we need to find the source by which the contaminated water is spreading. I do not know who the index case was or how the well became contaminated. But don't you see?

It doesn't matter. If the pump water *is* contaminated, the important thing is to stop people using it.'

'What have you found so far?'

'Of the eighty-nine deaths registered due to cholera last week,' he said looking at his papers, 'eighty-three occurred on Thursday 31st August, Friday 1st or Saturday 2nd September. I have, so far, visited about two-thirds of those addresses.'

'And?'

'In about three-quarters of the cases, the victim either *always* or *sometimes* drank from the Broad Street pump. In a few cases, I could gather no information as the families were dead or have fled. Some professed not to drink the pump water, but they may have done so unwittingly: in the public houses mixed with spirits, in the coffee houses or dining rooms, or in friends' houses. That means that so far, more than three-quarters *just of these cases* had a definite link to the Broad Street pump. I will visit the other addresses today. We don't even know about the deaths that were not registered by last Saturday, or those local cases removed to hospital.'

'But supposing you find that three-quarters of the deaths had a link to the Broad Street pump: is it enough? There are other features which link the cases: they share the same miasma, they live in poor and overcrowded conditions, they have the same nutrition or lack of it; they share many aspects of their lives which make them susceptible to the same diseases. These objections will surely be raised by the board and others,' I said.

'You are right. I need to find a case or cases with a link to the pump, but in all other respects different. If I could find a case which did *not* share the same "miasma" or the same features of location, overcrowding and poverty, but drank from the pump and contracted cholera; that would greatly strengthen the argument. Or conversely, if I could find people who live in these streets but have *not* used the pump and have *not* contracted cholera,' said John. 'There must be such a case that lends weight to the argument, one that makes the case more compelling.' He stared at his list again.

I said nothing. I knew how much this meant to him. He had already devoted months of work to it this very year. Now he had left that work, to examine the epidemic in Soho, on our own doorstep. What satisfaction John would feel if he was finally proved right, and if the proof lay in his own neighbourhood. I admired John's sense of purpose; he strove for the truth and my quiet, serious, diligent friend was simply sure that he was right. If I but had such strength to challenge the accepted view.

'How can I help?' I said, eventually.

'You could read my notes, to see if I have missed anything?' said John, looking up with a weary smile. 'Some refreshment might help us think.'

I went to make some coffee. Mrs Hook was not back; it was not safe for her to return yet. I had seen fewer new cases today, but I'd seen five hearses carrying eight coffins earlier. I was exhausted; I had never experienced a week like it. I peered out the window onto the arid backyard: the days were still baking hot, the air a fetid soup of flies, disease, smells and panic. As I waited for the pan to boil, I studied the water simmering within it. Was the water of life killing the people? I stood leaning at the sink, desperate for rest. Without thinking, I splashed water on my face. Then, as it touched my lips I experienced a moment of panic at the thought that those very drops could kill me. I hastily wiped my face on my sleeve; it was all getting too much. I felt myself teetering on the brink. I placed my hands flat on the counter and took deep calming breaths. I must help John. If he was right, it was imperative that they believed him; I had no choice. I returned with the coffee, to find him striding up and down in front of the fireplace, waving a sheet of paper.

'I think I have found something,' John announced slowly, with characteristic restraint.

'What?' I asked, setting down the tray.

'Gould's servant.'

'Gould?'

'Gould, the ornithologist. He draws birds. He lives at 20 Broad Street, almost opposite the pump. His servant was one of the first deaths registered on Friday 1st. Gould said his servant always drew water from the Broad Street pump. Gould was away and returned on Saturday 2nd to find his servant had died the day before. He sent for some water, but he didn't drink it because although it looked clear, it had a foul smell. He didn't drink it, and nor did his assistant, and neither of them contracted cholera. That is a control case: three people in the same household, one who drank water from the pump and died of cholera, and two who didn't drink it and were not ill. There are sure to be other such examples, if I look again through my notes,' finished John, a quiet excitement in his grey eyes.

I poured the coffee. 'Would it help to look not at the

individual cases we know of, but at houses and buildings near the pump where there are *many* cases or those where there are *not* cases, to see if anything is different there?' I said.

'Yes, I have already conducted some investigations along those lines,' said John. 'The factory on Broad Street, Eley's: there have been many deaths of workers there. Young Mr Eley says the men drink from two large vats of pump water provided for the employees. It is tragic that an act of beneficence should have such a deadly outcome.'

'If one believes the pump theory. What about the atmosphere in the factory?' I said. I did not wish to be negative, but I knew what an uphill struggle John would face to convince the board. In my heart I wasn't even sure that *I* believed his theory.

'Why would the atmosphere suddenly strike down a dozen men with cholera, when they have worked there for years in good health?' said John, irritation creeping into his voice.

'Perhaps the miasma is concentrated in the factory? The heat makes it more infectious? The workers are rendered more susceptible to the effects of it by their work?'

'Do you believe that, Frank?' asked John, dismay in his eyes.

'I do not know what to believe. I am merely highlighting possible questions and arguments that may come your way,' I said, lightly.

'The workhouse on Poland Street,' John said, changing tack; 'how many live there?'

'Upwards of five hundred I think; I saw a patient there yesterday, but he did not have the cholera, I think.'

'Then why have there been only five deaths from cholera reported there?' said John. 'It is situated no great distance from the pump. Surely sometimes people draw water there?'

'Perhaps not, for they have their own well on the premises, to supplement the piped supply. The warden told me yesterday.'

'Then that is an argument on my side: only five of five hundred? Many more would be expected; they share the same miasma as the rest of Soho. Many would suppose the miasma to be *worse* there than in the surrounding area,' said John. 'Here is another example: the brewery on New Street. The proprietor told me he has over seventy men employed there, and not one has died of cholera so far. I asked him whether the men obtain their water from the pump, and he said that even the local men tend not to as he provides them with malt liquor, which they drink in preference to water. The brewing process involves boiling the water, and anyway, they have their own well on the premises. That is two examples where it would be expected that there would be a significant number of deaths, but there have not been. In both instances, albeit for completely different reasons, the people are not in the habit of drinking water from the pump on Broad Street. Can you not agree with me, Frank? I am certain I am right,' urged John.

'It is not me you need to convince,' I said. 'You build a good argument. But you need to be able to explain to them what *started* the epidemic. People have always used that pump; what is different *now*?'

'Yes, we need to find the index case: the first case, the case which infected the water of the pump well and started it all,' sighed John.

'Anyway, what do you wish the board to do?' I said.

'Why, remove the handle from the Broad Street pump, to prevent people using it,' stated John matter-of-factly. 'I want to persuade them to remove the handle, of course.'

THIRTEEN

Thursday 7th September

The Board of Guardians meeting of St James's parish

'So have you prepared what you are going to say?' John and I sat in my parlour, eating yesterday's bread with some ham, old cheese and chutney from trays on our laps. Since Mrs Hook had gone, I had slipped into spending most of my time in the parlour; she would be horrified that I was not eating at the dining table, but it was too formal for the meagre fare I was subsisting on in her absence. 'Have you put together a compelling case? Will you convince them?' I said, spearing a mouthful of ham on my fork.

'I hope so, Frank, I hope so. I have visited all the other houses where there has been a cholera death that we are aware of. I can but try to put the argument in as logical a way as I can. The rest is up to the committee. Will you come with me?'

'I will, John, for from what I hear of the committee, you will need some moral support. They are an insular bunch and rather full of their own importance, I've heard.' I felt quietly anxious about attending the meeting, for all my old fears about challenging those above me lurked in my mind, but I had to accompany John if he wanted me to.

'Well, I thank you for your support.'

'Can I tempt you to try some ham?' I tried, knowing John was vegetarian. 'It may boost your strength, you know.'

'Thank you, but no. I do not expect a young fellow like you to understand but I am not likely to change my habits now, at my time of life, Frank.' As so often, I was not entirely sure whether he was in earnest.

'Less of the "young", thank you; I am above thirty years of age now, you know.'

'That seems young to me, believe me,' John's grey eyes twinkled back.

I spent the morning visiting more patients. I felt so weary, I longed for a rest. But there could be no rest until the epidemic was over. There were signs it was abating. Each day there were fewer new cases, but the deaths kept coming. I was exhausted, physically and emotionally. Such tragedy everywhere; lives destroyed at every turn. I longed for some respite from the endless sickness; I longed to be able to think about something else. I longed for Mrs Hook to return and look after me once more; I was sick of bread and cheese, bread and ham, bread and tea. I longed to be free of the ever present dread that *I* would contract the cholera. I had been in contact with so many sick people it would be a miracle if I escaped. I had never felt so tested in my professional life. But, following John's recommendation, I had not drunk from the Broad Street pump, I had been scrupulous in my hand-washing and I had disinfected my hands with vinegar between patients. I could only hope my luck and my nerve would hold.

After lunch, John left for his anaesthetic practice in the afternoon, for surgery went on as usual in other parts of London. I thought it would do him good to think about something else before the meeting this evening. I knew what it meant to John. But I didn't know whether we would even be allowed in, for the meetings were closed.

I turned my mind once more to Nurse Irvine. I was intrigued by her: she was intelligent and capable, and yet there was a vulnerable side to her. Perhaps it was that which had troubled me so in my dreams. I sat on the wooden settee in my parlour, composing myself before the afternoon's work, and allowed myself a few moments thinking about her.

As I set off to meet John to go to the Board of Guardians meeting, a voice hailed me from across the street.

'Dr Roberts.' I turned and there was Constable Lewis.

'Constable. How is Daniel?'

'Oh, yes, 'e's quite a bit better, thank you. We're 'opin' 'e'll pull through. But I thought you'd be interested to know, Doctor, that we 'ave looked into the Wiltshire case and we 'ave found out that Wiltshire and 'Arrison were in the same regiment, twenty years ago; they were out in the Caribbean together, in Jamaica.'

'Really?'

'Yes, and do you know what else? The pair of 'em were dishonourably discharged. Wiltshire 'ad assaulted a native woman and soured relations with the locals, causing a bit of trouble. 'Arrison was there and it was judged 'e was equally to blame, as 'e was intent on assault too if they 'adn't been stopped. They were kicked out after another man testified against 'em at the court martial. That man was a William Bates and do you know, it seems 'e was a distant cousin of Albert Bates.'

'How did you find all this?'

'It's all in the army service records and we tracked down another fellow who was in the same regiment with 'em, a George Hartley, and 'e 'as confirmed it. But there's more: before Wiltshire and 'Arrison could be sent 'ome, William Bates was found drowned in a pond. No one was ever charged, but George Hartley says on the quiet, everyone knew it was Wiltshire did it.' I stood, taking this in.

'So did Albert Bates know Wiltshire was implicated in his cousin's death?'

'Hartley said when 'e left the army, 'e reported the word about the barracks and 'e'd thought the family would 'ave been told. Wiltshire 'ad gone by then, so 'e couldn't defend 'imself against it and 'e was never charged, as far as Hartley knows.'

'So Albert Bates might have put two and two together, if he'd ever met Wiltshire?' I said slowly, thinking. 'But would he recognise him? What of his finger and thumb? When did he come upon those injuries?'

'Hartley said 'e'd lost 'em in a brawl long before, when 'e was in the Foreign Legion.'

'So Bates might have recognised Wiltshire if he'd met him?'

'Most likely. 'Ave to say, it doesn't look good for 'im,' Lewis grimaced.

'Is Hartley in London?'

'Bermondsey, Peddlars Court.'

'Thank you for telling me; I must be on my way,' I sighed. 'Good luck with your enquiries.' I mulled over what I'd heard as I walked off. It didn't sound good for James and Emily's father: there was the circumstantial evidence with the body being found in the yard of their lodging, and his pipe, and now the police had a motive too. I wanted to help the family if I could, but now I felt a pang of guilt that I had in some way contributed to their troubles, by discovering Wiltshire's name and by drawing the attention of the police to the link between him and Samuel Harrison. It was a bad business. Of course I didn't really know the family at all; for all I knew, Albert Bates was guilty.

I resolved to pass on to James and Emily what I had heard; the least I could do was to keep them informed of the course of the investigation. What hope was there? Their father would, in all likelihood, hang. Then a thought struck me: Albert Bates couldn't have been responsible for the death of Samuel Harrison outside The Newcastle, for he was in the Newgate by then. Perhaps there was a glimmer of hope for him yet.

I met John outside his large house on Sackville Street. As a successful anaesthetist, he rented a whole house, in which he rattled around with his housekeeper. He didn't need the space, but it befitted his position and he sometimes entertained colleagues or held medical meetings in his rooms. Occasionally, some of his large family came to stay; he was the eldest of nine and his siblings were engaged in a variety of professions. Sometimes one of them would visit London from the north. I shook him firmly by the hand as I wished him well for the meeting ahead. As the last rays of the sun were going down, the streets were a blaze of deep orange. We walked the few hundred yards to the Vestry Hall in Piccadilly where the Board of Guardians of St James's parish were meeting.

'I know how much this means to you, John.'

'I have to persuade them to let me speak first, Frank, but surely they *must* listen to me. I have it all here, I am sure I am right. They could save lives if they will only listen to me.'

We arrived and John stepped through the door at the back of the hall. I slipped in beside him. Through the fog of cigar smoke and dim lamplight, I could just see a large table in the centre of the hall, with a dozen or so men around it. They all were dressed similarly, in dark frock coats and waistcoats, even on the warm summer night. I recognised Henry Whitehead at one end. The men were arguing and so loud was the din that they appeared not to have even noticed the arrival of two newcomers.

'Order, order!' a bespectacled man with an expansive beard was shouting, trying to restore some semblance of calm. He stood and banged a small wooden gavel on the table in front of him. 'Gentlemen, gentlemen, this is getting us nowhere. We should not be fighting, but working together to decide what is best.'

'We are going round in circles, Mr Wilson; we have heard the same arguments over and over, but we are no closer to agreement,' said a tall man, with a deep, commanding voice. 'The committee must decide a course of action. We must be seen to be *doing* something,' he said smoothly. 'The situation in Soho this week has been beyond words: more than four *hundred* residents have died already. There's almost no one remaining, people have died or left, and those who are too ill to leave will doubtless die in their lodgings. We have done practically nothing, the people see us as powerless.' The men around the table paused briefly to digest his words, before the clamour started again, several people talking over one another, the noise level rising.

'It is not true that we have done nothing. We have limed the streets, we've distributed pamphlets warning of the danger, we've passed on the advice from the Board of Health, we have posted quarantine flags warning of illness...' countered Mr Wilson.

'Aye, and we have distributed pamphlets and placards directing people to sources of help, for those left destitute,' added another.

'What is the use of those when many cannot read?' interjected another man, to catcalls of agreement from his colleagues, setting them all off again, speaking over each other, with no semblance of order in the proceedings.

'I agree; I have witnessed time and again the tragedy of this epidemic and I have never seen anything on such a scale before,' said Henry Whitehead, to more cries of agreement.

'Order, order!' repeated Mr Wilson wearily. 'The truth is: no one knows what would help or what we should do. We must wait for the miasma to pass to some other area of London and pray that it never returns to this district again.'

'But by doing nothing, we look impotent; there must be something we can do,' said the tall man from before; a view which was shared by many of the others, who broke into a babble of complaint and suggestion once more.

'What about face masks… that's what happened in some areas in '49?'

'Or carts for the sick to remove them from the city?'

'We must order mass burials in limed communal graves…'

'We should burn sulphur in the streets…'

The suggestions came thick and fast. Each was greeted with a mixture of agreement and "ayes", and cries about how ineffectual the measures would be. The atmosphere was charged and tense. The cigar smoke grew thicker and curled up towards the yellowed ceiling. I glanced at John and saw he looked utterly despairing that these were the men responsible for protecting the health of the public: they knew nothing. His hands in his pockets, he stood swaying back and forth on the soles of his feet, staring at the ground. I understood how frustrating their ineptitude must appear to a man who had devoted so many months and years of his life to his work on cholera, who thought he had the answer. But before I could whisper my thoughts to John, he had stepped forward and cleared his throat.

'Gentlemen,' he announced, in his low but commanding voice, and in a moment the men at the table turned to stare towards the door, mute with surprise at the intrusion.

'Who is there?' asked the chairman, unable to see across the smoke-filled room. 'Come forward.'

'My name is Dr John Snow,' announced John, approaching the table, 'and I beg you would allow me to speak, gentlemen. I cannot listen to your discussion without frustration as I have spent many years working with cholera cases, and I feel sure I have important information to offer. My only wish is to prevent more deaths and I beg you will hear me out.' He was interrupted before he could say more.

'The committee doesn't allow non-members to speak, Doctor. These are closed meetings,' announced one man in a superior, dismissive tone.

'Gentlemen,' John said, and I knew from the tone of his voice that he was struggling to remain calm. 'I tell you, I have this year been studying the cholera epidemic south of the river. This very *week* I have been engaged with Dr Roberts here, a local doctor whom many of you will know, visiting the cases, studying the outbreak in Soho and considering what can be done. Unless you gentlemen have formulated a plan of action, I would suggest that the committee has little to lose by allowing me to speak for a few minutes?' said John firmly.

'Let Dr Snow speak,' interjected Henry Whitehead. There was a ripple of murmurs around the table and Mr Wilson banged his gavel again.

'Very well Dr Snow. In these extraordinary circumstances, we will make an exception and allow you to speak, if you have information relevant to our discussion.' John approached the table and the men fell silent.

'Thank you.' John's shoulders relaxed as he began to tell his story. 'Gentlemen, I wish to summarise my work on cholera to date, and then move to discuss the current epidemic in Soho. As a young apprentice in the north many years ago, one of the first illnesses I witnessed in epidemic was the cholera in the collieries, and six years ago I worked in and studied the disease in some detail in the last epidemic in our city in 1848 and 1849. During these past years, I have collated information about epidemics from all over the country. Over my career, I have developed a theory that the cholera agent is, in fact, transmitted not through the atmosphere or miasma, but person to person and through contaminated water.'

There were some audible gasps at this point, a guffaw and murmurings of dissent, but the chairman banged his gavel emphatically. 'Silence, gentlemen; allow Dr Snow to speak.'

'I am all too well aware that this is in opposition to the widely held view. However, I have long reasoned that a disease which produces symptoms of the digestive system is likely to be contracted via that same digestive system. It makes no sense that some agent in the air we breathe should lead us, suddenly and violently to experience such extreme vomiting and evacuation of the bowels as are seen in the cholera. Does cholera cause coughing or irritation of the throat or lungs? It does not. Does it cause nasal discharge or breathlessness? It does not. What it *does* do is cause extremely rapid and toxic evacuation of fluid via the bowel, which leaves the patient in a state of dehydration and collapse. The essence of the disease concerns fluids and fluid balance.'

'The popular miasmatist view', he continued, 'states that cholera is inhaled, enters the bloodstream and produces generalised constitutional symptoms of fever, sweats, imbalance and collapse, and *then* localised symptoms in the gut appear. However, in my experience of cholera, the constitutional symptoms occur *later*, *after* the gastrointestinal symptoms, and the subsequent features of cramps, collapse and death can be accounted for by the volume of fluid lost from the gut. I reason the cholera agent must be ingested into the gut and acts to affect the gut lining directly. I believe the cholera is taken in by mouth, not inhaled. It is ingested through contaminated water.' At this point, I noticed that although there was still some shuffling and mutterings, the men were listening to John now. I listened too, feeling pride in his eloquence. As I listened, for the first time, it began to sink in that John's theory could actually be correct. He continued.

'In the epidemics and outbreaks I have witnessed, they have all occurred where the drinking water supply and the facilities for human waste are in close proximity and there is opportunity for contamination from one to the other. In the collieries in the north which I mentioned, the miners relieved the calls of nature and took their sustenance in the same confined space. Six years ago, I studied the areas in south London hit by cholera. I found the water companies who supplied the pumps and pipes in the affected areas drew their water from the stretches of the river downstream of where the sewers empty into the Thames.' He looked at the men, listening to him now.

'I postulated that contamination of the drinking water with sewage was the cause of the cholera spreading. I found, in one instance, that there existed a physical route whereby the drinking water could become contaminated by sewage: in a row of houses where an outbreak of cholera occurred after a storm, it was found that the rainwater caused a waste drain to back up and overflow, contaminating the drinking water. In another instance two rows of back-to-back dwellings were supplied by different water companies and in one row there were many cases, in the other there were few, despite the dwellings and the inhabitants being in all other ways similar. I have come to believe that the choleric evacuations from one patient come into contact with the water supply of others and this is how the disease spreads.'

'Do you have any proof?' said Reverend Whitehead, but he was drowned out by others.

'This is not the view of the Board of Health. Chadwick believed the miasma theory and I'll wager Hall does too,' stated another committee member.

'I do not believe it; it is well known to be the miasma…' said another.

'I declare you are quite mad, man; for many years it has been known that the miasma is the cause,' added another.

The objections continued. John said nothing until the furore died down and they sat in silence looking at him.

'I believe I do now have proof,' he said. 'I have been working this year examining cases south of the river. There is an area of south London where the houses on the streets are equally supplied by two different water companies: the Lambeth Company, and the Southwark and Vauxhall Company. At the time of the last epidemic in '49, both companies drew their water from the same part of the river, and the cholera affected all the houses equally. However, two years ago, the Lambeth Company moved its source and workings up river, to an area out of reach of the tidal range, and therefore free of pollution by the discharges of the sewers. This summer I have studied the rates of cholera in houses supplied by the two companies, and I find that houses supplied by the Lambeth Company water are now between eight and nine times *less* affected by cholera than those supplied by the Southwark and Vauxhall Company. These are streets where adjacent houses may have a different supplier, but are in all other respects identical. The housing is the same, the occupants are the same and the "miasma" is the same. The *only* difference is in the water supply. When I have finally prepared the figures, I believe they will substantiate my theory.'

'But your work is not finished?' queried one man, sounding doubtful.

'Not completely, no, but it is far enough advanced to make me confident that I am correct,' answered John, levelly.

'Not proper proof though?' retorted the man.

'What's this got to do with the miasma on our streets now?' said another.

'I tell you, I do not hold with the miasma theory,' reiterated John calmly. 'If instead, as I believe, the cholera agent is ingested, it can be transmitted from person to person by the faeco-oral route and it can be transmitted between groups of people or communities by contamination of the drinking water.' There were some incredulous laughs from around the table, as if his very credibility was questionable if he opposed the widely held view, taken by many as fact.

'All right then,' said the second man, 'what does all this have to do with the epidemic on our streets *now*? What have you done *here*?'

'In the current epidemic in Soho, I have obtained figures from Farr, the chief statistician at the General Register Office, which list the location of all the deaths from cholera in the districts of Golden Square, Berwick Street and St Ann's. I have visited the dwellings where a death has occurred and made enquiries about the water supply and usage of the street pumps. Due to the locations of these deaths, and the habits of the victims, I have a theory that the public pump on Broad Street is contaminated with cholera.' There was outcry at this suggestion.

'No, not the pump, it's well used and well liked with good reason…'

'I drank from it last week, and I am well…'

'Where else are the people to get their water if the pumps are the cause?'

'As I say, I have visited almost all the affected premises,' interrupted John, raising his husky voice above the noise. 'I have found that three-quarters of cases have drunk from the Broad Street pump, and others may have done so unwittingly. It is clear to me that the Broad Street pump lies at the centre of the area affected by this outbreak. In summary, I believe the cholera is spread in the water and that the cause of this current epidemic in Soho lies in the water of the Broad Street pump,' John finished.

There was at last some quiet in the hall. It looked to me as if no one knew what to make of this calm, serious doctor, who had stood up and so resolutely challenged the widely held view. What next? Would they believe him? I held my breath.

'So what do you believe we should do about it?' the chairman asked eventually, not willing to venture an opinion on this strange idea.

'I believe you should remove the handle from the pump on Broad Street, to prevent the people using it, while investigations are carried out. I believe it will be discovered, in time, that there is contamination of the water by choleric bowel evacuations, possibly due to a physical connection between the well and a sewer or drain. This has allowed the cholera poison to contaminate the water supply of the people. If the handle is removed, the people cannot drink the water and that will prevent more people dying.'

'But we cannot act without firm proof,' one man objected.

'Do you have any better suggestions?' said John, calmly. There was silence. The realisation was dawning on the assembled committee that this doctor was right. They had no better ideas; they had no other ideas at all.

At least it would look as if they were doing something. What if he was right? What if he was right and they failed to act?

'Doctor, we must discuss this for a moment, amongst ourselves,' said the chairman. 'If you will wait outside?' he said. John and I stepped outside. The breeze felt pleasant and fresh on our faces after the warm, smoke-laden interior of the hall and we breathed in the night air and looked at one another.

'Do you think they believed me?' said John, a half smile on his lips, leaning back against the wall.

'I think perhaps they did,' I said. 'You built a good case; and you are right, they have no better plan. Well done, my friend.' I gave him a playful punch on the arm.

'I hope so,' said John, as we both looked up towards the twilit sky, birds wheeling in the dusk, the first stars winking in the heavens. 'It will truly be a tragedy if I have offered them the means of halting the spread of the epidemic and they are too pig-headed to take it. Wouldn't it be wonderful to practise medicine in a time when there was a cure for all disease?' he said. 'We see so much suffering, so much death. I am sure there will be a time when men of our profession will be able to do more good and save so many more lives than we can now.'

'Do you think there will ever be such a time?'

'I am *sure* there will be. Those stars up there,' he said tilting his head back against the wall to look up at the universe, 'when they have been there for another one hundred, one thousand years, surely things will have changed? But those stars will have to be our witness, for

159

we will be long gone. There will always be progression of man's knowledge, in all things, not just medicine. I would love to see the day when cholera is treatable; or better still, a day when it is eradicated altogether. Until then, prevention is the key. That is why they *must* believe me now.'

'But until we understand the causes, how can we recommend preventive measures?'

'You are right, we cannot; which is why we must strive ever harder to seek the causes of disease. We must use whatever methods are at our disposal; we must use the evidence of our eyes and the logic of our reasoning.' There appeared at the door one of the committee to summon us back inside and taking a last deep breath of fresh air, I raised my eyebrows at John as we stepped back into the gloom. John strode up to the table and the chairman addressed him.

'Very well, Dr Snow; we will do as you ask. We will remove the handle from the Broad Street pump, and undertake some investigations there. However, I have to say, the committee is not convinced by your argument. Goodnight to you.'

'Thank you, sirs, I bid you goodnight and I pray this epidemic will end.' John bowed to the chairman and turned back towards me with an unusually wide smile. When he reached me, I shook his hand, congratulating him on his success and he hugged me to him in a rare display of emotion. For a success it was, persuading the insular committee to act on the advice of a stranger. As we strolled back towards John's house in Sackville Street, we were a merry and optimistic pair.

'We did it, Frank! We persuaded them!' he said, a spring in his stride.

'No, *you* did it, John,' I said, smiling fondly at his childlike excitement. We walked the rest of the way, each lost in our thoughts. In my good mood, before I knew it, my mind turned once more to Nurse Irvine. I wondered if she was thinking of me.

FOURTEEN

Friday 8th September

Miss Irvine visits Soho

I was out on my rounds early again. There were still many requests to visit victims, although the number of new cases of the cholera each day seemed to be getting smaller. I strode down the filthy, noisome Broad Street longing for things to get back to normal: for the street sweepers to return, for the roads to be full once more of the normal chatter and buzz of everyday life. I had been too busy to realise how much I missed it; how I craved an easing of the pressure of work. As I passed the corner of Broad Street on my way to Berwick Street, there was a disgruntled gathering of people around the pump.

'Where's the 'andle gone?' a man grumbled.

'Who's taken it?' one woman complained.

'We'll have to go to the Carnaby Street pump now…' moaned another. A young girl swung her empty bucket looking unsure and then brightened as she followed two women to another pump. The guardians had been as good as their word: the handle had been removed. John had achieved his aim; but would it make a difference to the cholera cases? I saw Sarah Lewis, empty bucket in hand, among the crowd.

'Good morning, Sarah,' I called.

'Oh, Doctor, I need water but the 'andle's gone. My Thomas is not well today,' she said, distractedly, wiping her forehead with the back of her hand. My heart lurched for her; not her husband too?

'Would you like me to see him?'

'I won't worry ya yet, Doctor; I'm trying to get 'im to drink and 'e's not too bad,' she said, looking weary despite her hopeful words. Londoners were inherently optimistic, an admirable quality that perhaps was essential just for survival. I felt guilt that, even in my preferable circumstances, I sometimes succumbed to melancholia in a way they could not afford to. If many of my patients stopped to think, they would simply starve. As she spoke, beyond the pump I saw James Bates struggling to carry two full buckets of water towards the door to his lodging.

'As I said to Mr Bates there, Sarah, I have a colleague who thinks there may be something wrong with this pump at the moment.' I called to him. 'Mr Bates.'

'Dr Roberts,' he panted, putting his buckets down, flexing his hands. 'I've been to the pump on Warwick Street, but it's a long way to carry the water and Em won't go. She's minded to go and make a fuss to the parish 'bout the 'andle being taken off.'

'It may be for the best,' I said.

'It is a long way though,' worried Sarah, 'and I don't like to leave Thomas and Daniel.'

''Ave some of mine, if you like,' said Mr Bates, pouring water into her bucket.

'Oh, James, you're a good lad. I'm so sorry about your mother. My Thomas is sick now and I must get back to 'im.' She turned away but stopped and looked back at James, biting her lip. 'It's not really me place, but I jus' wanted you to know, Thomas feels terrible 'bout your father, James. I'm sorry.' She left us and I turned to Mr Bates.

'What news of your father?'

'The bobbies told us Wiltshire and another feller, 'Arrison, used to be in the army together, years back; and they knew me father's cousin, William. Me and Em are trying to find out what this Wiltshire feller was doing 'ere *now*, see if that'd 'elp. We went to the old master of the workhouse and 'e said 'e *'ad* been there, asking about a boy, "Elijah".'

'Oh yes,' I broke in, 'the boy on Poland Street, where Wiltshire stayed: he said about "Elijah" and also something about Christmas. Sorry, I meant to tell you but with the cholera, it slipped my mind.'

'That fits 'cause the old master, over in Peter Street said 'e didn't know of no "Elijah", but 'e *did* remember an "Eliza"; a baby left on the doorstep of the workhouse one Christmas Eve.'

'Eliza? Who was she? Did Wiltshire find her?'

James Bates hesitated. 'Well, I'm not sure meself, but Em wondered if it could've been our mother. 'Er name was Elizabeth, but she called 'erself Betsy. She was left at the workhouse as a baby and she grew up there. They gave 'er to a young woman who 'ad another daughter, and she took care of 'em both like sisters, see. That "sister" was 'er best friend, Mary Parker. But why the dead feller should 'ave been looking for Mother we've no idea. 'Sides, it doesn't 'elp Father none, does it?' he finished, his eyes on his worn shoes. "'E's still waitin' for the Court of Sessions to look at 'is case to see when 'e'll be tried. But 'e'd never seen the feller before in 'is life and 'e'd no idea 'ow 'is pipe got there…' his voice trailed off.

'What a puzzle. It's not much to go on, is it?' I frowned. I had no way of helping James Bates and I could see what a desperate situation he was in. His father could be hanged for murder, his mother and two siblings gone and just him and his sister left. He was a good lad, and took his responsibilities seriously, but as with many of the poor, it was always a fine line between coping and oblivion. What if they couldn't pay their rent? It was a short step to begging, thieving or whoring for the two of them. I sighed. 'Well, I can only wish you luck and that something turns up to help your father, Mr Bates. Good day to you.' The dark clouds were gathering over what remained of the Bates family.

As I came back down Broad Street later that morning, I noticed a carriage and two white horses opposite the pump. I felt my pulse quicken; it was surely Miss Irvine's carriage. Perhaps she was back to visit Emily Bates? When Soho was so stricken and disease was everywhere, I couldn't quite understand her seeking Miss Bates; it must be something more than a professional interest in her recovery. I went into The Newcastle on the corner and ordered a small beer. I could see if there was any news on the murder last week and if I sat by the window, I would have a view of the carriage. I saw her face in my mind: her clear eyes, her delicate features, her lip, dear to me now. Would I be bold enough to invite her to a recital or a concert, once the epidemic was over? But who knew if or when I would see her again? This was an opportunity I could not afford to miss.

After twenty minutes the door that led up to the Bates lodging opened and I saw Miss Irvine coming out. She looked elegant and poised, in a fine gown of cornflower-blue, her hair neat under her cream bonnet. She indicated to her driver that she was ready to depart. I stood up, knocking over my glass in my eagerness to catch her before she was driven away.

'Sorry, Daisy,' I called over my shoulder as I hurriedly left. As I stepped through the door onto the street, she was climbing into her carriage. 'Miss Irvine,' I called, fearing I would lose her, 'Miss Irvine!' She stopped and turned, a loose curl escaping from her bonnet and fluttering across her face as she did so. I thought her eyes warmed in recognition, as she stepped down and turned to greet me.

'Dr Roberts, good day to you,' she said, smiling at me.

'Miss Irvine, I am very pleased to see you again,' I said, trying to sound calm, but feeling as if I was blushing to the roots of my hair. 'What brings you to Soho once more?'

'I have business again with Miss Bates,' said Miss Irvine, 'and please call me Cassandra; I am not in uniform now,' she smiled. 'A moment, Hopkins,' she said to her driver.

'Miss Cassandra, what a pretty name; I had a Great Aunt Cassandra, and I have always liked the sound of it.'

'But perhaps not the connotations?' she said, raising

her eyebrows and pulling a face. 'You know my poor namesake's fate was to never be believed?'

'Indeed, but thankfully times have moved on from classical mythology now,' I smiled.

'Can I ask how the cholera is progressing? Are there any signs that the worst is over?' she asked. 'I hear Miss Nightingale has been sent to the Middlesex to supervise the nursing of the cholera patients there. Apparently, every half-hour patients are brought in from Soho and she has been up day and night tending them, destroying their soiled clothes and putting them in clothes soaked in turpentine. She believes it provides some disinfection. It sounds terrible, indeed.'

'Yes, it is; I have never witnessed anything like it in my professional life. But I am optimistic that the worst may have passed. My friend and colleague, John Snow, believes the pump here is to blame and this morning he will be very pleased as he has persuaded the Board of Guardians to remove the pump handle, as you see, so the people cannot use it.' She raised her eyebrows as she looked towards the pump.

'That is an unusual idea. We must pray that you are right, Doctor, but how can the pump be implicated? I thought the origin of the disease lay in the miasma? Miss Nightingale teaches us that we must promote ventilation and orders the windows open all the time, regardless of the elements,' she said, holding my gaze with her clear blue eyes, which, I thought distractedly, matched the colour of her dress. Blue: the colour of solidity, safety, reliability. I could feel my own colour rising again as she looked at me, and I struggled to appear calm.

'I know that is the commonly held view, but Dr Snow has worked for many years with cholera patients and he does not believe the miasma is the cause. He believes the symptoms indicate the gut is primarily affected by the cholera agent, causing loss of fluid leading to collapse and therefore it follows that it is likely the agent is ingested, not inhaled. When Chadwick ordered that the sewers discharge into the river to improve the miasma a few years ago, Dr Snow thinks he made the cholera much worse, by polluting the water which the people drink. But this is no discussion for a lady,' I said, suddenly embarrassed.

'But it is a discussion for a nurse,' she replied with interest, still looking at me levelly, not at all squeamish or unsettled by the subject. 'I can see it is logical, what he is saying; how interesting.' She looked thoughtful, as if digesting what I had said and I found myself admiring her intelligence and informed opinion.

'Let us talk of something else. How is your business with Miss Bates progressing? She seems to have made a quick recovery from the cholera, and her brother has taken my advice and he seems to have escaped it.' Miss Irvine's face clouded over for a moment, before she recovered her composure.

'It progresses slowly; she's a determined one, Emily, for sure.' She felt her wrist absent-mindedly. 'Mama wanted to see Emily's locket, so I have exchanged it for my own bracelet, as a surety. But I am sorry, I should not be telling you this,' she said, suddenly flustered and unsure.

'Forgive me, I did not mean to intrude,' I said. 'They

are a good family, I think; James Bates came to my aid when I was set upon by a group of young ragamuffins a couple of weeks ago and his sister seems a strong character.'

Miss Irvine sighed. 'It is a difficult and complicated business, and I am uncertain how to resolve it…' she murmured.

'I am at your service, if I can ever be of assistance.'

'Thank you. You are most kind,' she said, and I wondered whether I detected the merest hint of a blush as she smiled up at me, holding my gaze for perhaps a moment longer than she needed to, before looking away. 'I must return home; Mama does not know that I am out. As I told you, she has forbidden me from nursing while the cholera is raging; it is all over *The Standard*, you know. She could not bear another loss, I think, so I must obey her.'

'Has your family suffered loss from the cholera?' I asked. 'I am very sorry, if so. It is a terrible disease. My mother and brother died of it many years ago.'

'I am very sorry to hear that. No, not the cholera, but my younger sister, Jane, died of fever last year. She was fifteen and Mama also lost three of her children in infancy. She could not bear to lose me too. My older brother, Edmund, is to be sent to the Crimea any day now, for he is an officer, and she fears for him greatly.' She sighed again. 'It must be very hard to be a mother.' I offered my hand as she climbed up into her carriage and, taking a deep breath, uttered the words that had been forming in my head.

'I wonder if, when this epidemic is over, you would

allow me to escort you to a concert or the opera one evening, Miss Irvine? Do you enjoy music?' I waited, my heart in my mouth, unsure what her response would be. She looked at me, appraisingly, and paused.

'Thank you, Dr Roberts, I do enjoy music and I would like that.' She gave a shy smile.

'It's Frank, Frank Roberts,' I said, relief flooding through my veins. 'How will I contact you, Miss Irvine; Cassandra?' I felt myself blush as I spoke her name.

'Send word to 12 Grosvenor Square, Mayfair. Good day, Dr Frank Roberts.' Turning to the driver she ordered 'drive on', the carriage pulled away and she was gone. I stood on the corner, looking after her, and I felt a glow of happiness within me for the first time that week. I felt taller as I looked about me, congratulating myself on my nerve. Even the sky seemed a richer blue: not scorching, unremitting, but gentle and full of promise. I wrote a note about the pump handle on a page of my pocketbook and accosted a passing street boy.

'A penny to deliver this to Dr Snow, lad?' I offered. He took it and sped off.

FIFTEEN

Saturday 9th September

I am called upon for assistance and a possible clue

For the first time in days, I woke naturally from my slumbers. I had been in a deep sleep, my first decent night's rest since the cholera epidemic began. I had not been called to any new cases overnight. Perhaps the epidemic had peaked; perhaps, finally, I could draw breath. I breakfasted on all there was in the house, tea, wishing that Mrs Hook would return. Maybe soon I would feel confident enough to send for her. I had some visits planned this morning, but not an onerous load and I stepped out onto the street my stomach rumbling. After buying a pastry at the baker, I went on my way. However, my optimism was premature as over the course of the morning my visits yet brought five new cases and eleven patients who had died overnight. It was not over, but at least it was on a different scale from last Saturday. I stopped for a meat pie at Mrs Bootle's, where the clientele was a much depleted and more sombre group than at my last visit, and then I headed home.

I woke a little later to an urgent knocking and I looked around, confused and disorientated, my heart thumping. The sun was still high, slanting in through the windows and I had fallen asleep in an armchair in my parlour, my teacup perched precariously in my hand. I put it down and went to the door. I opened it to find a boy on the doorstep.

'Dr Roberts?'

'Yes.'

''Ad to ask around, see where you lived, sir,' he panted. 'Please, sir, Miss says can you come? To Broad Street, sir.'

'Is someone unwell?'

'Not ill, sir, but attacked. Miss says can you come now?' said the boy.

'*Attacked?* Very well, I will come; do you know who it was that sent you?'

'Miss Irvine, said 'er name was, sir.' I was immediately wide awake.

'Miss Irvine?'

'Yes, sir, been knocked over, sir.'

My heart was racing as I fumbled in my pocket for a penny for the boy, who scurried down the steps. Then I pulled out another penny, and called the boy back. 'Boy, another penny to run back and tell Miss Irvine I'm on my way. Make haste!'

'Yes, sir,' said the boy who ran off. I turned to pick up my bag and then I ran down the steps and up the street, my heart pounding. I rounded the corner into Silver Street, then ran up Cambridge Street to Broad Street. Within two minutes I was pushing my way through a crowd of onlookers to Miss Irvine's side. Her gown was dirtied from the filth of the street and one of her shoes lay forlornly on its side.

'Just pushed 'er over, tryin' to get 'er bag,' a middle-aged woman said. 'Poor thing, she's not from round 'ere. I've sent to The Newcastle for a drink for 'er.' She held a handkerchief to the patient's forehead. A boy arrived with a cup of wine and the woman held it to Cassandra's lips with her other hand.

'Thank you, that is enough,' said Miss Irvine, her voice trembling. 'You are very kind.'

'Two of 'em, there was, I saw 'em scarper up Poland Street,' said a man.

'Looks well-to-do, if you ask me...' There were comments from others, the crowd always up for a spectacle and intrigued by a well-dressed woman in their midst.

'Thank you, I am a doctor, I will tend to her now, I thank you for your kindness,' I said as I reached her.

'Yes, thank you,' murmured Miss Irvine, with a faint smile at the woman beside her.

'Very well, Miss,' said the woman, who stood to leave; her bloodied handkerchief falling onto the cobbles.

Miss Irvine was sitting on the ground by her carriage, propped against the step. My first glance took in the gash and blood on her forehead, her hair escaping her soiled bonnet and her left wrist lying cradled by her other hand in her lap.

'Miss Irvine, what has happened, where are you hurt?' I cried. I knelt down beside her and took her wrist gently in my hands, feeling for areas of tenderness or deformity. There was some bruising, but the joints appeared to move and I breathed a sigh of relief.

'It is my wrist; but what of my poor driver Hopkins?

He tried to protect me,' she said, craning her neck to see where he was lying on the ground behind the carriage, but the movement hurt her wrist and she turned back again, wincing. I knelt up to look towards him.

'I'll see him in a moment, let me help you first. I think it is a sprain, not a break; but what of your head?' I asked, looking up at her forehead and the trail of blood which ran down the left side of her face, onto her collar. I couldn't help myself looking into her eyes, where the normally confident blue looked so crushed and vulnerable; my heart turned.

'Oh, Dr Roberts, I am so glad you are here. I am all right, but can you please send all these people away? I am not a spectacle,' she whispered.

'Of course,' I said. I turned to the small crowd who had stopped to witness the trouble. 'You heard the lady, move along, there is nothing to see here; move along, thank you,' I said and I was glad when they started to move off.

'Just seeing if we could 'elp, mate,' said the man at the front.

'Yes, thank you, you are most kind. But there is nothing more to do now, and I can help the lady, thank you,' I said firmly. I turned back to Miss Irvine's wrist.

'I will strap your wrist for your comfort, Cassandra, and then see to your head,' I whispered, abandoning the formality of her title for the first time in the intimacy of the moment. I took a bandage from my bag and wound it around her wrist. Her skin was so soft, so pale; I was reluctant to remove my hand from hers. 'Now, let me look at your head; were you knocked out?'

'No, I was pushed to the ground and my head hit the pavement, but it is more my pride injured than my head,' she said, rueful. 'It will clean up, I know, but will it need a stitch or two, do you think?' I studied the beautiful, smooth skin of her forehead, streaked with mud, noticing even in her state, that at her brow there were soft wispy strands of hair framing her face. I had never been so close to her before. I felt a rush of warmth as her lip curled at the edges as she spoke. I found myself thinking how beautiful she was and I had to shake myself to examine her injury with a professional eye.

'It is quite superficial I think; you were fortunate. It will clean up well, if we dress and bandage it. You will look like an old soldier, for a while at least!' I said, so relieved that she had not sustained more serious injuries. 'But what happened?' I asked, as I got some gauze from my bag and set about cleaning and dressing her wound.

'A ruffian tried to grab my bag from around my wrist, as I stepped from the carriage. It tugged at my arm and I fell backwards from the step. Hopkins saw the fellow off and I managed to hold onto my bag. But then his accomplice hit Hopkins over the head with something and he went down like a stone. He has not got up yet, is he injured?' she asked, leaning forward to look at him again. I turned to see the driver who was now lying on his side, groaning. While I was looking over towards him, James Bates appeared and he knew Miss Irvine, presumably from her previous visit.

'Miss Irvine, what 'as 'appened to you?' he said, his eyes full of concern.

'Mr Bates, I have met with a little trouble, shall we say?' she said, her voice shaky.

'The streets are not safe for an unaccompanied young lady,' I said, retrieving her shoe and placing it back on her slim, stockinged foot, a gesture that felt oddly intimate. I looked at James Bates. 'Perhaps Miss Irvine could rest with your sister while she composes herself and recovers?' I suggested in a low voice. 'Can you take her inside, while I help this fellow?' I said, gesturing at Hopkins. Mr Bates nodded and went to Miss Irvine's side.

'Miss Irvine, would you like some tea and to sit with me sister?' I heard him offer as I gathered my things.

'Thank you, Mr Bates. I confess I would be pleased to wait away from the street until I see whether Hopkins will be able to drive me home. I was on my way to see you both, to return that which I borrowed yesterday. I fear I nearly lost it for you just now but I could not allow that to happen, for I had given you my word I would return it,' she said, looking levelly at James. I helped her up and after pausing to steady herself, she thanked me, held her head high and then she and James walked across the road to number 19 and disappeared.

When Hopkins had come round, I was not confident he was fit to drive, so I paid the fellow who'd been holding the horses and I hailed a cab. When Hopkins was installed within, I knocked at the Bates lodging to escort Miss Irvine, Cassandra, to the cab. James Bates opened the door, and I went up. Emily Bates was holding her locket of silver metal and Miss Irvine was fastening a bracelet around her own wrist.

'How are you, Miss Irvine? I have hired a cab for I

do not think Hopkins should drive you home. Perhaps your father would send someone for the carriage? I have paid a man to mind it and I will send to ask the constable to keep an eye on it. Are you well enough to make the journey home?'

'Thank you; yes, Miss Bates here has looked after me well. I have been trying to interest her in training as a nurse. What do you think, Miss Bates?'

'Oh I dunno, Miss,' Emily looked pleased. 'I do a bit of sewin' to make a few pennies. I don't think me father would like me as a nurse. Mind, I am nearly of age and then I can decide for meself.' Emily certainly knew her own mind and if she was set on something, she would do it, I thought.

'Well, nurses will always be essential; they do good and important work. You should consider it, Miss Bates.' I turned to Miss Irvine. 'I will see you to the cab where Hopkins is waiting and you must both go straight home, for you have had a shock.' I caught myself thinking how I longed to go with her; to take her under my wing and look after her, protect her. But I had work to do, and it was not my place.

We went down and I helped her up the steps to her seat. As she settled opposite a now slumbering Hopkins, I could not resist asking, 'I hope you had a pleasant talk with Miss Bates?' A cloud passed across her bright eyes and she looked down at her hands in her lap.

'Yes…' she said softly and then she tore her eyes from her lap and looked at me, a disbelieving, puzzled look on her face. 'Do you know, the Bates family and I are related?'

'Related?' I stopped. 'How can that be?' But she glanced towards Hopkins, flushed and looked embarrassed.

'I am sorry, I have said too much; I am speaking out of turn,' she said, biting her lip.

I bit back my curiosity. 'If you need a willing ear, I am ever at your disposal.' As I bowed, I wondered if she knew their father was charged with murder, but I pushed the thought aside as I stepped back. She commanded the cab driver to drive on and I watched as the wheels cut through the street, the milky lime splashing up as the wheels turned and she was gone.

Late in the afternoon, I went for a walk to The Newcastle. I was exhausted from my week, bone weary and cheered only by having seen Miss Irvine earlier. I craved a refreshing pint of ale.

'It's quiet, Daisy,' I said as she pulled the pump, for there were only a couple of lads in the place. She looked troubled.

'Aye, it's not good for me business, this sickness, Doctor. When's it gonna let up, then?' She pulled a face and cast her auburn hair over her shoulder as she put my glass down.

'That, I'm afraid, I can't say, Daisy. But I am hopeful we are over the worst. It has been a terrible week for everyone.'

'I know, I shouldn't complain. Just 'ave to 'ope me and Jimmy don't get it,' she grimaced.

'Maybe your ale is good for you after all?' I said, half joking.

'Just you go and tell that to the folks 'round 'ere, will ya?' She jabbed a finger at me.

'Thank you, perhaps I will.' I took my drink and sat at the window. The beer was cool and strong and I felt it refresh my shattered limbs and deaden my tired mind. I sat back and rolled my head on my shoulders, easing my aching muscles and wondered how Cassandra was faring. Increasingly, she seemed to fill my thoughts. I looked out on Broad Street and saw the pump, handle-less. A few people approached unaware it was out of use and stood with consternation and indecision, taking in the news. James Bates crossed the street, pot in hand. In a trice, he was at the bar, getting porter to take home.

'James Bates,' I called.

''Allo Doctor, 'ow is Miss Irvine doing?' he said, as Daisy filled his pot.

'She is recovering at home.' I beckoned him over and lowered my voice. 'I wanted to say I have some news on your father's case.' He looked expectantly at me. 'You know the police told you Wiltshire was in the army years ago with another fellow from around here, Harrison? Harrison was murdered too, outside this very establishment, last week. They both knew your father's cousin, William, and another fellow, George Hartley.'

'I remember father talking of 'is cousin William but I never knew 'im; 'e died years ago.'

'Well, George Hartley has told the police it was rumoured at the time that Wiltshire was responsible for William Bates' death…'

'No… but that makes it look even *more* like Father did Wiltshire in,' James broke in, dismay in his eyes.

'Yes, but listen. Although William and the other two are dead, George Hartley is living in Bermondsey. I wondered if you wanted to go and visit him to see if he could tell us anything. I could come with you.'

'Yes, anythin' that could 'elp Father…'

'I have a bit of time on Monday; I am not quite so busy with the cholera now. Shall we say I'll meet you here at six?'

'Thank you, sir, I'll swap me shift; I'll find a way to be 'ere.'

'Until then.' He picked up his porter and left. Shortly after he'd gone, the door swung open again and Mr Eley came in, his head down, shoulders slumped.

'Afternoon, Mr Eley, sir,' said Daisy. 'What can I get ya now?' Mr Eley scanned the bottles behind the bar.

'I'll have a whisky, Daisy, please.' I saw Daisy raise her eyebrows as she turned away from him to pour it, but she said nothing.

'There you are, sir.' She put it on the bar, and he picked it up and toasted the air.

'To my dear mother,' he said, looking at Daisy, and then he downed it in one, wincing as the smoky amber liquid hit the back of his throat. He gave a little shake and put down the glass heavily. 'Another, please. She has gone. Caught the cholera and gone from this world, in an instant.'

'I'm sorry to 'ear that, sir,' said Daisy, pouring another measure. 'This cholera is a terrible thing, I was jus' sayin' to Dr Roberts there,' she motioned at me. 'She went to live in 'Ampstead didn't she?'

'She did. But now she is no more,' he said with an air

of finality. He downed his drink once more and stood, his head bowed, gripping the bar. He looked so dejected I went over to offer my condolences.

'Mr Eley, sir, I couldn't help but hear you and I am sorry for your loss. The cholera has spread like wildfire in Soho these past days. Is it rife in Hampstead too?'

'No, sir, she was unlucky, for it seems it has not reached that way yet, and my mother and her niece are the only two to have come down with it. I can't believe she is gone,' he slurred. 'Many of our workers too: we've lost twenty or so these past few days. That's twenty families with nothin' to eat, assuming they're not all dead too.' He slammed the bar with his fist. 'Damn it, man, why can't anyone do anything to stop it?' His red-rimmed eyes looked beseechingly at me, as if I knew.

'It is a terrible disease; nobody knows what causes it, so it is hard to know how to stop it.' I thought of John and his endeavours, but Mr Eley was not in the mood for theories. 'For what it's worth, I am hopeful that it is past the peak. I am seeing fewer people sick with it than a week ago.' My words sounded hollow.

'That, Doctor, is little consolation.' He spoke slowly and deliberately, his grief raw.

'Indeed, forgive me.' I felt chastened and hung my head.

'Don't worry, it isn't your fault, is it?' he checked himself. 'You've been worked off your feet, and you've done your best. I'd best get back now. Good day to you.'

I watched as he walked unsteadily down the street, and then I bought another drink and sat back at the table for a while longer, putting off the moment I would have to go home to my empty house. Unconsciously, my mind turned once more to Cassandra Irvine.

*

The next morning, the bell towers of London were ringing out the morning. I had woken early with the first peal. Unusually, though, I had drifted back to sleep and only awoke with the call to church from the nearest, St Luke's. The spire, with its great bell, was but a short distance from my house, and there had been many a Sunday morning when the sound had interrupted breakfast on my day of rest, but the week had caught up with me and I was more tired than I realised. When I finally came to it was after nine which was unheard of for me; I grimaced to think what Mrs Hook would say if she knew. I leapt up, as John was coming to breakfast with me.

After a brief toilette, I dressed and went downstairs just as John arrived at my door. I settled him in the parlour and went to make some tea and on my return, John already had his map and his notes spread before him. Still waking up, I took a mouthful of tea and smiled as I studied my friend, who had one hand at his ever-receding hairline as he examined his papers.

'I am pleased about the pump handle, but the Board of Guardians didn't believe me, did they?' he said, not looking up.

'Perhaps not,' I conceded, 'but they did what you wanted.' I helped myself to a bread roll, which he had picked up on his way.

'So, Frank, where are we? Are there fewer cases: is the epidemic in decline?'

'I can only tell you what I have seen,' I said, between mouthfuls of warm, moist bread, 'but, yes, I am hopeful that it is. I saw five cases yesterday; I saw ten times that number last Saturday. I met Dr Rogers of Berners Street yesterday and he said the same. Mind you, there are still a number of deaths. Take some bread, it's delicious,' I added. 'How I long for life to return to normal.'

'Later,' said John dismissively. 'I read that *The Times* is calling it the "blue death"!'

'The blue from the peripheral shutdown and cold extremities, I suppose; I have to say that many of the bodies I have seen do have a blue tinge to the skin.' Blue for solidity, reliability; not this blue, I thought, not the blue-grey of cyanosis and death.

'I feel the wording is a little overdramatic, nonetheless. Mind, the paper is also supporting rumours that the epidemic is linked to the old plague pit off Marlborough Street.'

'How is that implicated: it was two hundred years ago and a different disease?'

'They say that noxious substances from the plague bodies have found their way through the soil and up through the gulley vents of the new sewers that run through the area, causing the miasma to spread,' said John. 'You know my views on miasma, Frank.'

'I do. But it is as well to be informed about what the papers say and what the people are thinking, is it not?'

'I suppose so,' agreed John. 'But better to be well informed ourselves, I believe, so let us continue. I do not have this week's figures from Farr yet, but you have your records and I have spoken to the undertakers.' We got to work, adding the cases to our list. John added bars to his map, a black mark indicating where each death had occurred. When we had finished, we sat back and studied the map.

'I would say,' I said, looking at the map, now with scores of black bars on it, 'that a walk of less than three minutes would take you from the epicentre of the outbreak to an area free from cholera.' He was right; the deaths were definitely clustered around a point.

'Precisely; and the epicentre is... the Broad Street pump,' said John emphatically. 'The water of that pump is the cause of this outbreak: the evidence is in front of our eyes.' John reached into the wrapper and took a bread roll, breaking a bit off and rolling it in his fingers.

'I agree, it looks persuasive,' I said. 'Oh John, I must tell you,' I said, remembering with a jolt, 'I saw Mr Eley last night. His mother has died of cholera in Hampstead.'

'I didn't know there was cholera there, too?' said John absent-mindedly.

'That's it. He says there isn't, but do you know what? I met him in the street not long ago and each day he sent her a flask of the Broad Street pump water, as she liked it so much. Could that be the case you are looking for?' John froze, eyes staring at me, the hunk of bread halfway to his lips.

'That could be it, Frank! When did you see him?'

'Must be ten days ago now, before the epidemic started. I stopped to speak to some acquaintances at the pump and he was there.'

'I must go and question him at once; this is most important.' John's eyes were shining as he folded his map and was on his feet. 'Farewell, I will come to tell you what I find.' I finished the rolls myself.

Later, the doorbell rang and I opened it to find John in a state of excitement.

'Frank, Frank, I have seen Mr Eley; I caught him on his way back from church,' he said, striding into the hall uninvited with uncharacteristic bluster.

'And?' I said, excited myself, but doubly so when I saw the excitement which lit up John's normally serious countenance.

'It is as you say. Every day, the Eley brothers sent a flask of the pump water from Broad Street to their mother in Hampstead, as she liked the taste. They sent a flask as usual on Thursday 31st August and she was struck down with the cholera on 1st September. She died the next day, on the 2nd. Furthermore, her niece from Islington was staying and she, too, partook of the water and after returning to her home, she also succumbed to the cholera and died. Mrs Eley is the only case of cholera reported in Hampstead and her niece the only case in Islington! They are the cases we have been looking for: cases with a link to the Broad Street pump, but in all other respects different.' He threw his arms wide, his face alight.

'I am pleased. Perhaps you are right after all?'

'I know I am right, and this certainly strengthens the case.' John paused, the implication of my words sinking in; he looked at me quizzically, his arms slumping to his sides. 'You never really have believed me, have you?'

I chose my words carefully. 'I am a traditionalist, I agree. I do not challenge what I am taught. But I have always had faith enough to believe your work worthy of support. I confess I was sceptical at first. But I have never known such thorough and methodical research. You have left no stone unturned, no death unvisited. You *have* convinced me that your theory is correct. You *have* built a compelling case. I believe you now, sincerely I do.'

John was quiet for a moment, rubbing his chin before looking up at me. 'Well, you are indeed a true friend, Frank, to have supported me despite your scepticism. I thank you.'

SIXTEEN

Monday 11th September

A meeting with James Bates and two women learn of my address

I met James Bates in The Newcastle as arranged to take a cab to Bermondsey. He had told Emily what the police had said and they were worried to find their father more strongly implicated than before. Emily had wanted to visit Mr Hartley too, but I thought he might speak more plainly, man to man, so we left her in Soho.

We alighted from the cab in a run-down alley and found Peddlars Court. It was a lowly kind of place where the sun never penetrated; back-to-back hovels, rubbish piled high in the yard. A couple of mangy cats hissed at us as we entered the alleyway and there was a pile of excrement to one side. Three filthy barefoot children played with a hoop, their clothes rags. The oldest, a boy of eight or nine looked at us suspiciously and I was glad I'd left my bag at home. George Hartley had fallen on hard times.

I knocked on the door at the address I'd been given and after a minute a short, crippled fellow appeared. He was missing one leg below the knee and supported himself on a stick. His hair and eyebrows were bushy and unkempt.

'Yes?'

'Mr Hartley? We're here about an old friend of yours, William Bates.' The man's eyes were wary.

'My, my, I 'aven't 'eard that name for years and now you're the second lot askin' 'bout 'im in as many days,' he said. 'Old Batesy; that was a long time ago now.' His eyes glazed as he thought of years past. 'What is you fellows wantin' to know about 'im then?' James stepped forward.

''E was me father's cousin.' Mr Hartley looked closely at James, peering through his metal glasses.

'Aye, ya look like 'im, lad, same eyes. Ol' William always 'ad those brown eyes that looked to the 'eart of ya. Goodness, I 'ave not thought of 'im these past years. Come in, come in,' he said, stepping back to allow us in. 'Ain't nothin' special, 'fraid,' he said, as he led us up the poky stairs. 'Mind, there's a step missin'.' He took us up to the first floor, where he occupied a room at the front, overlooking the yard. It was dark and sparsely furnished but tidy, perhaps from his years in the army. Three thin mattresses lay on the floor in the corner, a thin blanket folded on each.

'Take lodgers,' he said, pointing to the bedding. 'So whatcha want ta know?' He had only two wooden chairs, so we stood in the middle of the room.

'Sir, me father, Albert, 'as been arrested for the murder of a fellow called Wiltshire and it seems the police 'ave linked Wiltshire to knowing William Bates back in his army days. We wondered if you could tell us what you knew about the pair of 'em?' Hartley stood in thought for a few moments and then whistled.

'All those years ago, it was; thought it was long dead and buried. And then the bobbies come and now you two.' He looked at James appraisingly, his eyes alive with interest. 'Well, I'll tell ya what I know, 'cause I liked old William, I did,' he said quietly. ''Ave a seat, both of ya.' He motioned to the chairs and we sat as he paced the room.

'Back then, the four of us, we were mates, we were: me, William, Wilty and Sammo, or Samuel 'Arrison as 'e was. It was 'ard in the army, ya 'ad to stick with your mates. Anyway one night, out in Jamaica, we was off duty and we went to the local town, looking for a bit of fun, a break from the drudgery, ya know? We ended up in a bar with some women. We were young lads, we 'ad to 'ave our fun, eh? I think they thought we 'ad a penny or two to spend and they wanted some of it. They came on to us, and what were we to think? We'd 'ad a few too many and it all seemed like a laugh. We went with 'em and thought we were in for a good time.' He stopped, his eyes on the ceiling, thinking back to those days. 'Anyway, suddenly there was a couple of men sayin' they want our money; the women were theirs and we could only 'ave 'em if we coughed up the lucre.'

'What did you do?' I said.

'Well, me and William, we 'adn't 'ad so much to drink as the other two; we thought we'd bail out and go 'ome. But Wilty and Sammo were right up for it by then. We tried to pull 'em off, but they took on the men, put 'em both down with a couple of right hooks, out for the count they were. And then they took the women. Three of 'em ran off but they caught one and Wilty 'ad 'is way with 'er. Me and Batesy tried to pull 'im off, but 'e was 'aving none of it. The poor woman was 'eld down by

Sammo and Wilty attacked 'er. She couldn't even walk outta there when 'e'd done with 'er. Then a little kid comes outta the shadows, only four or five she was, and she was cryin' over 'er mother. It was not right, what 'e did, not right.' He sighed, thinking back to the night. 'Anyway, before Sammo could 'ave a go, a gang of locals arrived with knives and it was all me and Batesy could do to drag the other two outta there and back to barracks without 'em killing us all.'

'Then what?'

'It was terrible,' he raised his eyebrows. 'Next day, Wilty and Sammo were braggin' about it and Batesy felt bad. Anyway, when the trouble kicked off, the army 'ad to do something. The sergeant asked who knew what 'ad 'appened and Batesy told me 'e was going to split on 'em. When it came to the court martial, Batesy told tale in return for being let off any blame. I got a slap on the wrist and the other two were kicked out. But that weren't the end of it. The night before they were packed off 'ome, Batesy was found drowned in the water tank for the 'orses behind the barracks. Word was Wilty 'ad bribed the guard and got out and done 'im in.'

'Was he charged with the murder?'

'No. No one could ever prove it. But word got about after 'e'd gone that that's what 'appened. I can believe it too, 'e 'ad a terrible temper when 'e was riled, 'e did. 'E got sent 'ome and I never saw 'im again.'

'Did the army take the rumours seriously? Did they inform the Bates family?' I said.

'I don't know. There was no proof and Wilty was already in disgrace wasn't 'e?'

'I am not sorry that 'e's dead,' said James. 'But it is bad 'e was found in our yard. Me father would never kill a man, no matter what.' James was quiet.

'Thank you for telling us the story, Mr Hartley,' I said.

'It's dragged up things from long ago, but it seems right, somehow, that old Wilty 'as met with an early end. 'E was a funny character; well brought up 'pparently, but 'e went bad. 'E'd spent time in the Foreign Legion with the Frenchies; that roughed 'im up, I reckon. 'E never was one to be trusted, if ya ask me.'

'We must go now,' I said, standing. James stood too, still quiet, his brown eyes worried. Mr Hartley grasped him by the hand.

''Tis good to meet a relative of old Batesy; 'e was a good fellow, 'e was.'

'And it is good to meet a friend of 'is, sir,' said James, looking into the man's face, as he returned the handshake.

We left and made our way back past the cats and the children, out of the court and back into the street. It was still searingly hot and the air close and malodorous and I felt a pang of pity for George Hartley. All those four young men, in the regiment in the prime of their youth, and now three of them were dead and the last one crippled and living in grey poverty in a godforsaken hovel. Would they have foreseen the future? I thought, not for the first time, that it was a blessing that we could not. It didn't help Albert Bates though. James was silent on the journey home.

★

On Friday I called early at the Institute for Gentlewomen, as Mrs Hobson had admitted herself again, after receiving news of her son's death in the Crimea. I had spent a difficult half-hour trying to convince her she had no physical ailment, but rather was suffering from the physical effects of grief, to no avail. I had extricated myself to hear her demanding of the nurse that Dr Berners be consulted for a second opinion.

I was about to leave when a door in the hallway opened and Miss Irvine appeared. She didn't notice me and I studied the fine hairs escaping her chignon at the nape of her neck as she turned to close the door.

'Miss Irvine, Cassandra, I thought you had ceased your employment here,' I said, and she spun around. Her face suffused with colour as she looked at me.

'Dr Roberts, good day to you. I left my instruments here, including my favourite bandage scissors,' she held up a bag, 'so as I was passing, I asked Hopkins to stop for a moment. Did you see him outside?'

'No, I have been here some time, with Mrs Hobson. She was here the day we first met, do you remember? But how is your wrist?'

'I do remember. It is much better, thank you. I am mending well. Hopkins is much recovered too. It was an unpleasant incident, indeed, but there is no lasting harm done.'

'I am glad of that; you were fortunate.'

'But you were in my thoughts, as Mama and Papa would like to meet you. Mama would like to thank you after you tended to me last week.'

'I would be delighted to meet them, Cassandra.' My

stomach felt full of butterflies at the thought of meeting her parents.

'Mama wishes to invite you to lunch the Saturday after next. Please say you will accept,' she looked at me, her soft eyes anxious.

'Of course I accept, thank you. Your family live in Grosvenor Square, you said? I confess I have never had cause to visit that part of town.'

'Yes, we live in an old house on the square, number 12 it is, if you remember.'

'I do. Thinking about it, I did know of a Lord Portman who lived in that area, I think. You mix with a fine class of people,' I joked. She blushed and looked down at her hands in her lap. 'What is it, what have I said?' I felt myself a clumsy oaf, sensing I had somehow upset her; I was little used to female conversation.

'Maybe I should tell you something of my family, Frank, before you meet them,' she said, uncertainly.

'Please tell me anything you wish, you know I will listen.' She pulled me to sit beside her on the bench in the hallway and looked into my eyes, hesitating, before speaking.

'My parents are Lord Sidney and Lady Rose Irvine. My father inherited the title and his place in the House of Lords from his father, on his death. He was a lawyer, but now he sits in the Lords when it is in session and tinkers with the law as a pastime. Our house is large, too large in fact for the four of us, but we have servants.' She blushed as she spoke, as if embarrassed to admit her wealth.

'Why do you fear to tell me?' I said, for although I

was surprised, it was hardly something to be ashamed of. Although even as I thought this, at some level, I felt my chances with her slipping away; we would be hopelessly incompatible in the eyes of her father. I was nobody. It started to sink in and she must have seen the look of dismay on my face. She took my hand, her glove soft against my skin.

'I fear you will think us unsuited, Frank,' she said, 'and although I have not known you long, I believe I would miss your company.' She blurted out this last phrase and looked down once more, her cheeks red with her boldness. I was silent as I digested her meaning, but eventually I found my voice, choosing my words carefully.

'*I* do not think us unsuited, Cassandra, but it may be that your parents would think me unworthy, for my background is very different from your own,' I said quietly, her words ringing in my ears. A nurse came down the stairway and Cassandra lowered her voice.

'I pray they will not think so. Tell me of your family, Frank.' I thought back to my childhood, with all its difficulties. How could I tell her? What would she think of me? But I could not lie, so I studied my hands in my lap for a moment, took a deep breath, looked up into her earnest face and began.

'My mother loved me very much. She and my father met at a dance in York, where we lived. He was a farmer of sorts; he worked land on the edge of York, not far from where we lived and sold his produce at market. It was on a small scale, but he made enough to live on. He rented a tiny house and when they married she moved in, and my older brother, William, came along. My mother had four more children, all of whom died as babies. She must have spent years carrying a child or mourning one.' I thought of my mother and her warm embrace so long ago now and I felt a sudden emptiness. 'Then when she was carrying me, my father was killed in an accident. He'd hitched a ride to a neighbouring town for market day with a friend and the cart turned over on the way home, killing him outright. I was born a month later and named for the father I never saw. So it was the three of us: Mother, William and me.'

'How did your mother manage?' said Cassandra, her blue eyes intent on me.

'It was hard. Mother did what she could, but we relied on the charity of our neighbours and Mother's sister, my Aunt Maria.' I couldn't help a shudder at her name, but Cassandra said nothing. 'My aunt had married well you see, and her husband had a sizeable fortune. Out of religious duty, she helped my mother with handouts. But she was a hard woman and she never liked William and me. I used to dread her visits, when we'd have to wash our faces and be polite or see our mother suffer her disapproval. But we got by and Mother was a loving soul, devoted to us boys.'

'What happened next?'

'We managed until 1832, when I was nine. The cholera came to York, from the ports of the north-east, they said, on ships from the continent. I got it and Mother nursed me and somehow I recovered. But no sooner was I better than William was struck with it; he died within a day of falling ill. The next day,

Mother died too. I was left alone.' I stared at the fern by the newel post; a luxuriant jungle green. It came back to me; my loneliness, the desolation of everyone I loved being gone. I looked up at her and continued. 'Nearly everyone on our street died and I didn't know who to turn to. I stayed at home for a few days, but then I had to venture out, looking for food. I managed for a few more days, stealing and begging, going home to sleep at night in the silent house. One morning, my aunt came and took me away. I never saw the house again.'

'So you went to live with her?' said Cassandra.

'Yes. She'd heard my mother had died and I had nothing to eat, no one to look after me.' I could feel a lump in my throat. 'I didn't want to go but I had no choice. Aunt Maria had no love for me, but she felt a duty to care for her dead sister's child. I moved away, outside York and I was fed and clothed, at least. It was a handsome house, large and well furnished. I had a tutor at home, I was not allowed to mix with the local boys and it was a solitary existence. I would dream my mother was alive but I would wake to find myself in Aunt's cold, uncaring house each morning.'

'When did you leave?'

'My friend John Snow, who's ten years older than me, was my saviour. He had been friends with William since childhood and they were inseparable. His uncle had arranged for him to train as an apothecary-surgeon in Newcastle and he, in turn, arranged it for me. He had sent me letters and come to visit me a few times while I was at my aunt's and I looked forward to his visits more than anything. He was kind and I remembered him so clearly from my childhood, sitting with William as I climbed trees or the two of them taking me for a dip in the river. I had many happy memories of my former life and he reminded me of them.'

'So you went to Newcastle and then came to London?'

'Yes, I went when I was fourteen and when I'd done my five years, I followed John to London to finish my surgeon's training. John has always looked out for me.' I was silent. 'So, after all I've told you, your father may not think me suitable company for you,' I smiled sadly, feeling quite wrung out to have related the story. She pressed my hand gently.

'You are a respected doctor; you keep your own house. You have much to be proud of and all the more so considering your unfortunate childhood,' her voice tailed off.

'Aunt Maria left me her estate when she died, for she had no children of her own. So, in a material sense, I am comfortably situated. I choose to work in Soho for I have great admiration for those who live in poverty and make a life for themselves despite the obstacles before them. I have advanced in life through the good fortune of connections and I try to repay that good fortune by doing my bit to help others.'

'But your patients from Soho do not come to this hospital, surely?'

'No. My aunt recommended me to some of her acquaintances who moved to London and so I have some patients who can afford to pay for my services. She provided me with a legacy in more ways than one. I must be grateful to her, but in truth, I feel little gratitude. She was a very different woman from her sister.' I thought back to Cassandra's words. 'You said your house is too large for four, but if I remember, your brother is soon leaving for the Crimea?'

'Yes, Edmund, who is four years older than me, is shortly off East to join our forces. We have rather rattled around in the house since Jane died, and with Edmund gone it will be even quieter.' The conversation had strayed into gloomy territory and I tried to lighten it.

'I would be delighted to meet your parents and I promise to be on my best behaviour!'

'I think, I hope, that you will like them.'

'And I hope that they will like me. Send word of the time I am to present myself to 25 Great Pulteney Street and I shall attend with pleasure.'

We stood and left the building and I escorted her to her carriage. As Hopkins drove her away, my false gaiety disappeared. Lord and Lady Irvine; Cassandra Irvine hailed from the aristocracy. How could I possibly hope to win her hand?

That afternoon, as I walked down Broad Street on the way to Edward Street, I noticed the door to the Bates lodging open and a bowler-hatted man appeared. His face was glowering, suffused with red and he wiped his right knuckles up and down on his waistcoat. Then he pulled a red handkerchief from his pocket, wiped his brow and was gone, looking back once over his shoulder. I thought little of it; perhaps it was another resident of the building, although I had not seen him around before.

Later, I strolled home in the early evening down New Street, past the great Lion's Brewery. Emily Bates stepped from the entrance, head down, and turned towards Broad Street, nearly bumping into me. She ploughed on, oblivious to my presence.

'Emily? Miss Bates?' She half turned towards me.

'Sorry, Doctor, can't stop,' she mumbled, adjusting a shawl around her neck to cover her jawline and walking on. Something in her hunched demeanour concerned me and I caught up with her.

'Emily? Stop a moment; are you all right?' She kept walking, eyes down and I put my hand on her arm.

'Geroff of me!' she snarled in a low, warning voice I had never heard before.

'Emily, stop, what is the matter? Can I help you?' I insisted, planting myself firmly in her path. Eventually she stopped and looked me in the face. Her pretty face was spoiled by a large swollen bruise which extended over her left cheek and jaw. Her lip was cut and I saw she had dried blood at the corner of her mouth.

'No, you can't help me, right? Leave us alone; we're on our own, me and James, on our own.' Then her fierce eyes softened and she looked down, tears welling.

'Emily, who has done this to you?' I said gently, looking at her spirited young face and feeling such pity.

'Landlord sent his 'eavy round, didn't 'e? 'Aven't paid the rent this week, 'ave we? I've fallen behind on the sewin' so I've lost me job. Poor James is doing 'is best, but it ain't enough, see?' She looked at me, her

199

expression bleak. 'Thank the good Lord I'd taken me mother's locket off or 'e'd 'ave 'ad it.' I thought back to the man I'd seen emerging from their building earlier. The brute. At last I found my voice.

'I see. Let me clean up your face at least? And where is James?'

'I'm all right. I've just seen James in there,' she motioned back towards the brewery. 'Went to tell 'im 'e's gotta ask for his wages early; the feller's coming back tomorrow and then we're out. I'm gonna see Becky, see if she can borrow us any; though I don't see 'ow 'cause all 'er family 'ave died of the cholera now too, 'cept Jo.'

'Can I give you the money?' I fumbled in my pocket. 'How much do you owe?' She hesitated, battling with herself before her usual spirited air returned and she shook her head.

'No, we gotta sort it out ourselves; ain't no one can 'elp. It'll be all right, James'll fix it, you'll see. But thank you.' I could see her pride and resolve returning and I didn't push it.

'Well, if he can't, be sure to come and see me at 25 Great Pulteney Street.'

'Thank you, Doctor.' She repositioned the shawl around her face and was off. I stood looking after her, feeling such pity for the Bates family. It was a hard life, being poor.

PART III

SEVENTEEN

Saturday 23rd September

I meet Lord and Lady Irvine

Nearly two weeks had elapsed and the cholera was finally in abeyance. There were still a few new cases, but the peak had passed and the hearses carried fewer coffins. Life was starting to get back to normal. People who had fled the epidemic were starting to return and, although not back to the pre-epidemic level, the streets were once again starting to buzz with trade and gossip. Life seemed more colourful once more. The huge mound of rubbish outside The Newcastle had been cleared and the stench on the streets had lessened. The black clouds which had threatened to bring me low had passed, blown out of my sky by Cassandra Irvine. The dark dog was tamed.

I had come across James Bates from time to time and there was no more news on his father's case; the next Court of Sessions was not for another two weeks. James was working double shifts to pay their way and Emily had recovered and had got a bit of work for the bonnet maker on Silver Street. John continued to follow up the deaths from cholera; I knew he would not rest until he had convinced the Board of Health and the profession that his theory was right. For my own part, I was heartily relieved the epidemic seemed to be over. The last death

I had seen, sadly, was Constable Lewis, a few days ago. He'd battled it for ten days and I thought he'd pull through but he, too, had succumbed.

Importantly, to me personally at least, I was invited to luncheon to meet Cassandra Irvine's parents. The people of Soho could do without me for an afternoon. I felt nervous and excited in equal measure. I selected my best frock coat and striped grey breeches, my good silk waistcoat and a modest necktie which I hoped would give the impression of a sincere and responsible gentleman. Would I be good enough? Since my talk with Cassandra, my qualms about being introduced to them had increased tenfold. I could not bear to think what would happen if they did not approve of me; I so desperately wanted to impress them. I called at the barbers early for a proper shave and trim.

Eventually, it was time and I hailed a cab in Silver Street which took me to the address in Mayfair, where I alighted at one o'clock. Cassandra's friend, Mabel Foster, and her fiancé, Dr Edward Summers, were also invited. I had not met them before, but I was comforted that I would at least have something to discuss with a fellow medical man. After a late luncheon, the six of us were making up a party to go to *The Magic Flute* at the Opera House that evening. At least for that part, I would be on firm ground.

It was another bright, sunny bronze autumn day as I stepped from the cab and stood on the pavement in the leafy square, gazing up at the house. I had never seen a house like it. It was one of a row of similar houses: a huge, white marbled structure, with ornate railings and steps up to a magnificent black front door. The house had four storeys and on every level plants grew in boxes on the wide windowsills. The street on this side of the square was broad, with oak and elm trees bordering the road, their leaves a patchwork of yellow and rich orange. A magical looking garden formed the centre of the square: enclosed by railings, with huge trees shedding autumnal leaves onto the grass, and two iron benches, one on each side. It was like another world. It all fell into place: Cassandra's quiet self-assurance, how she held her head high, despite her disfigurement. She was no ordinary nurse, she was a Lady.

I took a deep breath and knocked at the polished brass door-knocker, shaped like a lion's head. Almost immediately a smart footman opened it and I was shown into a large marble hall, with ornate mirrors to each side and striking black and white tiles on the floor. A huge chandelier hung from the high ceiling and there was an air of calm luxury such as I had never experienced. My stomach churned.

'Dr Frank Roberts, for Lord and Lady Irvine,' I said awkwardly.

'This way, sir; his Lordship will be a moment.'

I was shown into the drawing room and the door closed behind me. I looked around, taking in the surroundings. It was a very grand room, with two deep gold-coloured sofas on either side of the marble fireplace, and thick luxurious red and gold curtains that reached the floor at the long windows. Red, gold: the colours of wealth. The floor was carpeted in a deep red pattern with a Persian rug at the hearth and another elaborate chandelier hung from the high ceiling. A grand piano filled one end of the room, with an enormous pot plant in a brass urn next to it. The scent of a large bowl of roses filled the room.

After a moment, the door opened again and a middle-aged couple came in, accompanied by Cassandra. Lady Irvine was tall and elegant in a fine lace-collared violet gown which rustled as she walked. She looked very much like Cassandra, sharing her soft blue eyes and delicate features. Her veined hand rested on her husband's arm. Lord Irvine was shorter and walked with a slight stoop, his hair greying and his eyebrows bushy. A heavy silver chain hung from the watch in his pocket, the links disappearing beneath the folds of his coat into his waistcoat. A trim grey beard framed his jawline. They came over and Lady Irvine took my hands in hers, looking at me intently.

'Dr Roberts, you are very welcome. I am delighted to meet you and I must thank you for caring for my daughter recently.'

'You are very kind, your Ladyship, it was a pleasure to be of service,' I bowed. Lord Irvine shook me firmly by the hand.

'Dr Roberts, Cassandra has told me much about you and it is good to meet you. Apart from saving my daughter, you have been working on the cholera, I hear?'

'Yes, sir, I have. It has been a terrible few weeks, but happily, the epidemic seems to be over now.'

'Yes, I can't stand all this medical business, I must say. Give me a statute book or a piece of case law any day. Far less messy, I say.'

'You are a lawyer, sir?' My mind flashed to the Bates case and I thought how Albert Bates could never afford defence counsel; the law was heavily weighted against the defence and even more so against a poor defendant.

'Indeed, indeed, called to the Bar, I was, although I do not practise much now. I prefer to pontificate with my esteemed friends and the honourable gentlemen in the House these days. The House of Lords, you understand.' His old eyes twinkled up at me in self-mockery from under his fine eyebrows. 'But what of the cholera, sir?'

'Papa, Dr Roberts perhaps does not wish to discuss medicine on his day of rest, do you Frank?' Cassandra interrupted, smiling at me. I was saved from answering by the door opening and two further guests were announced.

'Miss Mabel Foster and Dr Edward Summers,' announced the footman.

'Mabel, Edward,' enthused Cassandra, giving her friend a kiss on the cheek and offering her hand to the gentleman. 'Papa, Mama, you know Miss Foster is soon to be Mrs Summers?' she smiled fondly at her friend. 'Dr Roberts, let me introduce you: Mabel Foster and Dr Edward Summers.'

The introductions were made and the butler arrived to announce that luncheon was served and we made our way to the dining room. It was another fine room, with deep green walls and plum silk curtains. A large sideboard of dark wood displayed family portraits in silver frames and a long oval table of the same dark wood, mahogany I think, took pride of place in the centre of the room. The table was set with silver cutlery and an alarming array of glasses and in the centre stood a silver salver on which was arranged a collection of exotic fruit. A pineapple, some pomegranates, lychees: yellows, oranges, browns and purples, tactile and three-dimensional. I was seated between Lady Irvine and Mabel; Mabel, a pretty girl with dark auburn curls and grey-green eyes, could perhaps tell I was nervous, as she was attentive.

'I have heard much about you this past fortnight, Dr Roberts. You have made quite an impression on my friend,' she murmured, glancing down the table to the other end, where Cassandra was laughing at some story Edward Summers was telling. Her lip rucked as she laughed, making her whole face look uneven, but I saw only the sparkling blueness of her eyes, and the delicate blush on her cheeks as she laughed. I smiled at her briefly, before she bowed her head to her plate. My heart beat faster at the knowledge that Cassandra had spoken of me to her friend.

'I feel I have known her for so long, yet it has been but a short time. You have known her all your life, I understand?' I said, as Lady Irvine spoke to Edward Summers on her left.

'Yes, our parents are old friends and we played together as children. Papa is in the Lords with Lord Irvine,' said Mabel.

'Goodness, I am in esteemed company; I had no idea when I met Cassandra in Harley Street that she was so well connected. I fear I cannot match her expectations.'

'I believe you should leave her to be the judge of that,' said Mabel smoothly, 'and,' she murmured, leaning in slightly towards me, 'she is not all she seems; life has been difficult, you know.' Lady Irvine interrupted our conversation and we turned to other matters. We lunched on pheasant and potatoes, with creamed carrots and green beans, followed by an exquisite syllabub with candied gooseberries. Fine wine was served in fine cut glasses and the luncheon passed very merrily.

Later we travelled to the Opera House in two carriages. I had always loved Mozart, and I realised how I had missed my musical evenings these past weeks. It seemed appropriate also that the hero and heroine must face trials together, protected by the magic flute. Perhaps a magic flute had been protecting me from the cholera during these past weeks? Not that I could call myself a hero.

As the last note rang out, the crowd rose to tumultuous applause. I looked at Cassandra, who was on her feet, her eyes shining, applauding the performers. I thought back to Mabel's comment and thought again that her disfigurement, perhaps, had not been easy to bear. But I was bewitched by her; her clear countenance, her intelligent eyes, her calm, self-assured manner, her vulnerability. I clapped rapturously and I couldn't remember a day when I had enjoyed myself so much. The music, the atmosphere and the delightful company of this enchanting woman were intoxicating. I felt alive, I felt energised; I was in love. Yes, I loved her. I had never experienced the feeling before, but I knew at that moment that I loved Cassandra Irvine, and all was well with the world; reds, purples and golds, stars and light filled my breast and my heart brimmed with happiness.

'You know, Frank, I hope to be able to tell you soon,' she said cryptically, as we made our way to the carriages, her clear eyes looking up at me.

'Tell me what, Cassandra?'

'How I am related to Emily Bates,' she murmured.

'How could you be related to her family? They seem like good people, but surely from another world to your own class,' I said, watching her mouth as she spoke, the little ruck of her scar catching as she formulated the words and twisting her lip slightly. I found her captivating; I couldn't stop looking at her. Cassandra continued and I wondered if she was aware of my pleasurable thoughts.

'It is a long story, which I cannot tell until Mama has given me permission to do so. It has been a strange few weeks,' she said, troubled, looking down at her hands thoughtfully and placing one gloved hand over the other, falling silent.

'It has, indeed, been a strange few weeks. If you wish and when you are ready to tell me, I am interested to hear how you could possibly be related to the Bates family. In the meantime, I have very much enjoyed this evening,' I said. Lord and Lady Irvine joined us and I gave Cassandra my hand as she stepped up into the carriage.

'I have also very much enjoyed the evening, Dr Roberts, I thank you for coming,' she smiled back at me.

'Lord Irvine, I must thank you for a splendid luncheon and such a fine evening,' I said, shaking him by the hand. He looked into my face and I would have given my arm to know what he was thinking of me. I turned to his wife. 'Lady Irvine, it has been such a pleasure to meet you; I thank you,' I bowed.

'It has been a pleasure to meet you, Dr Roberts. I hope we shall meet again soon,' she said lightly, as she stepped into the carriage. 'Farewell.' Lord Irvine followed her, the door was shut and as I watched the carriage leave, I could still feel the touch of Cassandra's glove on my hand. I hailed a cab, feeling suddenly alone as the yellowy-orange gas lamps illuminated the streets of London as I journeyed home.

EIGHTEEN

Monday 25th September

The question of the sewers

As I made my way up Great Pulteney Street on my way to the Westminster, I saw the inspectors from the Board of Health on the other side of the road. Their top hats and surtouts made them stand out on the streets of Soho. I had seen them from time to time over the past three weeks, as they went about their business, collecting information from every residence, in accordance with Sir Benjamin Hall's instructions. It was doubtless not their remit to draw conclusions, but they must have developed an impression: their own views about the cause of the epidemic. They had worked hard to gain an intimate knowledge of the people of Soho; they had been more meticulous, even, than John Snow. I crossed the road to speak to them.

'Good day, gentlemen; Mr Fraser. I am Dr Frank Roberts; you may remember we spoke on the first day of your investigation? I wonder how it is progressing? For my part, it has been the hardest few weeks of my working life. I have never seen such a rapid and fatal spread of disease through a community. Have you formulated any ideas about the cause from your work?'

'Good morning, Doctor. We have all but completed

our investigation, I am happy to report,' replied Mr Fraser.

'What have you found?'

'We are not at liberty to divulge the findings until they have been examined by the Board of Health,' he said, with an air of self-importance, but I was not to be put off.

'Of course; I only thought that you, of all people, as the head of this vital work, must have developed your own opinion? Who could know the streets of Soho better than you, sir?' I flattered. Mr Fraser drew himself up and gave a self-congratulatory nod. 'Have you visited every residence, sir?' Mr Fraser softened and took my arm, speaking in low tones.

'Doctor, between you and me, I can tell you that we have visited eight hundred houses,' he said. I feigned looking impressed and, in reality, I *was* impressed.

'That is a huge enquiry, sir.'

'Indeed, indeed. Well, we had a schedule and we stuck to it. We took our questionnaires and we gathered the information. We found a terrifying number of odours in all locations affected by the cholera.'

'Odours from the sewers, sir? Or from the cesspits? You find odours are the cause?'

'Personally, I believe the gullies for the ventilation and escape of noxious gases from the sewers are to blame. These noxious exhalations have been made worse by the stagnant atmosphere due to the heat of the summer, and therein lies the cause,' he finished.

'I see,' I said, hoping Mr Fraser would elaborate further.

'We have noted, you see, that many of the houses

213

closest to the gulley holes have been the most severely hit by the cholera, whereas the *corner* houses, being in the best ventilated positions, have often escaped,' he declared. I thought of John and his records over months and years working in epidemics; I wondered what he would make of it. Although the work had collected a huge volume of information, this conclusion reflected a vague notion after three weeks' work by someone with no prior knowledge of cholera. Furthermore, it was surely predicated on a miasmatist viewpoint, rather than an objective study of the findings. These men had not questioned the view that miasma was to blame, they had merely deduced what they thought was the source of the miasma. Perhaps Hall's team at the board would be more open-minded in their analysis, but I doubted it.

'I have seen many cases on Broad Street; is there any suggestion as to why there have been so many afflicted there? The pump, for example; have you considered whether that is a factor?' I said.

'Yes, we have gathered information about the water supply as part of our survey. After the handle of the pump on Broad Street was removed, a surveyor investigated whether there was leakage from the sewer which could have infiltrated the water. He inspected the brick lining of the well, which appears intact, and Mr York the engineer informs us that the sewer there runs a good distance away from the pump well, lying ten feet away, and twenty feet underground.' He stabbed the end of his cane in the dirt of the street and drew a line sideways and then another line twice the length in a downwards direction to indicate his point. 'Anyway, we have found a great number of cases who do not use that pump; I am confident it is not the cause. It is the sewers and the odours escaping the gulley holes, you mark my words,' finished Mr Fraser, scrubbing out the diagram with his cane.

'Well, it is most interesting to hear of your work,' I said. Mr Fraser looked suddenly uncomfortable, fingering his beard and looking shiftily into my face.

'Perhaps you will keep our talk confidential, Doctor? Until the official report comes out; I would not like to speak out of turn, you know.'

'Of course, sir, I was merely interested; of course I will await the final report from the Board of Health. But it is good to hear it from the horse's mouth, as they say,' I said, and Mr Fraser looked gratified.

'Good day to you, Doctor,' said Mr Fraser, and the men continued up the street. I stared after them. What would John say? I would have to tell him what the surveyors had found at the pump well. It was strange if there was no breach in the well lining, through which contamination could have entered the pump water. No doubt John would dismiss the finding as incorrect. There was also an investigation under way by the new Commission of Sewers; they would doubtless refute any implication that the sewers were the cause. John continued to face an uphill struggle: he had won the battle over the pump handle, but the war was far from over.

As I walked homewards after a day spent with Mr Williamson, my attention was caught by the headline of *The Standard* at the paper seller on Silver Street: "Drowned in cesspit: Body in Broad Street, local man charged". I bought a copy and read as I walked. "The coroner has released the body of a man who drowned in a cesspit in Broad Street. It is understood that the body was discovered some time ago, but with the recent scourge of cholera which has swept Soho, details have only now emerged. The victim, understood to be one Matthew Wiltshire, was in his late middle age and had suffered blunt injuries before drowning in the pit. A resident of the building, Albert Bates, 38 years, has been charged with murder and, if indicted by the Court of Sessions, will stand trial at the Old Bailey in the coming weeks". I thought of young James Bates and his sister and wondered what would become of them if their father was tried, found guilty and hanged.

I turned my thoughts to more pleasurable ones. I was taking Cassandra out this evening, with her friends, Mabel and Edward, to a concert of chamber music at the Royal Academy in Hanover Square. Lord Irvine had offered the services of Hopkins for the evening, and I was to call for her at six-thirty. It had been a remarkable few weeks, in every way. The cholera was unprecedented, but from a professional point of view, I had managed to rise above my fears to help my patients and I had staved off the melancholia that often followed exhaustion and fatigue. In a strange way, I felt the deaths of my mother and brother would finally be avenged and I could lay my terrors to rest, if I was able to help John in his work to defeat the cholera. On a personal note, for the first time, I was in love. Indeed, I could not believe how I had grown to love Cassandra Irvine in such a short space of time. Even thinking her name sent the blood rushing to my head. I could not believe my luck.

But I checked myself. The people of Soho had experienced the worst few weeks in living memory; many families were decimated or gone forever and the medical profession had been able to do little to help. The Bates family had suffered and remained in a desperate situation. The lad, Jonny Harrison, in Poland Street was left alone, as were the many other children orphaned as I was by the cholera. I shared John's frustration at the lack of consensus about how the cholera was transmitted, at the lack of effective treatment, at our inability to do anything much apart from give empty advice. The Board of Guardians had removed the pump handle, but no one really believed his theory. Everyone, from the Board of Health down to the man on the street, still believed the miasma was the cause. I sighed: there was a long way to go. I had to consciously put the thought to one side and think instead about the coming evening.

*

The next morning, I woke and stretched in bed. My mind immediately filled with memories of the previous night; what a wonderful evening it had been. I thought of Cassandra at my side, beautiful in a sage-green gown which displayed her figure most pleasingly. At the concert, in the carriage afterwards; how right it had felt. How I longed to take her sweet face in my hands and kiss those beautiful lips, her beautiful lip. Had anyone kissed her lip before? I no longer even noticed it when I looked at her. All I saw was her strength, her inner beauty; I already longed to see her again. My pleasant reverie was broken by a knock at the door. I must send for Mrs Hook, the epidemic was over. Until then, though, I must push thoughts of Cassandra from my mind, get up and go to see who wanted me at this hour. I donned my gown and went down to open the door; I breathed a sigh of relief that it was John Snow.

'Good morning, Frank,' he said lustily, as if he had already been up for hours. 'Cooper, the sewers man, is presenting the findings of his investigation this morning; we must go and hear what he has to say,' announced John, breezing past me into the hallway.

'Good morning to you, too, John,' I said, standing in his wake running my hand through my dishevelled hair, vaguely irritated today at my friend's single-mindedness. Did he never stop thinking about cholera? For myself, I was sick of it. 'And who is Cooper?'

'Edmund Cooper, the chief engineer for the Commission of Sewers. He works with that Bazalgette fellow who wrote to the papers this week refuting that the sewers are to blame for the cholera. There's a meeting in Greek Street this morning to report on his findings.'

'I didn't know the commission had completed their investigation, too.'

'Yes; that's three so far: the Board of Health, the Commission of Sewers and our work. No doubt they will blame the miasma,' said John, with a hint of a smile.

'Let me get dressed and I will tell you that I met Mr

Fraser from the Board of Health enquiry yesterday. I will tell you what they have found,' I said, taking a deep breath to calm myself and retreating up the stairs to dress.

'Don't tell me,' John called after me; 'their findings corroborate the theory of one Dr John Snow: the water from the Broad Street pump is the cause of the epidemic?'

'Not exactly,' I called down the stairs. 'They say there's nothing wrong with the pump. It's the miasma from the sewers.'

'Now why does that not surprise me?' muttered John, and I had to smile at his usual understatement.

John and I went to the offices of the Commission of Sewers in Greek Street. A small gathering of people had come to hear the findings of the report, mostly general practitioners like myself, or members of the Board of Guardians committee. I recognised Mr Wilson, the chairman of the meeting at which John had persuaded the committee to remove the pump handle. For most of the populace, the meeting was an irrelevance: either they knew nothing of it or they had little interest in it. The cholera seemed to have gone, and even if it hadn't, the people themselves could do little about the water and drainage, sewage and ventilation. They were at the mercy of the authorities on such matters.

The chairman, Mr Jebb, sat at a large desk in front of three rows of chairs, squashed into a small room. We took our seats, two of less than a dozen in the audience. Mr Jebb called upon the chief engineer for the Commission of Sewers to present his findings. Edmund Cooper stood up; an insignificant looking man in a brown jacket, with a small moustache and a severe centre-parting in his brown hair. Everything here felt brown, somehow: the desk, the chairs, the walls, the officials. Cooper shuffled his papers before placing them on the table and looking at the audience.

'Gentlemen, thank you. I would like to outline the work I have conducted and to summarise the relationship of the metropolitan sewers to the recent cholera outbreak in this district. In so doing, I shall draw conclusions about the cause of that terrible epidemic, the worst visited on London in living memory,' he announced. He then proceeded to relate in some detail, the extent of the sewers in Soho, their vintage and condition, his investigations into the proximity of cholera cases to the sewers and to their ventilation gullies, and the relation of the old plague pit to the sewers. He spoke for twenty minutes or so and I watched as John listened. At the end of his talk, Mr Cooper unveiled a map of the area covered on an easel behind him, on which he had drawn the locations of the sewers and the houses where there were cholera cases or deaths. He pointed with his cane at the map as he reported that the houses nearest the sewer gully holes had no greater numbers of deaths than did those further away. Very few deaths had occurred near the old plague pit and the sewers from that region drained northwards to Regent Street, where there were also few, if any, cases. The sewers were not to blame.

'In conclusion, gentlemen, I find that the cause of

the recent outbreak is the miasma pertaining in areas in which there are poorly maintained drains and cesspools and a lack of linkage to the sewer system. The miasma stems from local drainage arrangements in the areas affected, the sewer system in those areas being in good condition and therefore, not the cause of the epidemic.' He sat down and Mr Jebb stood to take the floor.

'Thank you, Mr Cooper. You have conducted thorough and important work, and the commission is indebted to you.' He turned to the floor. 'Are there any questions?' John Snow was on his feet.

'Has the commission noted the high number of cases and deaths on Broad Street?' he asked. Mr Cooper was up again.

'Yes, sir, we have noted that Broad Street has been severely affected. Broad Street is served by two non-connecting sewers, one of recent vintage and one which is, admittedly, rather old, but the numbers of deaths are equally divided between the portions of the street served by the two different sewers. I therefore reiterate the conclusion that it is not the sewers, but rather the poor state of local drains and cesspits and their lack of linkage to the sewer system in many places, which gives rise to the miasma which is, in turn, the cause of the cholera.'

'Has the commission considered that the epidemic may be caused by an agent not related to the miasma? In the water, for example?' said John. Mr Jebb interjected before Cooper could speak.

'Sir, it is well known that the cholera is in the miasma,' he said patiently, as if explaining to a child the irrelevance of such a suggestion. 'The important question before us is "where does the miasma originate?" Mr Cooper's excellent work shows beyond all reasonable doubt that it does not arise from the sewers.'

'I would contest that view,' said John, sitting down. I knew what he was thinking: the commission had made up its mind before it started that the sewers were not to blame. It wasn't an open enquiry, merely an exercise in self-exoneration. The miasmatist view was so entrenched that people spent their time considering where the miasma originated, instead of considering that it might not be the miasma at all. I could only commiserate as we left.

'It is what we expected, John,' I said, quietly.

'Indeed it is, Frank. It is frustrating once more, for the evidence was there before them, on the map: the concentration of deaths around the corner of Broad Street and Cambridge Street – the precise location of the pump.'

We walked up Greek Street, through Soho Square and across Dean Street back to Mrs Bootle's coffee house. The days were finally turning cooler and a warm blast of the rich and delicious aroma of good coffee and hot food met us as we went in. The place was alive with people, a riot of colour, and Mrs Bootle was in fine form, much relieved her custom had returned. We took a booth at the back and ordered coffee.

'Well, John, it seems the outbreak is over. I have seen no new cases these past three days and not a coffin on the streets this week.'

'That is good news. But I am afraid I have not

succeeded; the waterborne theory is not believed,' said John. 'You heard the commission this morning, you heard the Board of Health inspectors: the popular view has not changed. I have not convinced them,' he said.

'You convinced them to remove the pump handle, didn't you?'

'Yes, but they say no defect was found in the well lining. I do not believe it; I am still convinced the pump was the source. Our map clearly shows that the closer people lived to the pump, the more people contracted the cholera. Then there is the evidence of Mrs Eley and her niece, who both contracted cholera in an area free of the disease, after drinking water from the Broad Street pump. The workers at the Lion's Brewery did not drink from the pump, and they were unaffected. The workhouse is close to Broad Street, but hardly any were stricken. I am convinced it all points to the Broad Street pump as the cause.'

'You build a good case, my friend. But if the outbreak is over, does it matter?'

John looked at me with a shocked, wounded look in his eyes. 'Frank, of course it matters. It matters profoundly: to prevent the next outbreak, the one after that and the one after that. If people continue to believe in the miasma theory, there will be no action to improve or regulate the water supply. There will be no action to improve drainage of sewage and waste. If there is no recognition that the cholera is waterborne, there will continue to be epidemics and people will continue to die,' he said, reaching across the table to grip my forearms. His grey eyes bored into mine, willing me to understand. 'Do you not see?' his voice tailed off and he released me and looked away.

'I know you are right; but if the pump well had shown some defect, or if we knew how it had become infected, it would make a more cogent argument. We still do not know who the index case was.'

'I know; I know. But I hear there is to be another enquiry, by the Vestry Committee at St Luke's. The Board of Guardians of the parish has sanctioned it. Perhaps *they* will corroborate my view,' said John. 'Never have there been so many investigations; I sincerely hope all these deaths are not in vain. For my part, I do not need further investigations. I have made a compelling case. I plan to publish the findings of my work south of the river, and our work here in Soho. Perhaps when it is in print, people will finally believe it.'

Mrs Bootle brought the coffee and we turned to other matters.

'How is your Nurse Irvine, Frank?' asked John.

'She is not "my" Nurse Irvine, John,' I blushed. 'But I confess I look forward to seeing her again. We went to a concert of chamber music last night at the Royal Academy.'

'Well, I am happy for you, Frank. It is high time you settled down and found someone to share your life with,' said John.

'She has asked me to be present at a meeting on Friday between her mother and some acquaintances of mine. Her mother wishes to meet James and Emily Bates; apparently there is a connection between them, although I cannot imagine how it can be so.'

'Well, Miss Irvine sounds like a fine woman and I should like to meet her. A trained nurse could be a great help to you in your work.' He paused, swirling his coffee and staring into the depths of his cup. 'I confess I sometimes wish I had a wife to talk matters over with, just occasionally, someone close, who understood me.' He paused again, unusually sober, before rallying himself and looking up at me. 'But there we are, I have made my choices, and I have a thoroughly interesting and stimulating life. Besides I have many siblings, you know, and they have populated the country with children enough between them. But I certainly wish you all happiness, my friend.' He smiled his generous, open smile.

'John, she is not my wife yet,' I blushed.

'One day, though, perhaps?' his eyes twinkled at me. I sipped my coffee, and did not reply. A delicious feeling of warmth spread through me, which I doubted was due to the coffee.

NINETEEN

Friday 29th September

I attend a meeting where I learn of a secret

I had cancelled my appointments for the afternoon as I had been asked to attend a meeting between Lady Irvine and James and Emily Bates. I was invited to luncheon once more at the house in Grosvenor Square.

'Thank you for coming, Frank.' Lady Irvine took my hand, anxiety in her eyes.

'It is a pleasure to see you again, Lady Irvine.'

'Cassandra tells me you are acquainted with the Bates family?'

'A little; they are good people and they have experienced much hardship of late.'

'So I have heard,' she said, still sombre and unsmiling. I wondered what the meeting concerned, but I said nothing.

'Lord Irvine is away from home today, I understand?' She twisted her hands and a shadow passed across her face.

'Yes, he is at the House this afternoon. He knows not of our meeting today.' Cassandra came to my side.

'Shall we go in for luncheon, Mama?'

'Yes, let us eat, for Mr and Miss Bates are coming at half past two.'

We sat in the pleasant dining room, the three of us dwarfed by the large table with its white damask linen. We were served cold meats with potatoes and salad, which I had to stop myself wolfing down and remember my manners. Lady Irvine, I noticed, worried the food around her plate and barely ate anything.

'Mama, are you not eating?' Cassandra said at one point, and I noticed a tight smile pass from mother to daughter. Lady Irvine pushed her food to one side, put her knife and fork together and resigned her efforts.

'No, I have no appetite today.'

'I find the luncheon to be delicious,' I said, spooning some more potatoes onto my plate. I was still no clearer what the meeting concerned; all Cassandra had told me was that she was related to James and Emily Bates. I was mystified.

We took coffee in the drawing room and as the mantel clock struck half past two we saw Lady Irvine's carriage draw up, bringing James and Emily Bates to Mayfair. Lady Irvine rung for the footman to clear the cups and, tight-lipped, she asked Cassandra and me to greet them. As I left the room to go into the hall, Lady Irvine was composing herself before the mirror, taking deep breaths and smoothing her dress.

As the footman opened the front door, I saw Emily and James on the step. James was wearing a jacket that was too small for his muscular frame and he wore a necktie, an item I had never seen him wear before. His hands fidgeted and he seemed the more nervous of the two. Emily wore a striped day dress, which had been ironed and her silver locket hung at her slender neck. She stood straight-backed and undaunted and, with her abundant curls pinned back, she looked altogether quite different; older, somehow. I could tell her eyes positively gaped as she took in the surroundings of the house, admiring the trappings of wealth. She gave a little smile and spoke first.

'Miss Irvine, good day,' she said, taking extra care to pronounce her words precisely.

'Mr Bates, Miss Bates; James, Emily; do come in,' Cassandra welcomed them, taking Emily's hand and pressing it in hers. 'You know my friend, Dr Roberts?'

'Yes, Miss; Miss Irvine, Dr Roberts,' said James Bates. I nodded.

'Let us go to the drawing room, Mama is there.' Emily held James' arm as Cassandra led the way through the wide, spacious hall. I watched as Emily looked around in awe, her brown eyes taking in the scene, as Cassandra led them towards the drawing room. I followed, smiling at her fascination.

Although I had seen the room before, I saw it now through Emily Bates' eyes. I could see her drinking in the grand surroundings: the plush sofas, the rich colours, the marble fireplace and the thick luxurious curtains. Emily stared at her feet, which sunk into the deep pile of the carpet and I could see how she marvelled at the softness of it. She gazed up at the elaborate chandelier as if she had never seen one like it. The grand piano lid was propped open and sheet music sat on the rest. The scent of blousy roses, pink today, filled the air.

'May I present my mother, Lady Irvine. Papa is out this afternoon,' said Cassandra to James and Emily as Lady Irvine turned from the fireplace.

'Miss Bates, Mr Bates, thank you for coming,' said Lady Irvine. Emily let out a gasp of recognition at the likeness between Cassandra and her mother. As Lady Irvine looked into Emily's face, she gave a slight nod and her hand went to her mouth. Without a word, she looked across at Cassandra, who nodded back to her mother.

'Miss Bates,' said Lady Irvine, regaining her composure and taking Emily's hands in her own, staring into her face intently. 'Miss Emily Bates. You are the graven image of my dear departed daughter, Jane,' she faltered. 'I am Rose Irvine and I am happy to meet you.'

'Yes, m'lady,' said Emily, looking into her face.

'And Mr Bates,' said Lady Irvine, taking James's hand in hers. 'Thank you both for coming today.' She paused, looking uncertain how to proceed. 'You are wearing the locket, I see,' she said, her eyes fixing on it.

'Yes, m'lady,' said Emily and without a word she reached to the nape of her neck and unfastened it. Lady Irvine took it in silence. As she turned it over in her hands, I could see her eyes welling with tears and Emily put her hand on Lady Irvine's arm. Lady Irvine closed her own hand over Emily's.

'It is as I remember. I am sure it is the one,' she said eventually, staring at it. The autumn sun streamed through the window and caught her lined face, highlighting the small hairs on her fine skin, illuminating her eyes, red-rimmed and shining with tears.

'Can you tell us about the locket?' said Emily.

Lady Irvine took a deep breath and looked Emily squarely in the face. 'I will. It has been so long in the telling, it is a relief that this moment has come. I never thought it would. Come and sit with me, child.' She motioned for Emily to sit on the sofa and sat down next to her, James hovering by. Cassandra and I sat on the other sofa and melted into the background and as we listened, I felt drawn in to the story.

'It was many, many years ago. I was younger than you are now, just fifteen. My parents took me for a week to a spring house party at the country estate of some friends. I was young and although meeting me now, you may find it a little hard to believe,' she smiled down sadly at the hands folded in her lap, 'I was once spirited and impetuous. I fell in love with their son; at least, I thought I was in love. I had never been in love before; never had feelings towards any man.' She gazed out of the window, her mind transported back to another time. 'We eluded my governess, snatched moments alone and engineered secret trysts. It was so exciting; I felt young and alive. He encouraged and enticed me, and we had an idyllic week.' Her eyes were far away in the past and for a moment I caught a glimpse of her as she must have been as a young woman, strong and wilful, bright and confident. Lady Irvine's eyes hardened and she returned to the present, her gaze resting on Emily's rapt face.

'At the end of the week we parted, but within a month I realised I was with child.' She looked down at her hands in her lap and her face flushed, the shame flooding back. 'It was a difficult time. I was the daughter of a lord and lady and I had brought disgrace on myself and my family. I didn't know where to turn. The gentleman was in Europe for four months with his family and I longed for his return. But he was no gentleman,' she said bitterly. 'When I saw him and told him of the pregnancy, he denied any responsibility; he abandoned me to my fate.' Her face hardened and a solitary tear escaped her eye. 'Can you imagine?' she whispered to Emily, looking into her face, lip shaking, imploring. After a moment, she regained control and continued.

'I had no choice but to tell my mother. I wasn't showing, but it could only have been a matter of time. My mother and father were outraged: furious with me, but more so with the man. My father went to his father but, like father, like son, the father defended his decision that he did not wish to marry me. He had developed a taste for young ladies in France and he did not wish to be tied so young. I was alone with a child on the way. My parents decided the birth must be concealed and the child, if it lived, be given away. They sent me to a relative in the country and two weeks before Christmas, the child was born: a girl, whom I named Eliza. I returned to London on Christmas Eve, to celebrations that I was home for Christmas. The baby was hidden from the servants and within hours of arriving home, Mama instructed her maid, Anna, who was like a sister to me, to take the baby that evening and leave her at the workhouse.' She paused, the memory of that night still raw, her grief etched on her face all these years later.

'Our mother...' said Emily, Lady Irvine's words sinking in.

'Yes, Emily, your mother. She was perfect, the most beautiful thing I had ever seen. Her little fingers and toes, her cherry lips, her soft, dark wispy curls, the smell of her,' she said, another tear rolling down her lined, powdered cheek and falling from her chin onto her aging bosom.

'What 'appened?' whispered Emily. After a moment, Lady Irvine continued.

'I begged and begged but I couldn't keep her. I longed to, but Mama and Papa absolutely forbade it: they said I would be ruined. My honour and reputation in shreds, I would never make a good marriage. They told me the only way to save my honour and safeguard my future was to take her to the workhouse where she would be cared for. They ordered that I must never think of her again and get on with my life. I cried my eyes out all afternoon. Then it had to be done. I fed her and wrapped her in a blanket. I was supposed to be lying in after the birth and Anna was meant to take her. But I couldn't let her go alone so I crept out and we took her together, under cover of darkness, and left her on the doorstep of the St James's Workhouse on Poland Street. I wrote her name on a piece of paper and tucked it into her blanket. Anna's family were from Soho and she knew a little of the workhouse there. Christmas Eve: I have never liked Christmas since that night.' She shuddered and stared into the distance, lost in her memories. 'As I walked away, I turned around to see her being taken in and I felt my heart would break. It took me a year to recover; I cried all the time, pining for my daughter, Eliza.'

'How terrible; I cannot imagine the pain,' said Emily softly. 'To lose a child to God is one thing, but to 'ave to *give* one away…' Lady Irvine looked at her intently.

'Yes, Emily. I spurned my parents for a long time; I was sure they were wrong and I am not sure I ever forgave them.' She looked bitterly at her hands and seemed unable to go on, but after a minute, she continued in a tone of resignation. 'But I was young and, over time, I came to acknowledge that I would have been ruined if I'd kept her. As it was, it was all kept secret and apart from my parents and Anna, no one knew.'

'What of the man? Did 'e know when the baby was born?' asked James, speaking for the first time. Lady Irvine looked up at him and held out her other hand to him.

'For many years he didn't. Although supporting his son cost his father the friendship of my own father, he knew he had done wrong. He punished his son by sending him to Africa, to join the Legion. To make a man of him, he said. It wasn't until many years later that he found me and came here.'

'And what of Eliza?' said Emily.

'I tried to push her from my mind. In time, I was introduced to suitable gentlemen and then I met Cassandra's father, Lord Irvine. I thought I could be happy with him, so when he proposed, I consented to the marriage. My parents were very pleased. Little did they know that, two days before the wedding, I took my one last chance to try to find out what had become of Eliza. I visited the workhouse to see if she was still there.'

'Did you see 'er?' said Emily.

'I saw her, yes. I made up a story and I was taken to see her, although I didn't speak to her. She was playing in the yard with a friend and she was bright and spirited, with soft brown curls and a pretty face. She called herself Betsy as she couldn't say Elizabeth or Eliza.'

'Betsy, Mother…' whispered Emily.

'Yes. She looked well and she seemed happy; I suppose she knew no different. The warden said the night I left her another girl in there with a young daughter already, had a baby that died, so she was given Eliza to care for as her own. She did a good job; she was a better mother to her than I was,' she tailed off, as if she was back in the past, so very long ago.

'That was Ivy and 'er daughter, Mary, was Mother's best friend all 'er life,' said Emily. 'What about the locket?'

'The locket. Before I left that day I paid the warden well to take care of my locket and to give it to Eliza when, or I should say *if*, she left the workhouse. He kept his word. Since that day, I never saw Eliza again; although not a day has passed when I have not thought of her, my little firstborn. Last year when my Jane died and dear Cassandra was lamenting the loss of her only sister, I told her the story I had never told anyone. I thought it right that she should know that she had a half-sister, although I knew not whether she still lived.'

'Jane was your other daughter?' said Emily.

'Yes, my dear Jane. It was my punishment for giving away my first daughter, to have another daughter taken from me. Jane died of the fever last summer, when she was fifteen. She looked just like you,' she said, remembering another terrible event in her past. They sat in silence for a moment, lost in thought. Lady Irvine turned the locket over and over in her hands. As she toyed with it, she pressed the mechanism which opened and a scrap of paper fell to her lap.

'Oh, there is something inside it,' she said, absentmindedly picking it up. 'Writing, look. "Rev Whitehed". What does that mean?'

'He's the curate at St Luke's; why's that there?' said Emily, taking the proffered scrap of paper and looking at it. 'It looks like Mother's 'and; what do you think, James?' She handed it to him.

'You're right, Em.'

'But what does it mean? Maybe she wanted us to see 'im?' Emily was quiet for a moment and then seemed to push the thought to one side, as she put the scrap in her pocket and continued speaking to Lady Irvine. 'Shall I tell you about my mother's life?'

'I would like nothing more,' said Lady Irvine, her eyes wet but her expression resolute.

'Well, me mother was a good mother to us. She always told us she was brought up in the workhouse by Ivy, who was a kind mother to 'er. She 'ad wondered who 'er real mother was and she tried to find out after she married but it came to nothing. Ivy was in the workhouse, 'aving no family 'erself and she brought up her daughter, Mary, and our mother like they were sisters. But Ivy died when Mother was eleven and then she and Mary made up their minds to leave as soon as they could. When Mother was thirteen she met Albert Bates, the boy who brought the groceries in to the kitchen and eventually, when they married, she left the workhouse. Mary left a year later. Mother lived in Soho ever since, and she and me father 'ad five children: me, James here, Mary, George, and William who died as a baby.' Emily's shoulders slumped. 'But Mother and Mary and George 'ave all been taken by the cholera.'

'I am more sorry than you can ever know that your mother, my daughter, has gone. It is my final punishment that I have come so close to finding her, but have missed meeting her by a few short weeks. But perhaps it is better: how could she have understood what I did?'

'She would 'ave loved to know the story,' said Emily. 'She was 'appy; we are poor, but she was 'appy with me father. She loved us children,' said Emily, her voice faltering.

'I am so grateful for that,' said Lady Irvine, studying her hands in her lap once more, tears falling onto her silk sleeve. 'I have spent so many years wondering what became of the little girl I last saw when she was five. You cannot imagine the terrible lives I have imagined for her.' She paused as a sob escaped her, before composing herself once more and looking up at Emily's face. 'I am blessed that life turned out as well as I could have hoped for her.'

'So did you ever see Mother's father again?' said Emily. Lady Irvine paused and a worried look passed across her eyes, as she seemed to suppress a shudder.

'I did see him, yes. Many years later; last year, in fact, he tracked me down and he came to this very house. I nearly fainted with the shock of seeing him after all these years; I had pushed him from my mind. When he came here, he said he had been abroad for years and he was almost unrecognisable. He asked about the child. I told him it was a boy: the name was half spoken, when I changed it to Elijah. I couldn't bear the thought of him anywhere near my little Eliza, even if she was a grown woman by then. He wanted money and he tried to blackmail me by threatening to tell my husband, who knows nothing of this matter. Lord Irvine returned and he was thrown out, but that was not the end of it. A couple of months ago he came to visit again; he had discovered the child was a girl, and he had found her. He said he was going to visit; I don't know whether he did or not but I pray he didn't. He is a frightening figure, tanned with tattoos and a disfigured hand. She would have been terrified of him, I think. What?' Lady Irvine had stopped as a cry escaped Emily, as everything fell into place.

'A disfigured hand: missing a thumb and 'alf a finger?' said Emily.

'Yes, from his time in the Legion,' grimaced Lady Irvine. 'But how do you know?'

'A man was found in our cesspit a few weeks back, excuse me, m'lady, talking of such things; a dead man with a thumb and 'alf a finger missing, and a tattoo on 'is arm,' said James. 'Wiltshire, 'is name was.'

'Matthew is dead?' said Lady Irvine, colour flooding back into her face.

'Without a doubt, 'e is dead,' said Emily, 'for our father 'as been charged with 'is murder and is awaiting trial in the Newgate.'

'Murder?' Lady Irvine's hand was at her mouth.

'I'm sorry to tell you, m'lady, but 'e was banged on

the 'ead and put in the pit and drowned,' said Emily. 'So 'e was Mother's *father*, our grandfather, Matthew Wiltshire,' she whispered in awe. I sat in silence, spellbound by the story.

'Yes, Emily, he was your mother's father,' said Lady Irvine. 'What a way to end his life. God forgive me, but I am not sorry for his passing. He has been a spectre lurking all my life and now he is gone.'

'But even if we know who 'e was, it don't 'elp Father none, 'e's still charged with murder,' said Emily, her eyes downcast, her demeanour deflated. Lady Irvine reached out and placed her hand on Emily's.

'I don't know how to help you,' she said. 'But if there is anything I can do, I would like to help, to make amends of a sort. I would like to think that where I failed Eliza, perhaps I can instead help her children. I will have to tell Lord Irvine about it, the time has come,' she said quietly. 'I have kept my shame hidden all these years and I think it will be a relief. I will tell him the story and, God forgive me, I will accept his judgement on me, whatever it may be.' She was silent, ashen faced, a gamut of emotions playing out: relief, dread, hope, fear. 'Even if he cannot forgive me, I hope he will allow me to arrange for our lawyer to advise you. Your father is in no imminent danger, is he?'

'His case is to be 'eard at the Court of Sessions next week, to see whether 'e'll stand trial,' said Emily, looking up at her, some spirit returning.

'Then there is no time to lose. If he is indicted for murder, his case will be heard before the Grand Jury who will decide if there is enough evidence to proceed to a full trial. Once a case goes before the Grand Jury, the law is weighted in favour of the prosecution; the best hope is to get it thrown out before it gets that far. You see, I have learned something in my years of marriage to a lawyer,' said Lady Irvine, smiling ruefully. 'I do not wish to dwell on what is past, but look to the future. My past shame does not cloud my joy at meeting you two and the connection with my first daughter.'

Emily slowly let the breath flow from her, as her shoulders visibly relaxed and she took in what Lady Irvine had said. However, I saw Cassandra was pale and silent so I squeezed her hand, but said nothing. It was a lot for her to take in.

'Ring for tea, Cassandra, for my grandchildren,' said Lady Irvine, calm once more. 'You have a niece and nephew to celebrate, my dear,' she said, letting go of Emily and James and reaching up to kiss Cassandra's hand as she passed to ring the bell. As Lady Irvine asked Emily more about their childhood, soaking up every snippet of information about her daughter, Cassandra came to me. She looked strangely deflated and perplexed, as if the ground had been pulled from under her. I supposed that all she knew and had grown up with was a falsehood.

'I need time to understand all of this,' she murmured. 'But it is strange, I do feel in a way that I know them already, Emily especially.'

We took tea and talked some more. After a while, Lady Irvine looked from Emily to James and back, a resolute look in her eye. 'It will take time, but I will consider matters; I would like to help you both. I received a substantial inheritance from my own parents, so I have money of my own, in addition to my husband's fortune. However, I must broach this subject with Lord Irvine. He knows nothing of my first child and you must give me time to find the best way to tell him. You must understand that I did a sinful thing, abandoning my child, and I do not know what he will think. I hope and believe he will be forgiving and will allow me the indulgence of contact with my "other" family. But I have long feared what would happen if he ever found out. I will try to broach it this weekend.' She tried to smile, but there was an unmistakeable anxiety about her; she couldn't keep still, her expression a fixed smile, her knuckles white.

'Thank you, m'lady,' said Emily. After a time, we all stood and Emily and James bade Lady Irvine farewell. Cassandra and I saw them to the door. I shook James Bates by the hand and wished him well. Cassandra took Emily's hands in hers.

'I am pleased to discover I have relations close to my own age, Emily. I hope, over time, we can grow to be friends.' She still didn't sound her normal self, but I sensed she was putting a brave face on it for the sake of her mother.

'Thank you, Miss, I should like that,' said Emily.

'It's Cassandra.'

'Yes, Miss Cassandra.' She held her head high, smiling, the locket back in pride of place at her neck. 'Goodbye, Miss. Good day to you, Dr Roberts,' she said. Mr Bates shook hands with Cassandra and thanked her, gave me a little bow and they set off on foot for home. We watched until they were out of sight, then without thinking, I circled my arms around Cassandra's waist and tried to pull her towards me.

'Are you all right?' I looked into her eyes and saw her confusion.

'Yes, but although she told me a little last year, I confess I am shocked at all that Mama has related.' She looked at the ground and kicked the step. 'It may yet bring great shame on us all, you know.'

'Well, I would like to help,' I said, pulling her closer.

'But our family is connected with abandonment and now a *murder*.' She looked mortified, her face pale and downcast now we were alone. After a moment she looked at me. 'Be careful, Dr Frank Roberts, Mama will see you and scold us for such a public display,' she said primly, but her blue eyes twinkled ruefully despite herself. 'What a terrible thing Mama did: giving away her baby. She has hidden the secret all these years.'

'Indeed, it is a terrible story. Remember, she was given no choice in the matter, so do not judge her too harshly. I would imagine that in telling your father, a huge weight will be lifted from her mind. She will be able to live free of the burden of her secret at last. Hopefully she can finally gain some comfort from knowing James and Emily.'

'I just hope that Papa will forgive her, or we will be ruined. What would our acquaintance say if they knew? She would be an outcast and, by extension, so would I, her daughter.' Cassandra looked into my face and sighed. 'No matter what Miss Nightingale says, it is still a man's world.' Then she pulled away, placed her hand on my arm and we went back inside.

TWENTY

A visit from James and Emily Bates

There was a knock at the door and I heard Mrs Hook go to answer it. She appeared in my parlour, where I was catching up on reading the news which I felt I had missed for so many weeks. The papers were full of the Crimea, the new sewers' commission, the Board of Health, and the usual assortment of reviews, oddities and trivia. I was working my way through the pile of *Standards* and *Chronicles* which had accrued during my enforced absence from the happenings of the world beyond Soho.

'It's some people to see you, Doctor: a Mr and Miss Bates.'

'Show them in, Mrs Hook,' I said, surprised they were visiting me at home, although I had given them my address. James and Emily Bates entered and I stood to greet them.

'James, Emily, what can I do for you? Please take a seat. Would you like some refreshment: some tea?'

'No, thank you sir, we jus' wanted a word,' said James, his eyes worried.

'Yes? Does it concern your father?'

'Yes sir, it does, sort of. We went to see Reverend

Whitehead, 'bout that slip in the locket and Em was right; it was a message,' said James. Emily fiddled with the fabric of her dress as they sat.

'Yes?'

''E says that mother 'ad told 'im, when she was ill, that a feller who said 'e was 'er father 'ad been to see 'er. 'E'd found out that a baby girl name of Eliza 'ad been left at the workhouse. 'E'd asked around and 'e'd found 'er; 'e wanted money from 'er 'cos 'e'd fallen on 'ard times. But she recognised 'im as the feller who attacked Jo Parker,' said James.

'Yes, I remember.'

'Anyway, Mother told the reverend that when she didn't 'ave no money to give 'im, he threatened 'er and tried to steal our things: 'er locket, father's pipe, a few spoons and bits of clothes. She was scared of 'im and when she tried to stop 'im 'e 'it 'er. She 'it 'im with a pan and knocked 'im right out and got 'er locket back. She thought she'd killed 'im and she was terrified.'

'What happened?'

'She sent for 'er friend, Mary Parker, and between 'em they managed to 'eave 'im out of the back window and then they went down and 'id 'is body in the cesspit.'

'What were they thinking?'

'She was so frightened, she *wasn't* thinking. She didn't know what to do. She'd brought disgrace on 'er family, she'd be 'anged if she owned up; what could she do?' said Emily, taking up the story. 'It all fits as mother wasn't 'erself those last few weeks before she died.'

'But what of your father? What happened when he was arrested?'

'That made things worse for 'er. The reverend said she couldn't decide whether to own up and get 'im off, or to wait and hope they'd let 'im go. She'd brought shame on her family; all for a father she never knew. She didn't know what to do. When she got the cholera, she told the reverend that she saw it as 'er punishment.'

'So she didn't tell anyone else what had happened?' I said.

'No. But she didn't want to take the secret to 'er grave. She begged the reverend to keep it quiet and tell it only if it could 'elp,' Emily finished.

'So when did she put the note in the locket?' I asked.

'I think she must 'ave thought to confess to the reverend before she took sick,' said James. She knew Em would have the locket, find the note and 'e'd tell her the story.'

'What a burden to bear,' I said.

'Poor Mother,' said Emily.

'So what d'you think we can do to 'elp Father now?' said James.

I thought for a moment. 'We will have to tell Lady Irvine. It is unfortunate that she will have to know that her own daughter committed a crime, but I do not see that there is anything else to do.'

'But she may not want to know us any more, if she finds out,' said Emily in a tight voice, uncharacteristically unsure. I could see in her pale face the dread of losing the connection so recently established and the potential promise of a better life.

'She said she wanted to help, didn't she? She knows lawyers, who may be able to help free your father. I think you have to try; *we* have to try.' Emily's expression lightened at this last phrase.

'Would you be able to 'elp us, Doctor?' she said, her spirit returning.

'Yes. I will send word to Cassandra and tell her and then we can decide when to approach Lady Irvine. Leave it to me.'

'Oh Doctor, thank you; if you could 'elp us…' Emily gushed, the colour returning to her cheeks.

'I'll send word now, and let you know how I get on. It may take a day or two, mind.' I stood up and they did likewise. 'Goodbye, you'll hear from me as soon as I know anything.'

I saw them to the door and as they walked up the street, I hailed a cab to take me to Mayfair. There was no time like the present.

I knocked at the large brass knocker and Carter opened the door.

'Is Miss Cassandra in?' I blurted out.

'I believe so, sir.'

'Please could you tell her I am here and I must speak with her?'

'Very good, sir. If you'll wait in the drawing room, I'll see if she is available.'

As we crossed the hall, Lady Irvine emerged from a door. 'Dr Roberts!' she said, smiling, coming towards me.

'Lady Irvine, forgive my intrusion, I wished to speak with Cassandra.'

'It is a pleasure to see you, Doctor. But I cannot

allow you to visit her unchaperoned, as I'm sure you will understand. Might I ask the nature of your business?' I was flustered. Of course, how stupid of me, I couldn't just barge in and expect to see her.

'Of course, forgive my impertinence. I have news of the matter we discussed on Friday, that I wished to convey,' I said, aware of Carter's presence.

'Very well, you may communicate it to me, as well,' said Lady Irvine, guarded. 'Carter, send for Miss Cassandra, please,' she directed, leading me to the drawing room. She sat on the sofa before the fire and directed me to do the same. In a minute, Cassandra joined us and Lady Irvine's eyes flicked towards the closed door.

'Dr Roberts, this is unexpected, although a welcome intrusion,' Cassandra said.

'Dr Roberts has news of the Bates family; pray, do tell us,' said Lady Irvine.

'James and Emily came to see me and they visited Reverend Whitehead about the note in Emily's mother's locket.' I was aware the two women were looking at me. 'It appears that their mother had confessed before she died to the reverend, that *she* was responsible for the death of the man in the cesspit, Matthew Wiltshire.' Lady Irvine blanched and Cassandra looked shocked. 'I am sorry to have to tell you, Your Ladyship, but he had found out that she was his daughter and he had visited her wanting money. When he threatened her, she hit him over the head with a pan. Thinking he was dead, she and a friend manhandled him out of the window to the backyard, where they placed him in the pit. They could see no other way of getting rid of the body.' Lady Irvine placed her handkerchief over her mouth and looked as if she felt faint. 'I am very sorry to tell you so bluntly, Lady Irvine. James and Emily begged me to see whether I could do anything to help their father, in the light of the confession.'

There was silence for a minute, as Lady Irvine and Cassandra took in this news, both of them pale and still. Eventually, Lady Irvine spoke, her voice calm and resolute. 'I have informed Lord Irvine of the whole story. I will seek permission from him to consult with Thaddeus Chattoway, our lawyer. I am sure if anything can be done, he is the man to achieve it. I am horrified to hear what has happened, but I have much to be ashamed of in my own past, and it would not be right for an innocent man to hang.'

'Thank you,' I said relieved. 'You are most kind. I will leave you now, for I have intruded on your privacy too long already.' I stood, gave a little bow to Lady Irvine, and risked a look at Cassandra. She looked shaken and I felt a stab of pain to have been the bearer of such ill tidings. I left the room and the house and neither woman tried to stop me.

★

A few days later, on Saturday, I called at Cassandra's house. I had not seen her since Monday, and I was most anxious to know what had happened since our last meeting and to glean some news to pass to James and Emily.

It was a fine, crisp autumn day and Lady Irvine suggested we went out into the large walled garden, immaculately bedded near the house with roses and shrubs. Mature trees lined the walls and their leaves were turning orange and brown and starting to fall. A path ran around the perimeter of the lawn, which ran down to a wildflower area, unkempt but natural in style. Lady Irvine sat discreetly on a wooden bench near the house and I offered Cassandra my arm as we strolled around, admiring the sights and smells that assaulted our senses from every direction. I felt very much at home, happy in her company. When we were far from the house, she pulled me to sit on a circular bench beneath a huge horse chestnut tree. Our feet nestled among the shiny conkers on the grass.

'I must tell you of the Bates case. It is all happening very quickly,' said Cassandra.

'Do tell me, my dear,' I said and her cheeks flushed, her eyes bright, as she took in my address.

'Well, Mama told Papa the story last weekend. They were confined to the drawing room for the whole afternoon and Mama had left strict instruction they were not to be disturbed.'

'How did your father take the news?' Cassandra hesitated.

'He has not spoken of it to me directly, but from his demeanour, I believe he was shocked and saddened to hear of Mama's past,' she bent to pick up a conker, which she polished between her gloved fingers, 'but I think he has accepted it now. There was a day at first when I don't think they spoke to each other and Mama was most distressed; but the following day they seemed to have made their peace. Mama did not relate the details to me; she said merely that she had told Papa and although he found it hard, he was willing to forgive her. Importantly, he is willing to allow her to have contact with the Bates children.' Cassandra was quiet, contemplative. 'Poor Papa; I don't think he expected such a shock after all these years of married life.' She tossed the conker carelessly into the wildflower area beside us, then she turned to face me and her soft eyes locked on mine. 'I hope you will not conceal any such secrets from me.' It took me a moment to realise what she had said and by then she had started to speak again.

'Then, before Father had really had a chance to get to grips with the story, there was the news you brought on Monday. Papa allowed Mama to consult her lawyer about it and Mr Chattoway is a good man. He dotes on Mama, so I am sure he will do his best to help. Unfortunately, the case came before the Court of Sessions last Thursday and the indictment will be heard before the Grand Jury next week. Mr Chattoway is preparing his representations on behalf of Albert Bates.' At this moment, we could see Lady Irvine standing and setting off down the path to join us. We stood and walked to meet her.

'It is, altogether, quite a story,' I said. 'I hope we are not too late.'

'Well, for my part, what's done is done and an innocent man stands accused of a crime he did not commit,' said Cassandra. 'I believe we should look to the future and hope that Mr Chattoway can help Mr Bates.'

We reached her mother and she changed the subject. 'Mama, Dr Roberts and I have been studying the fine conkers from the tree this year.'

'Perhaps it's the heat of the summer that has caused them to blossom and grow, my dear,' replied Lady Irvine. I risked a sideways glance at Cassandra's beautiful face and thought how much she, like the conkers, had blossomed these past few weeks.

As I walked home later, I found myself fervently hoping that something could be done for Albert Bates. I knew from my own childhood how hard it was to make your way in the world without a parent and I felt desperately sorry for James and Emily. I was so lucky to have had John to keep an eye out for me; I really hoped Lady Irvine could bring the Bates' a stroke of luck too.

TWENTY-ONE

I meet Albert Bates and I attend another meeting

The next evening, I opened the door and James Bates stood there, his young face pale and anxious.

'I went to the Newgate after me shift, Doctor, an' me father's terrible sick and they won't do nothin' 'bout it,' he blurted. His strapping form was a shadow of its former self and his brow was folded into deep creases which made him look much older than his eighteen years.

'Of course, come in; what's the matter with him?' I ushered James into my parlour and he slumped into a chair, utter despair on his face as he looked up at me.

''E's got the fever; it's going round in there. One of 'is cell mates 'as died and now 'e's raving away like a mad man, can't talk sense. 'E's so hot 'e's burning up and I can't get 'im to drink nothin'.'

'I see. If it's the gaol fever, it could be serious. Let us go and see him.' Gaol fever, or typhus as it was sometimes called, had long been rife in prisons, where the squalid conditions encouraged its spread through the ranks of half-starved weakened men. 'I'll grab my bag and we'll get a cab.' Cholera, gaol fever, dysentery, the pox, the list was endless: there were many diseases which could strike men in an instant. I pulled James to his feet and we left.

In the early evening lamplight, we arrived at the great door to the Newgate. I had never been inside before and as I looked up at the huge edifice, even the metal studs in the wood of the great portal spoke of incarceration. After a softener to the guards of a few shillings, James and I were shown through the labyrinth of passages, dark, damp and uninviting. As we went, the air was filled with a heart-rending mixture of cussing expletives, men begging as we passed and the keening cries of the desperate holed up in the deepest depths of the prison. I had to suppress a shudder and I felt new respect for James, visiting this grim scene each day. Eventually we reached the place and the guard selected a key from a heavy ring of many; there was a clink and a grating rasp as the old lock turned.

'Ten minutes now,' he said gruffly and we went in.

It took time for my eyes to acclimatise to the gloom. There was no window and a dim oily lamp provided the only illumination. The air was warm and soupy with the smell of unwashed, sick men. The inmates stirred at our entrance; there were five shadows, bearded unkempt men whose very skin seemed to move. As I passed the first, slumped on the floor against the wall, I could see the lice seething through the hair on his bare chest. He didn't look up. James pointed at his father, lying on the pallet, murmuring to himself. I steeled myself and went over.

'Father, I've brought the doctor,' James said, his

hand on his father's. Albert Bates was a slight man, but in the dim light, the bone structure of his face suggested he would once have been as handsome as his son. He lay still on the pallet, his eyes open but unseeing, fixed on the blackness above. As I watched, he stretched one arm towards the ceiling, his hand closing around some non-existent thing. Again and again, he reached out to grasp something which was not there, murmuring nonsensical childlike babble as he did so. I lit a candle from my bag and looked more closely at him, although he screwed his eyes up in pain and rolled away from the light.

'How long has he been like this?' I whispered to James, who hovered next to the bed.

''E had a chill a couple of days ago and 'is 'ead was 'urtin', and then yesterday 'e was a bit out of sorts, didn't seem to know I was 'ere; but today 'e's ramblin' away and 'e's got spots, look.' I moved my candle to focus on his chest and amongst the wispy hair dark purplish splodges discoloured his skin. As I looked more closely, a louse scuttled away from the candlelight.

'I think he has gaol fever; it's oftentimes rife in here,' I whispered.

'Can you 'elp 'im?' said James, an unspoken pleading in his uneven voice.

'There is not much to do but wait it out. We need to get him cleaned up and I could try the leeches, and he needs to drink. It would be better if he was away from these other men; they are all in a filthy state and it's said the lice may spread it from one to the other. You see they are all infested?' James groaned.

'They won't move 'im, Doctor, they couldn't give a farthin' for what 'appens to 'em.'

I moved to knock on the door, and the lock rasped open. 'A moment, James,' I said and I stepped outside to speak with the guard. After a few moments I had accomplished what I wished and I returned to the cell.

'The guard will move him and then we'll give him a good scrub with carbolic, and I'll bleed him a little, to help reduce the pressure in his head.' James looked astounded.

'How did you get 'im to do that?' he said, his brown eyes wide with amazement.

'I just gave him my professional advice,' I murmured. 'Come; let us get him up between us.'

'Well, you are a wonder, Doctor, I can't believe it,' said James, going to rouse his father. Professional advice and two pounds, I thought to myself.

We lugged him, semi-conscious, down the passageway and into another, tiny cell. It was barely big enough for a man to lie down, but it was empty of others and it had a small window which admitted both light and air. The guard brought a bucket of cold water and soap for the payment of another five shillings, and in the candlelight we stripped Albert Bates and scrubbed every bit of his skin with a brush until it was red. By the time we had finished, the water teemed with flaccid bubbles and drowning insects. We dried him with the end of the threadbare blanket and laid him on the pallet, his feet hanging over the end.

I opened my bag and brought out my jar of leeches and the bleeding bowl. I positioned his right arm facing upwards and applied a leech to the crook of the elbow. In no time, the animal engorged and the dark blood trickled into the bowl. When I had drained a few ounces, I removed the fat leech and applied a swab to the wound. James held it in place as I cleaned up. Albert was calmer now and had stopped raving. He managed to take some water and then we left him, swaddled in the blanket. I had done all I could; we would have to hope that it was enough.

'Let us leave him to rest now, James. I have asked the guard to look in on him later and offer him water. We can do no more for now.'

'I can't believe you've done that, Doctor, thank you. I'll call back and see 'im first thing.'

A different key clunked in a different lock and Albert was incarcerated once more. We retraced our steps and emerged back onto Old Bailey Street. I offered James a lift, but he declined so I caught a cab home.

On Monday, after a day at the Westminster, I visited Albert Bates again. He was still very sick and I gave him laudanum and bled him once more, paying handsomely for the privilege. I just hoped he would survive until his case came before the courts.

*

As I breakfasted in my parlour on Tuesday, I sat thinking of the previous day. Mr Williamson had performed an amputation as I assisted. John had administered the anaesthetic, a great blessing for the poor old fellow on the wooden operating table. Williamson had learned his trade in the days before anaesthesia when speed was paramount and it had taken barely a minute, but the operation always made me feel a little queasy and one of the watching students had fainted; surgery was not for the faint-hearted.

I shook myself back to the present as Mrs Hook knocked and came in bearing a letter. She held it in her upturned palm as if it might suddenly be engulfed in flames. I didn't often receive letters, so the arrival of a stamped missive was always a source of interest for my housekeeper.

'I 'ope it's not bad news Doctor,' she ventured, hovering for me to open it. I indulged her and slit it open with my knife. It was short and to the point.

'I am requested to attend the Court of the Grand Jury at the Old Bailey this afternoon,' I murmured, taking in the letterhead from Mr T Chattoway of Chancery Lane. 'Thank you, Mrs Hook.' She took my cue and left, her eyebrows arched, intrigued. I thought of Albert Bates and how important it was to secure his release.

I held my normal surgery in the morning, patients attending the dispensary in Edward Street. It had been suspended during the cholera epidemic as patients were too sick to get there and no one wanted to be out on the streets. It was a relief to get back to the normal assortment of ailments, wounds and today, a boy who'd fractured his wrist falling backwards off the top of the omnibus. I'd splinted it as best I could but the lad was in a great deal of pain. I stopped at Mrs Bootle's for lunch and then I went home to change into smarter attire.

I stepped from the cab in front of the Old Bailey. I had never been there before, and I paused to look up at the three-storey edifice next to the Newgate prison. I had a vision of Albert Bates, sick, incarcerated, awaiting his fate. As I approached the gate, I could see a wall stretching between the two buildings; I knew there was a connection to allow for transfer of the accused to the courtrooms. "Dead man's walk" they called it. An officer of the court opened a hatch in the door to ask my business and I was admitted.

Thaddeus Chattoway was waiting for me in the anteroom before the Court of the Grand Jury. The court did not take place in the main courtroom, but in a smaller room on the ground floor.

'Dr Roberts, I presume? Lady Rose has told me all about you,' he said, coming to shake me by the hand. He was a large, jovial man, with hair which was thinning on the top but too long at the collar and his large round glasses gave him a rather mole-like appearance. His oversized stomach protruded over his breeches and stretched the fabric of his waistcoat, but he was all smiles and I warmed to him immediately.

'Mr Chattoway?'

'Yes, Doctor, that is my name and has been since I was a boy, hah,' he said. 'Thank you for attending at such short notice; I felt a character witness may be of assistance and a respected doctor like yourself will be just the ticket.' He clapped me on the back as he looked me up and down. 'Come, sit, I must ask you a few questions.' He motioned we sit at a wooden bench before the window. As I glanced out, I could see a prisoner in irons being led along the passage from the gaol, two burly guards at his side. The poor fellow was emaciated and dishevelled and wore a look of utter defeat. I was called back to the business in hand by Mr Chattoway.

'So, you know the Bates family?'

'Not well. I have come across James and Emily Bates several times in the last few weeks in the course of my work and I am fairly well acquainted with them.' A dark heaviness clouded my head as I thought of their father. 'I have met Albert Bates only recently for now he is very sick with the gaol fever.'

'Is he in danger?' I bit my lip before speaking.

'To be honest, I don't know how much longer he'll survive in there.'

'I see.' The lawyer's lips thinned as he took in my meaning. 'So what do you make of them all? Are they a good family?'

'Yes, I believe so. I first met James Bates when he pulled some young pickpockets, street children, off me. He seems like a lad who knows right from wrong and despite their poor situation they seem to have been brought up well. Emily is a feisty one, spirited you know, but in a good way. I cannot imagine either of them harming anyone; it's not in their natures. Those values must stem from the parents.'

'And you heard of Mrs Bates' confession from them?'

'James and Emily came to see me as a note was found in a locket of Emily's, while we were with Lady Irvine, in fact, which directed them to talk to Reverend Whitehead, the curate at St Luke's. They came to seek my help in the light of what he told them.'

'Yes, I have met with Henry Whitehead and I have his written testimony here.' He patted his inner pocket.

'It seemed to me from the start there was no evidence to implicate Albert Bates; just the circumstances of where the body was found and the pipe…' but I was interrupted as at this point the door to the court opened and a clerk bade us enter. Too late, I wished I had thought to question Mr Chattoway on the process before finding myself part of it.

The Grand Jury, more than a dozen men, sat in throne-like chairs around a huge oval table in the lofty wood-panelled room. At a side table sat a second clerk, with sheaves of papers and a pot of ink. Portraits of great men of justice adorned the walls, severe, unsmiling figures in their black robes and wigs. Black for death, I thought. The room had high windows down one side but was largely lit by a chandelier which hung low from the ceiling. There were no seats for us and the clerk who bade us enter indicated we should stand at the foot of the table. I shuffled my feet nervously as the man at the top of the table, the chairman, looked at his papers.

'We come now to the indictment of Albert Bates, thirty-eight years, for the murder of Matthew Wiltshire, August last. I shall summarise the case for the prosecution. The body of the deceased was found in the cesspit in the backyard of 19 Broad Street, Soho, on 26th August this year. At the time, the only family in residence at the building were the Bates family, comprising Albert Bates, his wife Elizabeth, thirty-seven, and their four children. A pipe was found with the body, which Albert Bates freely admitted to being his own, it being distinguished by a burn mark on the stem. Enquiry into the identity of the deceased found the man be one Matthew Wiltshire, fifty-six, and it has been ascertained from army records that Wiltshire was implicated in the death many years ago of William Bates, the cousin of the accused. Does anyone have anything to add?'

'Are we agreed the indictment should be for murder, or is there reasonable cause to indict for manslaughter?' said a bearded fellow halfway down the table.

'If a man is put in a cesspit, it must be with the premeditated intention of killing, must it not?' said another.

'But was he dead when he went in? If so, we cannot rule out manslaughter, we don't know what happened to lead to that point.'

'To conceal the body indicates an element of premeditated deception...' The discussion went on, until the man in charge called them to order.

'What did the post-mortem examination show?' He turned to the clerk.

'I have the report from the coroner,' the clerk consulted his papers. 'The lungs showed feculent material, indicating the deceased was still alive when he went in,' he said, reading my words. It seemed a lifetime ago that I had sat in Middleton's and written them.

'It has to be murder, then. We cannot indict on manslaughter in the circumstances. A trial jury may decide that the lesser charge is applicable, but we cannot make that decision. I remind you gentlemen, our job is to decide whether there is enough evidence for a true bill which will be tried by a full jury in open court. Does anyone have any representations to make?'

Thaddeus Chattoway cleared his throat and the men of the Grand Jury turned to look at us, unnoticed, it seemed, until now. 'Gentlemen, I am in possession of information which, while it does not change the nature of the indictment before you, profoundly alters, nay disputes, the role of the accused in the case.'

'Who are you, sir, and what is this information?'

'I am Thaddeus Chattoway, attorney at law, of Chancery Lane. I am in possession of a written statement from the Reverend Henry Whitehead, the highly respected curate at St Luke's Church in the heart of Soho.'

'How is this relevant to the case, sir?'

'Before her death from cholera but a few days after the body of the deceased was discovered, Mrs Elizabeth Bates, wife of the accused, Betsy as she was known, confessed to the good curate that *she* was responsible for the man's death. The deceased had visited her, due to a family connection which I will not trouble you with, and he had become violent, whereupon, in self-defence, she had struck him and he had collapsed. Believing him to be dead and panicking at the grave implications of this turn of events, she managed to push him out of the window. He fell into the backyard, from where she dragged him and concealed him in the cesspit. I would contend, therefore, firstly that the crime was manslaughter, for it was not a premeditated killing. However, of more concern today, I propose and request that the case against Albert Bates be dropped. From what is known, he is of good character and the evidence against him is but circumstantial. Furthermore, he is now in a dangerous condition with the fever in the Newgate.'

'And the pipe, Mr Chattoway?'

'It seems Mr Wiltshire attempted to steal various items from Mrs Bates when he visited, including the pipe and some jewellery. Mrs Bates recovered the jewellery, but not the pipe before she heaved him out of the window.'

'Do we know this Reverend Whitehead, gentlemen? Is he to be believed?' the chairman looked around the table expectantly. No one spoke. I cleared my throat.

'Gentlemen, if I may be permitted to speak? I am Dr Frank Roberts, a general practitioner in Soho, and incidentally, I undertook the post-mortem on the deceased. I am well acquainted with Reverend Whitehead, for I have many dealings with him in the course of my work. He is a fine man, a true man of God, who is as full of integrity as any man I have ever known. There is no doubt in my mind that he speaks the truth.'

Suddenly, the door flew open with a crash against the panelling and Emily Bates burst into the room, pursued by two officers of the courthouse.

"E didn't do it, you must let 'im go, it weren't 'im, and now 'e's *dyin'* in there,' she cried, as the officers tried to restrain her, one now gripping each arm. Her hair was wild, loosened from its tether in the scuffle and she had fire in her eyes. "E's me father and 'e's a good man, it weren't 'im. It ain't right, you've got nothin' on 'im, nothin', you let 'im go. 'E's got the gaol fever and 'e's like to die in there if 'e don't get out.' There was desperation and fury in her face as she looked at the faces around the table, defiant.

'Silence!' the chairman thundered and the whole room fell quiet. 'What is the meaning of this intrusion?'

Suddenly she noticed I was there and she murmured, 'Dr Roberts,' the fire gone out of her.

'Are you acquainted with this woman, Doctor?' said the chairman.

'Yes, sir, she is the daughter of the accused, Emily Bates.' I went to Emily and looked her in the eye. 'Emily, you are not helping. Go with these gentlemen and I will come to you when the hearing is finished.' She looked at me, indecision in her fierce brown eyes.

'I 'ad to do somethin', Miss Cassandra told me it was today and I couldn't sit back and do nothin'. 'E didn't do it, it weren't 'im, you tell 'em, sir.'

'Yes, Emily, we have, we've told them.'

'Take this woman outside and if she interrupts the hearing again, she will be charged with perverting the course of justice,' the chairman ordered.

'Go,' I mouthed to her and she bowed her head and was taken out.

'An intolerable intrusion; now, back to the case in question. Do you have the written statement of the reverend for this jury?' the chairman addressed Mr Chattoway.

'Indeed I do, sir,' he said smoothly, handing over a sheet of paper, which the chairman studied for a moment.

'Very well. We will conclude our deliberations in private; if you will wait outside.' We were thus dismissed and we went back into the anteroom, where Emily was sitting with one officer. She stood as we entered.

'Well, sir?'

'They're just deliberating, child. We'll have to wait,' said Mr Chattoway, patting her arm. 'I am not sure you did our case much good in there, you know.' She cast her eyes to the floor, chastened.

'Sorry sir. I jus' couldn't do nothin'.'

'Best leave it to people who are familiar with these things, eh?' he said gently. 'How did you even manage to get in here?'

'I came in with the charwomen this morning, tagged on the back of 'em, I did. Then I found out where they were meetin' and I listened 'til I heard they were talking 'bout me father's case. But they'd caught up with me by then.' She grinned to herself. 'Caused a bit of trouble, I did.'

'Mr Chattoway is right, Emily, we do not need more trouble.'

The door opened and the clerk came out. 'Mr Bamber says to inform you the case is dismissed: not enough evidence to go to trial and the likely perpetrator is dead. Now I should get out of here, all of you,' he added under his breath. I needed no second telling and I took Emily's arm and guided her away, anxious to remove her before she could cause another scene. When we three were outside the walls of the Old Bailey, I breathed a sigh of relief.

'So will 'e be set free now, sir?' Emily asked Mr Chattoway.

'Yes, Miss Bates. It may take a day or two for the

papers to be signed, but I will let Lady Irvine know when he is to be released.' Emily took his hand and grasped it with both of hers, looking up into his face, pleasure flushing her cheeks.

'Thank you, sir, for what you have done. We'll always be grateful. Me and James couldn't 'ave lost 'im too.' I was surprised to see that she was on the verge of tears, the strain finally showing on her young face. Mr Chattoway looked almost wistfully at her.

'I would have liked a daughter myself, you know; three sons we have. A daughter would be a comfort to me in my old age, I think. But there we are; we have what we are given.' He patted her arm again with his big ringed hand and drew himself up tall. 'I must report to Lady Irvine, for she was anxious to be informed of the outcome. I will bid you good day. Thank you for coming, Dr Roberts; it has been a pleasure to meet you, sir.' He hailed a cab from the ranks which passed the time of day in the wide street outside the Newgate and was off.

'Come, Emily, I will take you back to work, for we can do no more and you do not want to lose another job.' I hailed another cab, and we travelled back to Soho.

TWENTY-TWO

Thursday 12th October

I meet Cassandra's brother

Two days later, I met James in the street and Albert Bates had not yet been released although he was cautiously hopeful that his father's condition was a little improved. I fervently hoped he would make it until he was freed. Tonight, though, I had other distractions. The Irvines were hosting a dinner party in honour of Cassandra's brother, Edmund, and I was invited.

Edmund Irvine, Lord Irvine's heir, was an officer in the 30th Infantry Regiment. The situation in the East had dominated the news since the spring and the date of his departure had been set. The regiment was to travel by train to Portsmouth, where they would embark on a troop steamer. From there they would sail to Malta for supplies, before progressing across the Mediterranean Sea, through the Dardanelles past Constantinople and up through the Black Sea to Sevastopol. Weather permitting, the journey was expected to take six weeks.

I hailed a cab and journeyed through the rainy twilight to Grosvenor Square. I longed to hear if there was any news of Albert Bates' release and I was intrigued to meet Edmund as I had heard much of him from Cassandra; I knew she adored him. I fiddled with my

266

cufflinks as I travelled, hoping that he would like me. There still loomed the spectre of our different situations and I felt it would be a small victory if I could persuade Edmund of my worth. Before I knew it, the cab pulled up outside the house and I stepped down; chamber music flowed from the house, filling the night air. My stomach twisted in knots and I was surprised I was so nervous.

Cassandra met me in the hall and we went into the drawing room together. I was immediately struck by a tall, dark gentleman, bedecked in the dress uniform of the hussars. His tight-braided dolman and flowing pelisse enhanced the appearance of his athletic figure. His hair was darker than Cassandra's and it curled over his collar in rakish waves. He had the same clear cornflower eyes as his sister and he sported a fine curled moustache beneath his aquiline nose. He stood by the fire, the gold buttons of his jacket gleaming, a white sash across his chest and a fine sword swinging at his hip. His long black boots shone to perfection and set off his elegant legs in high-waisted trousers. He was talking and laughing with two other fellows, similarly attired, but it was plain that he was the centre of attention. Cassandra led me over and I took a deep breath, feeling acutely the difference in our situations, Lord Irvine's heir and myself.

'Edmund, I should like you to meet Dr Frank Roberts,' she said, taking Edmund's arm and giving it a light squeeze. I wondered if she was entreating him to be kind to me. He clicked his heels together, standing a good six inches taller than me, and held out his hand.

'Dr Roberts, I am delighted to meet you. Cassandra

has told me a little about you, but I am intrigued to meet you myself.'

'And I you, Mr Irvine,' I felt myself blush, unsure how to address him; was the son of a lord also a lord? I didn't know. 'Please call me Frank.'

'Edmund, it's Edmund,' he said as he shook my hand firmly and I felt my colour rise further under his keen gaze. 'You live and work in Soho, I hear?' There was a stifled audible intake of breath at this from one of his friends, whom I guessed was shocked at the connotations of the poor, working-class area.

'I do, sir, I am a general practitioner and my practice is largely in the poor streets of Soho,' I said, my head held high. I could not allow myself to be intimidated by these fellows who were half a decade younger than I was; I had nothing to be ashamed of.

'Frank has been working in the cholera epidemic there, haven't you?' said Cassandra, her silken-gloved hand on my arm. 'He has done wonderful work with his patients and has been a great comfort to them.'

'I am pleased to hear it,' said Edmund, his eyes still locked on mine. 'Cassandra has given up her medical work for now, have you not, my sister?' he turned affectionately to her.

'Yes,' said Cassandra, 'I'm afraid so, as Mama did not approve, but perhaps when you are in the Crimea she will see the value of women nursing. My old superintendent, Miss Nightingale, is setting up a hospital there at Scutari; you may meet her.'

'Only if we're damned unlucky!' said one of Edmund's friends.

'I am sorry, Dr Roberts, this is Mr Bainbridge, and this is Mr Collins, my fellow officers in the 30th Regiment; we sail together next week on the great adventure,' said Edmund, and I shook their hands in turn. At this point, Lady Irvine came over and Cassandra removed her hand as I bent forward in a bow.

'Frank, I am pleased to see you again,' she took my hand warmly, her grey eyes smiling. 'I see you have met my son, Edmund?'

'Indeed I have, Lady Irvine, I am honoured to make his acquaintance; I declare I will follow the news of our quest in the East with a personal interest from now on.' At that moment the footman arrived to call us in for dinner, and we took our places at the huge table. I was seated between Cassandra and an elderly friend of Lady Irvine, who was rather deaf, and I had to keep my wits about me to keep conversation flowing. I was seated opposite Edmund, whom I caught studying me intently from time to time through the candelabra between us.

We were twenty in number and the party included some of Edmund's friends, and Mabel Foster and Edward Summers, soon to be married, as well as friends of Lord and Lady Irvine. The host and hostess were seated at opposite ends of the table, as was the custom, but I detected a note of formality, of coolness between them; or rather, a chill emanating from Lord Irvine whenever his wife spoke. It was barely perceptible, but I was sure I was not mistaken. I caught Lady Irvine throwing her husband a wistful look which seemed to be full of longing, and I imagined her wishing the past undone. Lord and Lady Irvine presented a united front in professing excitement at their son setting off on such a journey. However, I often caught Lady Irvine looking at her son with fear in her eyes, as if she didn't want to let him go.

It was an enjoyable evening. I forgot all about the Bates case as we dined on seven courses and as many wines and the conversation flowed; Edmund and his friends were good company indeed, with their youthful exuberance and excitement at the upcoming campaign. Edmund was a fine young man of twenty-five; handsome and witty, with charming manners, an obvious affection for his sister and a filial devotion to his parents. I could barely stand from the table by the end of the meal and it required a force of effort to compose myself as the ladies left us and the port and cigars came out.

When the ladies had left, Edmund made a point of coming to sit next to me, a welcome companion after the deaf lady with her ear trumpet.

'Look here, Frank, I need a word about my sister,' he slurred, slapping me on the back as he sank into the chair beside me.

'Yes?'

'I just want you to know that if you break her heart, I'll personally come home from the Crimea to break your nose, old chap,' his eyes were swimming and he could barely enunciate the words, but he was obviously serious.

'I can assure you, my intentions are honourable, sir,' I slurred back. 'But I have not known her long; I do not know her own heart as yet.' He ignored me and ploughed on with his own train of thought.

'My sister's heart is a precious thing and it has already been broken once… I will not stand for it again,' his voice trailed off as he fumbled with his cigar, trying to light it and then puffing smoke rings into the air as he sprawled back in his chair.

'No?' I said biting back my curiosity, feeling it would be rude to enquire further. I watched as his smoke ring hit the ceiling and fanned out across the ceiling rose.

'No,' he said flatly, and I looked at him again. 'Three years ago, a scoundrel broke her heart, and never again, old man, you hear me, never again. Engaged she was, and crushed when she found he was seeing another lady; she blamed her appearance for the whole affair. Father called it off and she was very down, very low.' His arm lunged around my shoulder and he breathed fumes of alcohol into my face. Before I could respond, three of his friends lurched over and as one sat on his lap, the other two tried to divest him of his jacket. The four of them fell about laughing, intoxicated by the wine and by the power they imagined they would wield as officers off on a crusade. The moment was lost and I could ask no more about it. It was the first I'd heard of Cassandra's past, but I resolved to say nothing of it unless she told me herself, if she ever did.

The next day, I met John at Mrs Bootle's at lunchtime; it was back to normal and buzzing with life once more. The smell of coffee and fresh bread and cigar smoke filled my nostrils and the chatter of the clientele rung in my ears. Despite the after effects of the wine, I felt on top of the world; life was good. John stood up in the booth to greet me.

'John, it is good to see you.' I clasped his hand in affection.

'And you, Frank,' he smiled back.

'So what is occupying your time now the epidemic in Soho is over? Do you have time for leisure, at last?' I joked, sitting down.

'Ah, you know me, Frank, leisure and I do not mix; just the occasional swim, that's leisure enough for me. No, I have been finalising my work on the cholera in south London, in between my anaesthetic commitments. I have been asked if I will join Lankester's enquiry into the cholera for the Vestry Committee of the Board of Guardians of the parish, you know. *Another* enquiry. And I am planning to publish my work; I will not give up. Who knows, if I speak loudly enough, one day…?'

'I hope so.'

'Oh, and they've invited me to become president of the Medical Society for London next year.'

'You are becoming positively famous, John, for your many talents!' I laughed.

'I don't know about that, Frank. But let's have some lunch and you can tell me of your Nurse Irvine; have you asked her to marry you yet?' he said. I was silent for a moment.

'You jest, but one day, I might just do that,' I said quietly, looking into his earnest grey eyes. 'But I have little to offer her at the moment. Although her parents are charming, I fear they may not approve; they are of much higher rank than I will ever be.' This was the problem; I was not sure they would accept me, whatever my feelings, and I knew enough of the world to know that I would need their blessing.

'But do you love her, my friend?'

'I do, very much,' I flushed to be talking of such things. John put his hand on my shoulder.

'Well then, what could any man want for his daughter but a man who truly loves her? You are a respectable fellow, Frank, and a gentleman.'

'We will see; I am not sure it is as simple as that.' Mrs Bootle brought over our lunch.

'Ah, food,' said John, as she set down a large omelette for John and a beef and ale pie for me. I changed the subject.

'I don't know how you live without meat, John,' I said, taking a succulent chunk of beef which was dripping in rich gravy, and spearing a carrot on my fork.

'Well, it has suited me very well since I was but seventeen, so there we are. John Newton's essay "The return to nature: a defence of the vegetable regimen" persuaded me. You should read it, you know. He recommends that pure water, teetotalism and vegetarianism all make for a healthy body and an active mind. The regime has served me well over the years.'

'Well, I think we will have to agree to differ on that, for I believe one cannot better a good meat pie! Now let us enjoy our meal.'

On Saturday, I received word from Cassandra that Albert Bates had been released. Mr Chattoway had come in person on Tuesday to tell Lady Irvine that the case had been thrown out by the Grand Jury and then he had returned this morning to say the prisoner had finally been released the previous day. The Irvines had powerful friends indeed. I chuckled to myself as I thought of how Emily had interrupted proceedings. I felt genuine pleasure at the prospect of James and Emily being reunited with their father, and I resolved to pay them a visit soon.

*

As I made my way home from my surgery in Edward Street I took the long route, along Broad Street, down Berwick Street and along Little Pulteney and Brewer Streets to approach Great Pulteney Street from the south. I wandered along, thinking of Cassandra and what John had said. Would her family accept me; could I dare to hope? It was a bright October day, the last warmth of the sun of autumn before winter set in, and I felt quietly optimistic as I strolled along whistling "The Queen of the Night", lost in my own world. I reached my house and set down my bag in the hallway. However, before I had taken off my greatcoat, there was a knock at the door, and I opened it again.

'Doctor, there's been an accident, can you come?' A boy of eight or nine stood on the doorstep.

'Where, lad? What's happened?'

'Broad Street, sir, girl knocked over.'

'Very well, I am coming,' I said and I picked up my bag and hurried out. On the corner of Broad Street and Berwick Street a crowd had gathered. There were cries from the innermost onlookers and one woman staggered back, looking pale. A cab stood in the middle of the road:

the old horse wide-eyed and sweating, whinnying in fright, frothing at the bit as the driver tried to calm it.

'Stepped out, she did, wasn't looking where she was going,' a fellow said.

'Poor lass, she looks badly hurt,' a woman's voice said.

'Let's see then,' said another, in a more prurient tone.

'Get back, give 'er some room,' cried a deep voice at the front.

It was an accident. They were all too common on the busy narrow streets where pedestrians and traders jostled for space with carriages and animals. In the crush, the slops and filth of the road made it easy to lose one's footing at times. I pushed my way through.

'I am a doctor, can I help?' On the ground lay a slight figure I recognised. It was young Jo Parker, who had been attacked over the summer by the man in the cesspit, Matthew Wiltshire, and his accomplice. She lay motionless, her torso partially pinned under the wheel of the cab. Her abdomen was crushed, her blood and insides spilling onto the filthy cobbles. She was gasping short, terminal breaths, her eyes wide and staring. Two men were trying to push the vehicle backwards to release her, but I knew it would be too late. I knelt beside her young face, white and ghostlike, a trickle of blood running from the corner of her mouth, her blonde plait limp on the muddy road.

'Jo, Miss Parker,' I said softly. 'I am Dr Roberts. Easy there, try to take small breaths.' Her lips moved as if she was trying to speak. 'Don't talk, Jo, rest quiet,'

I comforted her, my hand on her grey, clammy brow. It would not be long. Her lips moved again and I put my head close to hear what she was trying to say.

'Tell Em… it was me.'

'Emily Bates? Tell her what?' I said.

'Was me, I killed 'im. Not 'er mother. Me; I was there. And the other one. Tell 'er. They both of 'em near did for me, but… I got 'em… I killed 'em both…' she took a deep gulping breath like a man drowning.

'The man in the cesspit?'

'Yes, and The Newcastle…'

'With the scissors?'

'Yes. They got me…but I got 'em. Tell Em…' Her throat made a gurgling sound and suddenly her mouth was full of blood, as she choked. I tried to turn her head to one side but it was no use. Her blood spewed onto the road and she died with her head in my hands. I sat back on my haunches, a sadness spreading through me for this poor young girl. A hard life and a brutal attack which sent her mad and caused her to murder two people; then a return from recuperation in the country to find most of her family taken by the cholera. What a pitiable life some of the poor were forced to lead. I closed her eyelids, my heart wrenching in pity for her. I thought of her sister, Becky, Emily Bates' friend, who had now lost another sibling. I felt sick to the core with the tragedy of life; the tragedy of death.

'God bless you, Jo Parker; God bless your soul,' I murmured, staring down at her lifeless face. Suddenly, there was a presence at my side and I turned to see Emily Bates.

'What's 'appened? I'm just on me way 'ome. Oh, it's Jo; poor Jo,' she shrieked as she took in the scene. She took her friend's head in her hands and kissed her white forehead. 'Oh my Lor', my poor Jo,' she muttered over and over, her face white with shock. I put my hand on Emily's shoulder.

'I am sorry; there was nothing I could do.' As I stood, the bobby had arrived, Constable Lewis's replacement; he looked even younger and greener than his predecessor.

'She's Jo Parker of 25 Marshall Street. I know her sister; I'll let her know. Will you send for Middleton's?' I said. 'Come, Emily, you can do nothing for her; I'll take you home.' She allowed me to give her my arm and she leaned heavily on me as I tried to comfort her. Despite the shock, she remained dry-eyed as we took a last look at Jo and left.

I took Emily to her lodging and set the pan to boil on the stove. I glanced around, noticing how clean and tidy it was, and how Emily had restored a sense of homeliness, with a jar of flowers on the table and some soup ready on the stove. Emily sat slumped in the armchair, silent. When the tea was made I sat beside her.

'Emily, I am sorry for your loss. But listen, I have news.' I took a deep breath. 'It was not your mother that killed Matthew Wiltshire; it was Jo. She just confessed to me as she lay dying and she wanted me to tell you. She also killed Samuel Harrison outside The Newcastle. He was the second of her two attackers back in the summer and she killed them both. They were bad men; they had attacked a woman before.' Emily looked up and stared at me.

'Not Mother?' Her brown eyes looked straight into mine, seeking the truth.

'No. Jo must have been here with her mother when Wiltshire came looking for his daughter, "Eliza". Jo knew him immediately as the man who had attacked her, and she must have gone mad and killed him when he started threatening them all. Your mother confessed the partial truth to Reverend Whitehead when she knew *she* was dying, to save her friend's daughter from the gallows. Your mother is innocent; her soul can rest in peace.'

'Mother; I am sorry for doubting her,' Emily said, her hands twisting in her lap, her eyes filling with tears. She sat for a few moments in silence. 'I'll tell Father when 'e wakes up, 'e's asleep in there.' She motioned to the back room. 'But poor Jo... and poor *Becky*, I must go and tell Becky, she must know...' She started up from the chair, but I put my hand on her arm.

'Wait, you have had a shock. Wait a while before you go.'

'Jo killed him...' she said, eventually. 'Not Mother. Not Mother.' It sank in, and the conflicting emotions showed on her face: the relief, the sadness, the horror of it all.

'No, not your mother; I will send word to Lady Irvine. It is over, Emily, it is over.'

As I walked home, I thought of the Bates family, I thought of the cholera epidemic and John's work and I thought how my own life had changed. For all of us, after this autumn, nothing would be the same again. What a couple of months it had been.

TWENTY-THREE

Wednesday 1st November

A garden at night and it is Cassandra's birthday

I was taking Cassandra to a concert that evening at St John's Smith Square in Westminster. It was probably my favourite of all the music venues in London; it had an intimacy which larger settings lacked and it was an elegant building. Cassandra had never been there before and I was thrilled at the thought of introducing it to her. She genuinely shared my love of music and she herself was a fine pianist. I had met with her often and those times enriched my week.

On our way home from the concert, Hopkins dropped us on the opposite side of the square as we desired some cool night air after the warmth of the concert hall. I opened the wrought metal gate to the secluded garden in the middle of the square, and we sat on the iron bench beneath one of the enormous oaks in the moonlight. Bats flitted and turned high on the night airs and an owl hooted its presence. The vast inky sky stretched above us as I held her gloved hand in mine and we sat in silence looking at the stars.

'Look, there is Cassiopeia, I was almost named for that,' Cassandra laughed. 'Luckily, Mama saw sense and named me for a goddess instead.'

'I rather like the name Cassiopeia and I think it would be fitting to name a child after an infinite part of the universe,' I said. 'People say they have infinite love for their offspring.'

'Well, I am not sure that "Frank" is part of the universe; it sounds very down to earth to me!' she said. 'Difficult as it is to be a mother, I should like to have a child one day,' she mused.

'Well, we will see what the gods have in store for you, beautiful Cassandra.' I looked at her pale face in the moonlight and I ached with love for her, feeling a deep pull towards her in the pit of my stomach. I broke my gaze at last. 'We should go in, your father would not approve of you out here, unchaperoned, my dear.'

'It has been a strange two months,' Cassandra said, ignoring me and staring up towards the stars once more. 'I have gone from nursing to being a lady of leisure; from having one brother to having one brother but also a niece and nephew my age and from having no sisters to nearly having met a half-sister who confessed to murdering a man when she was innocent. These are strange times indeed.'

'You are right, my dear,' I agreed. 'For my part, I have had the most harrowing time, professionally, that I can remember, but I have learned so much about the cholera and about the human spirit. I have witnessed acts of bravery and kindness, in families and neighbours caring for each other and I have witnessed great resilience in people whose lives have been devastated. I have, to a large extent, overcome my own fear of cholera and I have come to like and admire my old friend, John, more than I ever did before. I have gained, dare I say it, the affection of the most beautiful and sweet woman I have ever known.' I pulled her to me in the darkness and she rested her head against my shoulder and looked up at me, her face bathed in soft moonlight, her blue eyes looking into my very soul.

'And I have shed a mistrust of men and gained the attentions of a fine man whom I believe I can truly love and respect.' She lowered her eyes as if she had said too much. I placed my hand under her slender chin and raised her face to mine.

'May I kiss you, sweet Cassandra?' I said.

'You may, Dr Roberts,' she murmured, and I did. As I closed my eyes and felt her soft lips on mine, all else was forgotten.

Eventually, I opened my eyes and the moon shone onto Cassandra's face as she looked up at me. My heart beat faster. Now was the moment; I was never more certain of anything.

'Cassandra,' I said, 'I have something I wish to ask you.' I slipped from the bench to kneel on one knee and felt the damp of the grass seep into my breeches, as I composed myself. A ripple of breeze lifted the hair at my forehead and I felt my pulse throb in my head. She looked nervous, shy and hopeful all at once, and I could see the colour rise in her soft cheeks as she anticipated what I was about to say. 'Miss Irvine, sweet Cassandra, I wonder if you would do me the honour of accepting my hand in marriage?'

She looked down at me, her eyes suffused with emotion, soft and loving and shining with wetness. She gave me her hand. 'I will, Dr Frank Roberts, I will,' she said.

I sat next to her and we embraced, and I held her head at my chest; I felt I had finally arrived home. I could not speak, I merely held her tight, never wanting to let her go. Eventually she pulled away from me.

'When will you go to Papa?'

'We have not known each other very long; is it too soon?'

'It is my birthday in two weeks and Papa and Mama are to hold a party for me; perhaps that would be the time?'

'I will wait until then. For now I must take you in or I may not be invited!'

★

It was Saturday 11th November and the evening of Cassandra's birthday had arrived. I donned a hired tailcoat and white tie and put on my best shoes, which Mrs Hook had polished until I could see my face reflected in them. When I was ready, I studied myself in the mirror, the oil lamp kind to my reflection. I looked my thirty years, but with age I had gained a certain *gravitas*; my skin was still smooth and my hair dark and I looked, although not a young man in the first flush of youth, a respectable and genuine man. I had proved myself a successful doctor, liked and valued, so I hoped, by my patients. I looked confident of my place in the world, comfortable in my own skin. I had not been dogged by the melancholia for many months now, and I was starting to hope I had left it behind forever. I hoped it would all be enough.

The cab arrived and it cut through the rainy night to Mayfair. The party was in full swing when I arrived, and what a party it was. The house was brilliantly lit, and bright yellow-white light spilled from every window onto the square. As I stepped down and paid the cabbie, the sound of orchestral music floated out on the damp air. The front door was open and a group of people made their way in ahead of me. The women wore long evening gowns of sumptuous silks which gave off a soft sheen in the artificial light, their necks bedecked with pearls glowing and diamonds twinkling brilliantly. Chatter and laughter regaled my ears, as I checked my tie and followed the group up the steps.

Two footmen were greeting the guests and taking the travelling cloaks, and I handed my overcoat to one of them.

'Ah, Carter, good evening to you.'

'Good evening, Dr Roberts, sir,' he said. I looked around, not recognising anyone. 'Miss Cassandra said to tell you she's in the drawing room, sir.'

'Thank you, Carter.'

'Very good, sir,' he bowed.

I walked across the hallway as he greeted the next guests. The drawing room door was open and the room was full of people. I spied Cassandra, who looked stunning in a deep red silken gown, high-necked, with two gleaming strings of pearls at her neck. Her hair was pulled into a soft chignon and adorned with tiny pearls and her ear lobes sparkled with rubies. She was with her friend, now Mabel Summers, and I went over.

'Cassandra; Mrs Summers,' I bowed. 'How are you enjoying married life?'

'It suits me very well, thank you,' said Mabel, smiling.

'Frank, I have been waiting for you, for most of these people are even older than Papa,' said Cassandra conspiratorially, a twinkle in her eyes, our secret hopes unspoken.

'I am at your service,' I bowed to her. 'You look beautiful tonight; as do you Mrs Summers.' Cassandra blushed prettily.

'You are looking very well, Frank,' said Mabel, standing back and eying my appearance up and down. 'I believe formal wear suits you; I declare you look most distinguished, doesn't he, Cassandra?' she laughed, her hand on her friend's elbow.

'You do, indeed, Frank. You could rival Edmund, tonight, although he, poor fellow, I expect is very much wishing he could be here.'

'Have you heard from him?' I said.

'Not yet, it is too soon. Edmund did love a big party, though.' Edward Summers joined us.

'My dear Mabel, Cassandra, there is dancing in the ballroom, you must come! Ah, Frank, good evening to you, we must get you a drink, man,' he said, shaking my hand and then lifting two glasses from the tray of a passing waiter. I raised my glass, looking into the beautiful face of Cassandra, silently wondering if in but a few hours I would be able to call her my fiancée.

'Dancing, dancing, come!' urged Edward again, as the orchestra struck up a rousing tune, propelling Mabel by the arm towards the door and looking back over his shoulder at us.

'I'm afraid my dancing skills are a little rusty,' I said, but Cassandra would not let me off the hook.

'I'm sure you are too modest, Frank, come on,' she laughed, pushing me through the door after her friends, back through the hallway to the ballroom at the back of the house. As we went, she whispered to me.

'I must tell you, Mama has found lodgings for James and Emily and their father, in John Street, off Golden Square. It is a much better area, and more spacious rooms. They are to move at the end of the month.'

'Well, I am pleased for them and grateful to your mother. It is a stroke of fortune for them, indeed.' We arrived at the ballroom and opportunity for conversation was lost in the crescendo of the orchestra. I looked at the lead violinist and thought of my father's violin in its case, so long untouched of late.

Later, after the dancing and the mingling in the crush of guests who seemed to spill from every room, I could wait no longer and I determined to find Lord Irvine. I passed through several rooms, looking for him. If he gave his consent, I may soon be able to call her my fiancée, my *wife*. It was too much joy to comprehend. I felt butterflies swooping and soaring in my insides. Her face in the moonlight as she accepted me that night nearly two weeks ago was burned in my memory. I had no happier vision in the whole of my life. I found Lord Irvine standing at the fireplace in the drawing room, with two elderly gentlemen. I took a deep breath and approached them.

'Ah, Frank, come and meet my friends. Lord Palmerston, you will recognise, and Lord Granville. This is Dr Frank Roberts, Cassandra's guest. Frank works as a general practitioner in Soho, don't you, Frank?'

'Indeed, sir, I do. Lord Palmerston,' I shook the hand of the Home Secretary with a little bow; 'Lord Granville.' I tried very hard not to feel intimidated by these great men, but it was hard, remembering my own beginnings, an orphan, a nobody.

'Lord Palmerston may soon be wearing greater shoes, if the rumours are true, eh?' Lord Irvine chuckled and tapped the side of his nose.

'We shall see, Sidney, we'll see. But Soho, that's where the epidemic of cholera was, isn't it?' said Lord Palmerston to me. 'That must have hit your patients hard?'

'Yes sir. It was a terrible time; five hundred or more died in ten days back in the autumn, but it has passed now.'

'Gracious, I didn't realise it was so deadly. I know the sanitarians have been making their presence felt in the House; there is a growing movement that something must be done. The trouble is: what? No government can change everything overnight. We've committed £300,000 for the expansion of the sewers, you know, but such works take time.' Normally I was keen to discuss the cholera at any opportunity, feeling I had something useful to add, but I was not in the mood for it tonight. I had more pressing matters on my mind.

'Excuse me, gentlemen, but I wonder if I might have a private word with Lord Irvine?' I looked at him, and he must have seen the seriousness in my face.

'Very well, Roberts. We'll step into my study.'

'It was an honour to meet you,' I bowed a farewell

to their Lordships and followed Lord Irvine out of the room.

Lord Irvine's study was a small, snug, panelled room, with bookcases filling two of the walls. A fire was burning and a leather-topped desk stood before the window. He turned up the wick on the lamp and sank into his chair behind it. 'Take a seat, Frank.'

'I will stand, thank you.'

'What is it, man?' he said, his grey eyes and the silver streaks in his beard highlighted by the lamp. I took a deep breath.

'Lord Irvine, you can have little doubt as to what I am about to say. I come to request the hand of your daughter, Cassandra, in marriage. I can assure you that I love her with all my heart and I believe she returns my feelings. I swear I will do my utmost to make her happy and care for her most diligently for the whole of my life.' I stopped, my heart in my mouth, awaiting his response. He looked at me, then down at his desk, rubbing the fingers of one hand with those of the other. He said nothing, as if weighing up what to say. The clock on the mantelpiece ticked softly and struck eleven, the chimes seemed to stretch an eternity. I heard the strains of the music in the ballroom, the distant flurries of laughter, the rising cadence of a party in full swing. Still he didn't speak; he didn't look at me. After a couple of minutes, I could bear it no longer.

'Sir, what am I to assume by your silence?' I said, my voice sounding hollow and shaky. Had all my early fears come to pass? Was I not a suitable suitor after all? He was roused from his reverie by my words, and when he spoke his voice was soft and broken, pleading forgiveness.

'Frank, I am sorry, I do not know what to say. I know you are a fine fellow and I know Cassandra cares for you. But I should not have encouraged you, for I have my family's position to think of. Every generation of Irvines has married into the aristocracy…' his voice tailed off, and he looked ashen-faced and guilty.

'Are you not convinced of our regard for each other?' I said, in a small voice.

'I am. Lady Irvine, particularly, is certain of it, and she has encouraged me to allow your visits. But I have had cause of late to question her judgement, and now the moment has come, I realise that I should have put a stop to it a long time ago. I am sorry; it was not fair to either of you.'

I felt my blood turn to ice and I felt set to collapse into the chair, but fighting through my emotions, I knew I had to maintain my poise. 'Do I understand that you refuse your consent, sir?'

'I am afraid so, that is my decision, Dr Roberts.'

'Am I permitted to see her at all, if she wishes to maintain any sort of contact with me?' I said, my last vestige of self-control receding. He hesitated.

'As long as you both understand that I will not change my mind,' he said, gravely.

'Thank you, sir, I will bid you goodnight.' I bowed and scurried from the room, my face burning now I had turned from him. He did not follow and I closed the door, leaning back on it gripping the door handle tightly. I took deep breaths. Suddenly I was aware that people in the hallway were looking at me strangely. They had paused in their chatter and laughter to consider the stranger in their midst, an unknown, a nobody, clutching at a door for support. I looked at them all in their fine clothes, with their titles and their inherited social position, and I felt sick. I had to get away; what was I doing in this place? I stood and, mustering as much dignity as I could, I strode towards the front door.

Cassandra stood near the entrance with Mabel. I could hardly bear to look at her as I stumbled past. She put a mute hand on my arm, and all I manage was a small shake of my head. The fire in her eyes went out, but she maintained an outward expression of normality. I squeezed her hand and lurched out into the night.

TWENTY-FOUR

Sunday 26th November

I am confined to my house and John gives another lecture

I woke to the sound of knocking on my chamber door. Dim, cool light spilled around the sides of the curtains; it was after daybreak. I rolled over and ignored the sound. A moment later it came again, a gentle, persistent rap. I buried my head under my bolster and all went black. From my dark cocoon, I heard the door open and footsteps approach the bed.

'Sir? It's after nine and I've brought you some refreshment.' Mrs Hook's voice sounded reedy and uncertain. I didn't move. 'Sir? I've sent out for a pastry and got the *Chronicle*.' A pause. 'Won't you sit up, sir?'

I roused myself to speak. 'Leave it.' I heard her leave the tray on my side table and her footsteps retreating.

'Try to get up, sir, it's not doing you any good lying abed,' she ventured, her voice quiet. The door closed behind her. I cursed her; I was awake now.

The melancholia had returned. Everywhere was darkness and gloom. All was bleak; the clouds were grey, the sun failed to break the thick fog which sat heavy over London, heavy over my head. I could not remember when I had last eaten; I subsisted on flagons of coffee, pots of tea and bottles of wine. Mrs Hook had seen it before, but she could never just let me be, let me float away, fade into unthinking oblivion. I wished she would.

From time to time she came to tell me I had requests for visits, people needing me. Let them wait or seek help elsewhere. I was done. The exhaustion of the autumn, coupled with the perpetual state of nervous excitement which surrounded my every thought of Cassandra had done me in. It was all for nothing. I wasn't good enough; she wouldn't be mine. My patients would find another practitioner. The work with John had achieved nothing: what had changed? He, *we*, had convinced nobody. I lay in silence, my head cushioned from the world, hiding, and let sleep roll over me again; welcome oblivion.

The curtains were open and a few rays of feeble sunlight fell on my bed. The warm aroma of fresh coffee hit me and my mouth watered despite myself. I opened one eye and could see Mrs Hook fussing, tidying away a few bits of clothing strewn around the room. She worked quietly, but her head was alert; I could tell she was listening for any sound from me. I shifted my position, my lips dry and my head aching.

'Good day, sir, it's after lunchtime now, I've brought you some fresh coffee. Won't you have a drink, sir?'

I raised my head a little and shifted myself to lean against the bed-head. My mouth felt like sand. She came over and poured a cup of steaming coffee; adding a little milk and handing it to me. The richness and warmth hit my face as I raised the cup to my parched lips, and I took a sip. The bitter, hot liquid swirled in my mouth, delicious, for a moment.

'Can I get you anything to eat, sir?' she said. 'I've a meat pie, or some cheese and some of my chutney; or a milk posset?'

'Perhaps a little bread and cheese,' I said. Somehow I could not rouse myself for conversation. My brain was a dark sea of thoughts, images colliding and sinking, sinking into the depths of blue-black. I was squeezed between a deep ocean and a black, threatening sky; there was no room for me in between. I had no wish to think, or to live.

'Very good, sir,' she said and she scuttled away.

I sipped the coffee. I had lost track of what day it was and as I tossed the paper on the bed aside, I was surprised to find it was dated the 26th; more than two weeks had passed since Cassandra's party. I had no memory of what I'd been doing. I remembered getting home and going to bed, and then very little since. It had hit me like a sledge-hammer and knocked me for six. I'd succumbed quickly with little warning this time.

I threw the paper to the floor and finished the coffee. Then I lay my head back under my covers to block out the light and went back to sleep.

*

It was two weeks later, nearing the middle of December, and the melancholia was lifting. I was still not entirely well, but the quiet ministrations of Mrs Hook and the passage of time had produced an improvement in my spirits. I had ventured outside, finally, and had started seeing my patients again. Winter was setting in and

292

darkness enveloped the city by not long after four in the afternoon. It seemed the coalition government was struggling and it was rumoured that Lord Palmerston would be likely to take over as Prime Minister in the spring. With the festive season approaching and Soho back to normal, there was a buzz on the streets, a sense of optimism that the New Year and a new administration might bring change.

Personally I felt less optimistic. I was rocked by the force of depression which had hit me like a steam train and, now I was improving, I felt guilt retrospectively at my own self-indulgence. I had had no contact with the Bates family for several weeks and I had no idea how they were faring. I had not seen Cassandra since the fateful party and, when I could bear to think of her, I found I missed her very much. She had written to say she was bound to respect her father's decision. Mrs Hook had kept the letter from me until my mental strength had returned. I had belatedly written back to say I would respect her wishes. Back at work, I had been busy with the burgeoning numbers afflicted by influenza, always rife in the winter months, and I had been glad of the distraction. Whenever I was unoccupied, my mind filled with the image of Cassandra's crushed look as I had fled her house that night.

This evening, though, I was back to thinking about the cholera once more, for I was going to listen to John lecture on his work. Apparently he had called on me during my illness, but I had no memory of his visits. He had sent word inviting me to his lecture and I felt strong enough to go.

The small oak-panelled auditorium at the Hunterian was packed once more, a throng of erudite faces illuminated by the oil lamps at the ends of the rows. Again, people sat on the steps and craned for a better view. I recognised many of the same faces as at my last visit here, more than three months ago, and many unfamiliar ones. Many sanitarians and public health reformers had come to listen, in addition to physicians, general practitioners and representatives of the many parishes of London. I heard people before the lecture started, conjecturing about the talk with a ripple of excitement; word was the illustrious Dr Snow was to present to a wider audience his ideas on cholera transmission. I listened to the gossip and said nothing. I knew what he was going to say; but I didn't know what his reception would be. I felt quietly nervous for him. Once again John was dressed in a sombre black suit and dark tie and once again his quiet, husky voice commanded attention. His dark hair had greyed a little since the last time, but otherwise he looked the same as ever.

I watched as he placed his hands on the lectern and drew breath for the conclusion of his talk. His clear grey eyes surveyed the audience and I briefly caught his eye as he once again gave the merest of nods to acknowledge my presence.

'In conclusion, gentlemen, I put it to you that the miasmatist, anti-contagionist view of cholera transmission is outdated and incorrect. I have presented here the results of investigations conducted this summer in south London and in the Soho district. I put it to you that the evidence is before our eyes on this map of the Broad Street area: the cholera is transmitted from person to person through the water.' John pointed again to an enlargement of his map depicting the Soho deaths, which he had described in detail earlier in his talk.

He stepped back from the lectern to muted applause. There was a shuffling in the audience, whispered comments from each man to his neighbour. I looked around to see many of the gathered listeners looking doubtful or even embarrassed. Groups of onlookers broke into discussion and I overheard some comments from those seated nearest to me.

'It's a shame; an esteemed anaesthetist, but he's gone too far this time...'

'This'll destroy his reputation for sure; why, who will take him seriously now?'

'I'd heard he has a fixation with this idea of the water, when everyone knows it's in the miasma. He's in line to take over as president of the Medical Society of London, too.'

'It contradicts the Board of Health's view; waste of an evening, listening to this...'

John looked uncharacteristically uneasy, shifting from one foot to the other as he sensed the disbelief and hostility of the audience. I caught his eye fleetingly and I could see he knew it had not gone well. His eyes swept the hall once more, before he cleared his throat loudly, and invited questions from the floor. Several members of the audience stood, and he called upon one to speak.

'I believe the Commission of Sewers enquiry found the areas where there were odours from poorly maintained drains and cesspools and a lack of linkage to the main sewer system to be the worst affected by the cholera? Surely that confirms the miasma as the cause, does it not?' an elderly gentleman said.

'I would counter that by arguing that where the drains and cesspools are poorly maintained, there is a much greater likelihood of cross-contamination of the drinking water supply by waste, and that it is this contamination of the water that is the cause, rather than the miasma,' said John.

'But it is well known that the miasma is the cause of disease; did your work not consider *where* the miasma comes from?' called another speaker.

'Sir, I put it to you that if you have listened to my lecture at all, you will understand that I absolutely refute that the miasma is the cause of transmission of the cholera.' There was a ripple of disagreement at this, with audible "noes" and indignant cries. John flushed, struggling to make himself heard, his deep voice starting to sound ruffled.

'Gentlemen, gentlemen, I do not report my findings and propose my views on a whim; but rather after careful and detailed study of the cholera, over several epidemics and spanning two decades. I believe there needs to be a radical shift in our thinking away from the vague concept of the miasma to a more precise view of disease causation. I believe simply that the cholera is transmitted via a specific agent or poison and my work leads me to believe that the agent is carried in the water.' The crowd did not like this view, so strongly stated. The noise level was rising; people calling out that he was wrong, he had lost his senses, he should stick to anaesthesia and leave the question of disease causation to the physicians and sanitarians. A few people even stood to leave the lecture theatre, muttering crossly to themselves, the oil lamps guttering and flaring as they passed.

'A moment, gentlemen.' A tall man in a pale frock coat and elaborate necktie stood and spoke with authority, and the crowd quietened. I turned to see and I felt my stomach churn as I recognised the speaker: it was Edwin Chadwick himself.

'May I ask,' he said, 'is the esteemed Dr Snow familiar with a report commissioned by the Government twelve years back, written by myself and my colleagues, entitled "The Sanitary Conditions of the Labouring population"?' A ripple of laughter passed around the hall, as all men of the medical profession were aware of the document, which had underpinned the sanitarian movement.

'Indeed, I am, Mr Chadwick,' said John, recognising his nemesis.

'May I further ask: is Dr Snow aware of the link this report showed between poor living conditions and life expectancy, and the link with poor sanitation?'

'I am fully aware of the findings outlined in the report mentioned, and I am aware that draining the sewage of London into the drinking water of London was the outcome of the report.' There were more guffaws at what many in the audience saw as this blatant distortion of the report's recommendations. Chadwick stood stony-faced, his deep forehead framed by a strip of heavily receding black hair and his thin lips humourless beneath his thick moustache. When the audience was silent, he continued.

'Is Dr Snow aware that the report concluded the increased miasma which surrounds the poor to be the cause of the disparity in life expectancy?' he said, a chill in his normally plummy voice.

'I saw no direct evidence in the report which attributed the reduced life expectancy of the poorer classes to the miasma, no. I am, however, aware that the report resulted in a sewerage system which drains the waste of London into our great river; and it is well known that our drinking water is sourced from the same.'

'Whatever his own interpretations of the findings, is Dr Snow aware that the report and my investigations were instrumental in inspiring the Public Health Act of 1848, and the establishment of the General Board of Health, of which I was the first director?'

John was unmoved and spoke evenly. 'I am, sir, but what, may I ask, does this have to do with specific knowledge of the cause of transmission of the cholera?'

'My friend,' Chadwick replied icily, 'I can assure you that those at the top, both of the medical profession, and in government, are fully in agreement that the miasma is the cause of the transmission of all contagious diseases, be it influenza, typhoid or the cholera. Well known for your work on anaesthesia you may be, but I question your impertinence, Doctor, in challenging this basic tenet of medicine. I assure you, there is not a man in England who has conducted more thorough and rigorous work on the living conditions of the poor and the link with disease than I have done. I tell you, it is accepted fact that the cholera is transmitted in the miasma. Furthermore, I suggest it is arrogance of the basest nature to question your superiors and betters.' He sat down, to a mixture of catcalls and laughter, but I am sad to say the laughter was directed not at Chadwick, but at John Snow. John gripped the edges of the lectern, his lips pursed in a thin line, and waited for the furore to die down.

'And I suggest that the esteemed Mr Chadwick was forced to step down from public office last year due to his rigidity of thought and unpopularity in certain quarters, and therefore will have greater time on his hands to read and fully understand my work on the cholera. He will then, perhaps, be able to speak from a position of knowledge rather than one of prejudice.' There was a momentary silence in the hall and you could have cut the air with a knife.

Chadwick stood once more, paused and then with a dignified air, head held high, he merely said, 'You are wrong, Snow, you are wrong, and all your colleagues here know it.' He sat down, to whistling and calls of agreement, which were followed by the breakout of chatter and laughter at the interchange. Some members of the audience threw rolled up papers at John. It was all most unseemly, and I felt deeply sorry for John to be placed in such a position. It was rare for open hostility to be expressed in such medical meetings, which made it all the worse; usually disagreements were phrased in gentlemanlike suggestion and considerate questioning.

'Thank you, gentlemen, no more questions; thank you,' said John evenly, stepping down from the lectern and leaving through the panelled door at the back of the dais. I sat and watched the barely perceptible drop of his head as he went and I felt anger, real fury, for him. After the past weeks of dulled emotion and nothingness, I was stirred to feeling once more. All around me I could hear the audience talking, agreeing with Chadwick, belittling John, laughing at the interchange. I knew John disliked Chadwick and fundamentally would not care what he thought, but after all John's efforts over so many years, it must be humbling to be so publicly dismissed, and to be laughed at too. How could they throw their papers at him? I wasn't sure whether to follow him and commiserate or whether he would prefer to lick his wounds in private.

I sat in silence until the hall had almost cleared, and then I went out, to see if John was there. Unlike his last lecture here, three months ago, when everyone wanted to see him and speak to him, the foyer was empty and he had gone. I guessed he wanted to be alone, so I left. I felt furious at the way they had treated him, when I had seen how much work he had done, how much time he had devoted to the cause. They were wrong, and I hoped the great men in the audience this evening would live to rue the day they had ridiculed him. Big snowflakes were falling as I stepped out into the street and I kicked wildly at the kerb stones, spattering my boots with muddy slush as, chilled to the bone, I walked home.

★

It was nearly a week later and John had invited me out to a talk at the Medical Society for London and for a drink afterwards. After the last talk, I could not stomach another meeting of medical men, but I agreed to meet him at Wilkins for refreshment afterwards. I had not seen him since the lecture at the Hunterian, and I was anxious to see how he had taken it. We stood at the rail along the back, a platter of oysters on the counter and a port in my hand; John stuck to his coffee.

'I was so sorry to hear your reception at the Hunterian, John. They are fools. One day they will see that you are right and they will be forced to eat their words.' He paused, tight-lipped, debating what to say, and then his shoulders relaxed and he spoke.

'It is as it ever was; the establishment is remarkably slow to adopt new ideas.'

'You must have been furious with them; *I* was furious on your behalf. I know how hard you have worked,' I said.

'I was angry, but after a day or two I realised that they cannot be expected to change their minds on the evidence of one evening. I have always known it will be an uphill struggle and I riled Chadwick that night, I could tell. I stood up to him. I said things that many are too afraid to say. I am hopeful that it may have put the seed of doubt in their minds. From a seed, great things can grow. One day, Frank, one day.'

'You are remarkably patient.'

'What else can I do? I can only chip away at established thought, little by little. There is no other option. But I am so glad to see that you are up and about, Frank; I was worried about you for a couple of weeks. I gathered what had happened from your ramblings.' His earnest grey eyes looked into my face and I saw sincere affection and concern there. I looked down into the red liquid which swirled in my glass.

'I am sorry; the business with Cassandra hit me hard. I went from thinking I might marry the finest woman I know, to nothing. On top of the exhaustion, I sank without trace; it is frightening how rapidly I fell this time. But I hear you visited me: thank you, my friend.' I looked up at him, and he patted my arm.

'Don't give up yet, Frank. Perhaps he might change his mind, one day.' John had voiced what I had not dared to allow myself to think; was there, could there be any possibility Lord Irvine would ever reconsider his decision? I shook myself; it would do no good to speculate on things I had little influence over.

'Let us talk of other matters, John. Has there been *any* progress in the adoption of your theory?' I took a mouthful of port as John sipped his coffee. 'It was unbelievable, the scene at the Hunterian; I was truly shocked that they wouldn't even consider your ideas, they were such a prejudiced bunch.'

'Frank, that is not fair; they were a traditionalist crowd, I'll agree. But no matter, the truth will out one day. Besides, it was not so long ago that you were reluctant to challenge the accepted view,' he teased.

'Well, I have grown bolder, working alongside you, and I have changed,' I retorted. 'I hope the medical profession will beg your forgiveness one day. Has the Vestry Committee commenced its investigation for the Board of Guardians?'

'Yes; Reverend Whitehead and the committee have

plans for a very thorough survey, in greater depth than our work, but essentially covering the same ground. I visited the houses where there had been deaths from cholera, but the committee plans to seek full information from all the dwellings where there were cases, not just deaths. It should provide a more complete picture of this area than my work did. I told Dr Lankester I would join the investigation.'

'Who is Lankester?'

'He's the medical officer of health for the St James's district. He's to be in charge of the enquiry; a microscopist by background.'

'Well, at least he acknowledges your contribution.'

'Not really; can you believe the Board of Health is refusing access to the information they collected, so he will be in need of extra feet on the ground to repeat the work. So much for a coordinated effort; the people of Soho will be sick of answering questions. I confess, though, I am surprised that a second excavation of the pump well was undertaken and Mr Farrell, the engineer, informed me personally that he found no hole or crevice in the brickwork of the well by which any impurity might enter,' said John, puzzled. 'I feel sure the breach must have been missed; I remain convinced the pump was the cause.'

'Perhaps they did not excavate sufficiently?'

'I don't know. Anyway, they replaced the handle of the pump a week after the last case and the cholera has not returned to the district. I still hold that my theory was correct, but I did not make a compelling enough case. You know I presented the map at the Epidemiological Society meeting recently?'

'No, what did they think of it?'

'They thought the map was a novel approach, shall we say, but they were not convinced either.'

'When will the committee report the findings of their enquiry?'

'In the spring, I believe. We shall see: I take one step at a time, Frank. If the investigation refutes my theory, I shall just have to redouble my efforts once more,' said John. I marvelled, not for the first time, at this ever resilient and resourceful man.

'I wonder if they will identify the index case, the first case which started it all,' I said. 'If we understood how the pump well became infected, the case would be stronger.'

'More watertight, you mean? If you'll excuse the pun,' said John with a smile. 'I hope so, for I confess I am still not sure of the index case,' he said. 'I have studied the figures from Farr time and time again, but I do not know. But I must head home now; I am expected at the Westminster in the morning to see the patients for Monday's list. Goodnight, my friend.' He patted my shoulder and was gone. I picked at the last oyster, drained my glass, and headed out into the night.

TWENTY-FIVE

Monday 18th December

A call in the night

Two nights later, I woke, confused; the room was dark and quiet. What had roused me? Then I heard it again: an insistent knocking at the front door. As I came to, I heard Mrs Hook descend the stairs and, a moment later, her footsteps came back up to my room. I opened my door before she knocked.

'Doctor, there's a gentleman downstairs says you must come,' she said, her face half lit by the lamp light, her hair untamed.

'What gentleman?'

'Says he's Lady Irvine's driver; Hopkins.'

I was immediately alert, my heart pounding. What was Hopkins doing here in the middle of the night? Why had they sent for me, of all people? Was Lady Irvine unwell? Was Cassandra unwell? With no thought for propriety, I pulled on my breeches and shirt as Mrs Hook retreated. I buttoned my boots and threw on my coat and, grabbing a scarf against the cold night, I bounded down the stairs, to where Hopkins stood waiting.

'Hopkins, what is the matter?' I asked.

'It's Miss Cassandra, sir. Lady Irvine begs you to come. She's taken ill, sir.'

'Let's go,' I said, aware that Lady Irvine would not summon me in the middle of the night unless Cassandra's life was in danger. I marched out of the door and climbed in the carriage, my mind racing. What could be the matter with her? What would I find? Please God, I would be able to help.

The streets were quiet and it didn't take long to travel through the cold night to Mayfair. A damp fog hung low over the city and the light of the gas lamps created a confined blur, a yellow mist which didn't penetrate the darkness. I shivered and tightened my scarf around my neck. What could be wrong? I felt chilled to the bone with cold and anxiety and I blew on my hands to warm them. We arrived at the house, lit like a beacon in the dark night. Lady Irvine herself opened the door and ushered me in.

'Oh, Frank, it is Cassandra,' she whispered, grasping me by the hands and looking up into my face. 'She has a terrible sickness and purging and she is very weak. Lord Irvine's physician is out of the city and will come tomorrow, but I beg you, can you help her?'

'Take me to her; when did she take ill?' I asked, already on my way up the stairs as Lady Irvine indicated the way. I took the stairs two at a time, fleetingly wondering if Lord Irvine had given permission for me to attend, but I pushed the thought aside, not caring.

'Yesterday afternoon, Frank. She went out with Mabel and Edward Summers two days ago, then she was sick a couple of times after luncheon yesterday and today she has developed terrible stomach cramps and the liquid has been flowing out of her. She cannot get to the pot, she is so weak. Every hour or so, we have changed her bedding. She can barely open her eyes now.' We reached Cassandra's door and Lady Irvine opened it. As we went in, a maid came out carrying a basket of soiled sheets.

'We're out of fresh linen, m'lady.'

'Dr Roberts has come. Take the linen from the guest rooms, and then from my bed, if necessary, Lily.'

'Yes, m'lady.' She bobbed and was gone.

'Where did she go on Saturday?'

'To Hyde Park, then to Browns on Albemarle Street for tea; she had the almond cakes, she said…'

I went into the room, dimly lit after the brightness of the hall. A glass gas lamp stood on the table, and another next to the bed. As my eyes adjusted to the gloom, I saw that slumped on the pillows of her four-poster bed, lay Cassandra. On the floor were two buckets and two chamber pots. But Cassandra was beyond using them. She lay motionless, her features sunken, her face pale. Her beautiful lips had a bluish tinge to them, which made her scar appear livid, purple and prominent. Her soft brown curls lay limply at her brow, stray hairs damp with the hopeless ministrations of her desperate mother.

I sank to sit on the bed next to her. 'Oh Cassandra, sweet Cassandra,' I murmured under my breath, not caring what Lady Irvine thought. My heart wrenched at her appearance. I took her cool wrist and felt for the pulse, which was barely palpable. I was aware of my own pulse racing. I knew what it was. The signs were so familiar to me, there was no doubt. Cassandra had all the signs of cholera. Cholera: it seemed to haunt me. How could this be? Although there were always sporadic cases in London after an epidemic, I'd not heard of any locally. How had she contracted it?

'Is anyone else in the household unwell, Rose?' I asked, still holding Cassandra's wrist, for once abandoning her title. She was just a mother like any other, faced with the impending loss of her remaining daughter.

'No, Frank, although Mabel called yesterday morning and her Dr Summers is ill, too. What is it? What is the matter with her? Can you do anything?' asked Lady Irvine, a quiet desperation in her voice.

I thought hard. The tea in Mayfair: that was what linked Cassandra and Edward Summers. They had probably been served water with the tea. My mind was filled with an image of John Snow. Water; it had to be water. It was the cholera for sure.

'I fear she has the cholera.'

Lady Irvine gasped, her hand at her mouth, shaking in horror and sinking to sit on the chair. 'No, Frank. Please God, not the cholera.'

'I am afraid so.'

'But the cholera's gone, gone I thought...' she whispered, the colour drained from her lined face as she placed her hand on the brow of her daughter.

'There are often sporadic cases after an epidemic.'

'But the terrible epidemic in the summer: hardly anyone lived...' she whispered.

'That was a particularly devastating outbreak in Soho. Usually more people recover. We must get some fluid into her; she will be losing huge quantities from the gut. It is paramount she replaces that which she has lost.' I looked at Lady Irvine, to see silent tears falling. I transferred my hand to hers. 'Get some rest, I will stay with her. Leave me a maid in case I need anything, but I will nurse her. I will get her to take some liquid. Try to get a couple of hours of sleep before morning. I will look after her. I love her, too, you know,' I finished quietly.

'I know you do. But I cannot leave you, it is not proper, and my husband does not think I should have called upon you but I insisted,' she said, her wet grey eyes looking into mine.

'You can leave me; there is no one who will care for her more. Get some rest and I will do my utmost. She will be in good hands, I promise you.' I closed my hand over her hand.

'Very well.' She kissed Cassandra's forehead and made to leave, squeezing my hand as she looked at me. 'Please,' she implored. 'I will tell Lily to stay. Send for me if there is any change.'

'I will,' I promised, and she left. I held Cassandra's head and raised a cup of water to her lips. 'Cassandra, my love. It is Frank. Take a sip of water, you must drink,' I said. Her head was heavy in my hand and, although her eyelids fluttered, she made no other response. I put the cup down, and let her rest back on the pillow. I tried speaking to her more forcefully, but still there was barely a response. I sat for some time. I could not lose her; it could not happen to me again. My mother, my brother; please God, not the woman I loved. I would happily forgo any claim to her, if she would just live. There must be something I could do.

What would John do? John would say it was all in the fluid balance. I had to get her to drink. Cassandra's body gave an involuntary shudder and the bedding was soaked. I groaned, stood up and called for Lily. She and another maid came and I stepped outside as they changed her bed and clothing once again.

As I stood in the cool of the night corridor, I held my head in my hands. After all that had happened, I could not lose her from this world. She had to live. I felt raw and terrified; sick to my stomach. I felt an overpowering wave of empathy at the memory of all my patients last summer in Soho. Each household, each mother, each father, each husband or wife must have felt the same desperation that I was now feeling. I knew all too well how precarious life was, but I had never experienced it in such a visceral way. I felt so desperate to help her, so desperate for her to recover; so terrified of losing her. The maids came out with their load, and I shook myself. I must put my feelings to one side and behave in a more professional manner. What would John say if he could see me now? He would tell me I was doing Cassandra no good by dwelling on such thoughts, and he would be right. Fluids, she needed fluids. I took a deep breath, held my head up and went back to her bedside.

'Cassandra, Nurse Irvine,' I ordered, wondering if her professional title would bring any response. 'Nurse Irvine, you *must* take a sip of this; Miss Nightingale's orders,' I said, pulling her up less gently than before, and thrusting the cup against her lip. 'Rouse yourself, take some water,' I ordered. I kept speaking in this manner for a few minutes, willing her to wake and obey me. After a few minutes of abrupt orders, her eyes flickered, opening momentarily, and I felt a leap of hope. 'Take a sip, you must take some water,' I repeated sternly. Her lips parted and I was able to pour a trickle of liquid into her mouth. I watched her scarred lip as the tiny amount of water flowed under it. She managed to swallow, and I pushed the cup against her lip to allow her to take another sip, and then a mouthful. Some escaped and dribbled down her chin. I put the cup down and let her rest back for a minute, and then I tried again.

'Cassandra, a sip more,' I ordered sternly, and she managed a little more. I continued like this for several hours, in total getting her to drink a dozen or more cups of water. It was hard going, and required persistence and patience. Also, if I lapsed into soft tones she wouldn't respond, but would only do so if I spoke harshly, which I hated doing. But it was doing the trick: there were no more evacuations, and she gradually appeared less pale and death-like.

As the first wintry rays of light crept around the sides of the heavy curtains, her breathing was easier and her skin felt a little warmer. I sat in a chair next to the bed, holding her slim wrist in my hand. The next thing I knew, I must have dozed off, as I gave a start as Lady Irvine entered the room.

'Frank, how is she?' she asked anxiously, coming to the bedside. 'I hear from Lily that there have been no evacuations for several hours now? Is that a good sign?'

I looked at my patient and saw she was sleeping

peacefully, her features soft, her lips a better colour. 'I think she is over the worst,' I said. 'We must continue to get her to drink, but I hope she will recover.'

'I can never thank you enough, Frank,' said Lady Irvine, gripping my hands and staring up into my face. 'I could not have borne her loss,' she finished quietly.

'And nor could I,' I replied, the realisation sinking in.

There was a knock on the door. 'Come,' she said.

'Please your Ladyship, this has arrived for you. Boy said it's urgent.' A maid handed Lady Irvine a note, which she read, slumping down on the end of the bed. Her eyes filled with tears and she brought her hand to her throat and spoke in a constricted voice. 'Poor Edward Summers passed away in the night,' she said, her old face etched with grief at what might have been. She looked at me, desperation and gratitude in her face. 'I cannot thank you enough, Frank. Now if you believe she is out of danger, get some rest. I have had a room readied for you and there is some breakfast if you would like it. Lily will show you. I will sit with her for a while. I will encourage her to drink.'

'Dr Summers was a fine man; poor Mabel.' I stood, staring at Cassandra, thinking myself of what might have been. 'I will take a short rest, and I will return. Get her to drink as much as you can; you may need to speak sternly to her! She has a mind of her own, for sure.'

Lady Irvine insisted that I stay that day and the following night, until I was sure she was out of danger. I did not see Lord Irvine during my stay, and for that, I was thankful. She would live, that was all I cared about; Cassandra Irvine would still walk the earth. On the

Wednesday morning, I declined Lady Irvine's offer of the carriage home, and stepped out of the house into the cold December morning. A freezing mist hung over the street, damp and penetrating. I pulled my coat tight around me but despite the chill in the air, I could see only beauty in the world that morning. The houses on the square were bedecked with holly and fine Christmas trees were visible at some of the windows. She would live; she was nearly lost, but she would live. I offered a silent word of thanks to John Snow. As the snowflakes started to fall on my tired face, I smiled to myself and felt warm inside. I bought a steaming coffee from a street seller and headed for home.

TWENTY-SIX

Saturday 23rd December

A chance meeting, another invitation and some sound advice

I ventured out to buy a goose for the upcoming festivities, muted as they would be for, bachelor as I was, I liked Mrs Hook to cook a special meal at Christmas. Holly sprigs with fat red berries and white mistletoe decorated the shopfronts. The aromas of hot chestnuts and mulled wine made the juices in my mouth water in the chill morning air. The merry tunes of a group of carollers rang in my ears as I walked down Silver Street, and I hummed along. Suddenly, for the first time in many weeks, I saw James Bates across the road. I swallowed my guilt and hailed him.

'James, James Bates.' He saw me and came over.

'Doctor, Miss Cassandra told us a few weeks ago that you'd been sick; I 'ope you're better now, sir?'

'Yes, yes, thank you, I am; but what of your father?'

''E's much better, Doctor, and did you know we 'ave moved to John Street? Lady Irvine fixed it for us and it is a wonder; Em can't believe our luck!'

'How is Emily?'

'She's well. She's workin' at The Newcastle, which she prefers to the 'atters, although Miss Cassandra still says she should train for a nurse.'

'I think she would make a good one. Well, I am glad things have turned out well for you both.'

'Becky Parker's come to live with us, too.' His cheeks coloured, but he said no more.

'Well, send my regards to them all, won't you?'

'I will, Doctor, thank you.'

'I am sorry to rush but I am off to visit Miss Cassandra now for you may know she has been sick too, but happily she is on the mend. May I pay you a visit in the new year?'

'We'd all be 'appy to see ya.'

'Farewell and Happy Christmas to you all.'

'Happy Christmas to you, Doctor.' He walked jauntily off up the street and something in his demeanour made me suspect that he had formed an attachment to Miss Parker. I was pleased for him. It was a strange irony that *she,* unlike Cassandra, would need no permission to marry.

Since leaving Mayfair I had received twice-daily updates from Lady Irvine on Cassandra's condition. She was making a good recovery and, although still weak, she was out of bed and able to sit downstairs for periods at a time. Yesterday evening, I received word that she was desirous of seeing me, and I was invited by Lord and Lady Irvine for afternoon tea. My waking mind had been filled with images of Cassandra and my dreams tormented with nightmares of her, blue-tinged and cold, dead from the cholera. How I longed to see her.

I arrived in Grosvenor Square at the appointed hour and I was shown into the drawing room. Cassandra was alone, seated on the gold sofa by the flickering fire. She wore a soft silver-grey gown, a gentle grey, too large now for her cholera-ravaged frame, and a plaid blanket warmed her knees. She looked up as I was shown in, and I was struck by how thin her face was. Her cheeks were pale and her forehead had a ghostlike sheen, some small veins visible through the pallor of her skin. Her eyes were the same though, soft oases of cornflower, more vivid against the unnatural whiteness. She looked at me and I felt my heart melt with love for her. She stretched out her hand to me.

'Frank, come and sit with me; it is so good to see you again. Mama and Papa will be here in a moment,' her voice was soft and bird-like. 'I owe you a debt of gratitude, I understand.' I sat beside her and a lump came to my throat.

'You owe me nothing; it is reward enough that you are recovered. It is a joy to see you again,' I murmured.

'Poor Edward; Mabel came to visit yesterday and she is distraught at her loss. It seems some others caught the cholera at Brown's too; there is quite a scandal about it, Mama says.' She looked down at her hands, stroking one index finger with the other.

'I think it must have been the water; did you drink water?'

'Yes, I did, as we waited for our coats.'

'You see, John was right all along. When will they believe him?'

'I don't know; I am just grateful that you were here and I know Papa is most grateful too. He will be here in a minute to thank you in person. Poor Mama, I don't think she could have survived another loss…' her voice tailed off. A stone appeared in my chest at the thought of the last time I had seen her father, but I had no time to dwell as the door opened and Lord and Lady Irvine came in. I scrabbled to my feet to welcome them, aware that they might think it improper for me to sit unchaperoned with Cassandra. I stood next to where she remained on the sofa and they came over. Lord Irvine leant on his stick, frail as he held out his hand to me.

'Dr Roberts, Frank, how can we thank you for saving our Cassandra?' he said, shaking me at length by the hand. He had aged since the night of Cassandra's birthday party and he looked small and vulnerable, as he turned his head to cough, a deep guttural phlegm-laden cough. He stopped and pulled a handkerchief from his pocket, mopping his waxy brow with it. His wife supported him as she concurred.

'Frank, it is a pleasure to see you again. I shall never forget what you have done for us,' Lady Irvine beamed at me, her lined face alight with warmth, eyes shining. 'You see, Cassandra is making a good recovery; she will soon be up and about, I hope.'

'Indeed, she looks to be mending well, Lady Irvine. Nothing could give me more pleasure, I can assure you.' I looked down at Cassandra and there was a hint of colour in her cheeks, embarrassment at being the centre of attention. I felt my cheeks redden as I suddenly felt awkward, aware I was speaking out of turn.

'Shall we call for tea, Mama?' Cassandra said. 'I still have such a thirst.' Lady Irvine rang the bell and the footman took the order and left.

'One moment,' said Lord Irvine, raising his hand. 'Let us be seated, for there is something I wish to say.' I sat next to Cassandra, as her parents sat on the sofa opposite. 'Frank, I would like to say that I regret my words at our last meeting. I have always been a traditionalist, always done things the way they have always been done.' He paused to cough. 'Since her cradle, I have imagined a titled husband for my daughter, and all that goes with it. However, these past weeks have wrought a change in me. I have been forced to accept that everything does not always run to order, that nothing in life is certain, and that appearances can be deceptive.' Here, Lady Irvine blushed imperceptibly and pulled at a thread on one of the cushions. He continued. 'I have been unwell since you saw me last and, for the first time, I feel my own mortality. I will not live forever and it is my duty, as a father and the head of this household, to arrange matters for my family when I am gone.'

'Oh Papa, do not say such things,' Cassandra broke in. Lord Irvine held up a finger to silence her as he coughed again, and his old grey eyes were filled with love as he looked back at her.

'The truth is, Cassandra, none of us knows what may happen in the future. I do not know when I shall pass, I do not know whether Edmund, my son and heir, will return safely from the Crimea, I do not know whether the two women most precious to me may be taken from me.' He looked at his wife and then at his daughter. 'These are things that only God can know,' he said, in a soft, distant voice. He coughed into his handkerchief and I swear I saw a tinge of blood this time. 'I have come to a decision. Frank, you may have Cassandra's hand in marriage, if that is what she chooses. You are a respectable fellow, and I have come to believe that you do truly love her. What more could a father wish for his daughter? Times are changing and I, too, must change. What do you say?'

I looked at Lord and Lady Irvine, her hand on his leg, and her face relaxing, suffused with pleasure and relief. She gave a little nod, as if this was all that was needed to make the world right. 'Yes,' she murmured under her breath. I looked at Cassandra, whose eyes had filled with tears. Without a word, I took her cool hand and slipped to one knee on the floor in front of her. I looked into her eyes, into her very soul.

'Sweet Cassandra, I ask you again, will you do me the honour of accepting my hand in marriage?'

She grasped both my hands with hers, and her face flooded with colour as she looked to burst with happiness. 'Yes, I will, Frank Roberts, I will,' she said, our eyes locking, an unbreakable connection forever between us. I sat next to her and held both her hands and we stared at each other for what seemed an eternity.

'Bravo!' said Lord Irvine as, supported by his wife, they stood and came to kiss their daughter. In the midst of the celebrations, tea arrived and the footman could barely mask his curiosity at the four of us laughing together. When he had gone and we were left alone, Lady Irvine poured the tea and Lord Irvine spoke again.

'It has been a strange couple of months and there have been many changes in my family. My dearly beloved wife has persuaded me to see that I was wrong;

that love in a marriage will tide one through the difficult times. I have seen this myself, and I recognise that love is more important than titles and protocol. So I will raise my teacup for neither you, Cassandra, nor I, are fit for anything stronger: to my daughter and her fiancé!'

'To Frank and Cassandra,' said Lady Irvine. I raised my cup and looked at Cassandra.

'To us,' I said quietly.

'To us,' she murmured, her eyes locked on mine.

Later, I found myself thinking of my mother and how finally, all these years after I had lost her, I was truly happy again. I felt sure that, somewhere, she was happy for me; I knew she would love Cassandra as much as I did.

*

It was two weeks later, the first week of 1855, and John had come to congratulate me on my engagement for I had sent word on his return from visiting in the north. He brought with him a fine cognac, an admission that he had not yet converted me to temperance. We took tea in my parlour, warming ourselves before the fire.

'Frank, I am so thankful that Cassandra has survived the cholera. She sounds a fine woman and she will make a fine wife; I very much look forward to getting to know her.'

'Thank you, John. I confess it shocked me terribly to come so close to losing her. It brought it all back.' I sighed. 'She is still weak, although she bears it graciously.'

'It would have been a cruel twist of fate if the cholera

had taken her. All the work you did in Soho, all my work on cholera, it would have amounted to nothing.'

'Your work helped for I knew, beyond a shadow of a doubt, that fluid loss was the key. I forced the water into her mouth all night when she could not take it; I sat with her as she fought it. I feared it would be to no avail; I was terrified and I am a doctor. What use are we when so often we are powerless to help?' I said, staring back into my cup.

'It must seem like that, sometimes. But you *did* help the people of Soho,' he said. 'Miss Bates, for instance, and little Daniel Lewis and that boy on Poland Street; the countless others you gave comfort to.'

'But not my own family; very nearly not my own love?' I said. 'It is too hard. I declare I am almost minded to give up medicine and train for some other profession.'

'I understand how you are feeling, Frank. But the way forward must be to work harder,' John said. 'One day, we will be able to cure the cholera, and even sooner than that, the waterborne theory will be accepted and we can develop ways to prevent it.'

'But still there is so much that we don't understand in medicine, so much that we don't know.'

'Yes, but advances are being made all the time. The tide is turning. You saw it reported last month that Pacini, in Florence, has discovered a distinctive organism in the gut linings of cholera victims; he believes it is the causative agent. The miasmatists cannot hold the faith for much longer in the face of mounting evidence to support the view that the pathogen is ingested and not inhaled. For cholera, my theory will gain acceptance one day; it is just a matter of time. Do you know my book will be in print next week? I have called it *On the Mode of Communication of Cholera*. It will be available to buy for seven shillings but I will give you a copy.' His mouth twitched with his wry smile, but I was not to be placated.

'It will be too late for all the poor souls who have died in agony,' I said.

'You are a comfort to your patients and, even if we can't see it, knowledge of medicine *is* progressing every day. And Frank, when you are a married man, I will not allow you to succumb to your tendency to melancholia; you must fight it with all vigour.'

'You are right, my friend; it is sound advice.' The reference to Cassandra shook me from myself and I looked at him. 'Would you do me the honour of being my best man? We plan to wed when Edmund returns from the Crimea.'

'Nothing would give me more pleasure.' We sat in silence for a moment and then he patted my hand and spoke again. 'Shall we go for a walk? Get some fresh air? Let us go to Hyde Park for a while? I hear it is beautiful in the snow.' I hesitated, and then agreed. I had not visited the park since Cassandra had been there the day she contracted the cholera.

John hailed a cab and we rode to Hyde Park. We walked alongside the Serpentine, which was frozen solid in places. It was a bright, but bitterly cold, afternoon and people were skating on the ice. The sky was a cool grey, weak sun glinting on the frozen lake. There was the sound of excited banter between the muffled skaters and two young women squealed with delight as their menfolk raced each other around the ice. An old fellow wheeled his barrow with difficulty, leaving a warm chestnut smell in his wake. Some early snowdrops bent their delicate heads amidst the snow; new life for a new year. The freezing air was refreshing, invigorating; I could almost feel the icicles forming in my nostrils as I breathed in. I wrapped my scarf tighter to catch the warmth of my breath.

I imagined Cassandra's visit here that day. I could see her with her friends in my mind's eye: perhaps in her thick blue coat, her elegant hat, the fur at her pale, creamy smooth neck. Her cheeks rosy in the cool air, flushed from the exercise, her eyes full of life and happiness. It was just a few short weeks ago. I shuddered at what might have been.

John and I sat on a bench in our greatcoats and watched the people. Everywhere I looked, there was life: children running, rosy-cheeked, nannies pushing perambulators of swaddled babies, men with their young ladies, elderly folk in blankets nodding along, pushed by companions. It was unbelievable that only a few months ago, last summer, it had seemed that the world was ending. There was death and despair at every turn, in every house: the Bates family, the Parkers, countless others. But life went on, no matter what tragedies befell them, people carried on. There was no other way.

I closed my eyes and felt the cold breeze on my face. In my heart, I knew John was right. I could not give up my profession; it was my life and Cassandra would not want me to. But I recognised that after my experience,

I would be changed forever. I would practise medicine with an empathy and understanding for my patients that had been missing before. I had grown as a person; I had more understanding of myself and my place in the world. I had found the woman I loved. After half an hour in companionable silence, my feet were chilled to the bone and the light was fading. I looked at John, my supporter, mentor and friend and I felt admiration and affection such as I had never felt for any man.

'Thank you, my friend. Let us go home.'

EPILOGUE

I visit John Snow's house in Sackville Street

'John, John, rest back, do not trouble yourself,' I said. 'Lie back and be comfortable. Can I get you anything?'

But John could not reply. He slumped back against the pillow, the left side of his face drooped, his eyes vacant as he seemed to stare beyond me into the middle distance. I wasn't even sure he knew I was there. There was a soft knock on the door.

'Come,' I said, not taking my eyes from John's once fine face. It was Mrs Wetherburn, his housekeeper. She had found John collapsed in his parlour six days previously, and I had spent much of those six days at his bedside. There was little I could do. He had long suffered from kidney disease; I knew he had consulted his old friend Joshua Parsons, the nephrologist, over the years. His physician colleagues Drs Murchison and Budd were tending him diligently but he had suffered a stroke and there was little to be done but to wait and hope. But John was showing no signs of recovery. I knew in my heart that unless victims showed some positive change within the first couple of days, it was rare for there to be any significant improvement. John was forty-five; it was too young, especially for a man who had done so much for others.

'It's Dr Snow's sister, Mary,' said Mrs Wetherburn. 'Is it all right for her to come in?'

'Yes, send her in.' John's sister came and stood by the bed. 'Mary, good day to you. I will leave you with him for a while. I need to get home to my wife, Cassandra, anyway to see how our little John is doing. We named our son for him, you know,' I said, my voice hollow and unsteady.

'Tha's a good friend, Frank. He always spoke fondly of thee. John? Can you hear me? It's Mary.' John's eyes fluttered and he seemed to try to turn his head towards the voice, familiar from his faraway childhood. 'It's Mary,' she repeated. 'How are thee, my big brother?' she continued, with a forced smile. Nothing. A solitary tear escaped her eye, and she brushed it impatiently away with the back of her hand. She looked at me. 'Is he any better?' she whispered.

'I'm afraid not,' I murmured. 'I've sat with him for many hours over the last few days, and there has not been much change.' My heart was heavy in my chest.

'Thank ye for staying; it must be a comfort, to have a friend here.' She looked at John in silence for a few minutes, before she spoke to him again. 'Father always hoped tha'd make something of thy sen, didn't he, John? Sent us all to be schooled, but tha did best. Tha always liked learning, finding out things, knowing things. Father and Mother were so proud of thee when tha went off to become a doctor. Us just farming folk, too; so proud they were, so proud. It's a pity they never lived to see how well tha've done.' She looked at him, immobile in the bed, and faltered. 'He did do well, didn't he?' she whispered to me, as if suddenly unsure how much she really knew about her brother.

I was silent for a moment, staring at my friend. 'He did. He did so much for people, for medicine. His work on anaesthesia will be remembered. He was finishing his book on it when this happened, you know. His name will be known long after he has gone,' I whispered, trying to sound strong, wiping a tear from my own cheek. 'But do you know, I think one day his work on cholera will be even more well known.'

'Cholera? I know he were interested in it when he were young. He worked in a mining village once, years ago, I remember,' said Mary.

'He had a lifelong interest in the disease. I worked with him a few years ago, just a few streets from here. I have never seen a man so devoted to a cause. He spent years working on it: researching, gathering information from outbreaks, trying to build a compelling case that people would believe. He was convinced it was carried in the water, you see, but no one would believe him. But his work convinced me: it was the Broad Street water pump.'

'I remember him talking about it.'

'It took a while but eventually it was found that there *was* a breach in the lining of the well by which sewage from a drain got in,' I said, talking more to myself than to her. 'A baby had died of diarrhoea before the epidemic started and her mother had been washing her soiled linen into the drain. It was recorded as "diarrhoea", but actually she was the first case of cholera; the index case who started the whole epidemic.' I came back to the present once more. 'He said it was the pump, and he was right. He published a book about it. But do you know, the sad thing is, even after all his work, many people to this day still hold to the miasma theory.'

'Miasma?'

'Yes, you know, that disease is carried in "bad airs",' I said. 'Some diseases might be airborne, but not the cholera. He believed cholera was waterborne and he worked so hard to build the case. But one day everyone will believe him; one day, he'll be known the world over for his work,' I murmured. I took his hand and paused to look into his face, willing those grey eyes to open. 'Farewell, John. I will leave you with Mary and return later. Rest well.' I stood and walked to the door. As I turned back, Mary was sitting on the bed, holding John's hand.

'Do you remember that day when our pig Nelson got into Mr Jones' vegetable garden and dug up the lot? And Father sent William and thee to catch it, and old Mr Jones thought you two had wrecked his garden and chased you off with a scythe, while old Nelson had a doze back in his sty?' she chuckled to herself. 'And the rest of us kids were all lined up, laughing so much at you two, I thought we'd all wet ourselves!' She talked on animatedly as if they were back on the Yorkshire farm with their parents and siblings around them and John's friend, my brother William, was there. I could have been mistaken, but I thought I saw a flicker of a one-sided smile pass across his face. I closed the door softly.

When I returned that evening, John was gone. I allowed the tears to fall.

John Snow

THE LATE DR. SNOW

We announce with great pain and grief the death of our distinguished and estimable brother, Dr. Snow. He was suddenly seized with paralysis on Thursday, the 10th instant, and died on Wednesday the 16th, at his own residence, 18, Sackville-street, at three p.m. Drs. Murchison and Budd assiduously attended him to the last. Dr. Snow was only in his 46th year, and both on public and private grounds his early loss will be very greatly regretted. His name was known to the profession chiefly in connection with chloroform, to which subject he had of late years devoted a great deal of attention, and next to Dr Simpson he was most deservedly looked upon as the highest authority respecting the properties and administration of this agent. He had instituted at great labour a vast number of experiments for the purpose of ascertaining its effects on the lower animals, and the manner in which it might be given with the least amount of danger. His labours were fully appreciated by the profession, and for several years the leading surgeons in London constantly sought his co-operation. He was very successful in the administration of chloroform, and we believe that only one death happened in his hands from this agent. Dr. Snow's labours were not by any means confined to this subject; he is well known as having devoted great attention to the investigation of cholera, and his views regarding the propagation of the disease by drinking impure water are familiar to the profession. Dr. Snow was a man of high integrity and moral worth, possessing great abilities and untiring energy, with an unassuming disposition, and his loss will be deeply felt by many who appreciated his sterling character and valued his friendship. – *Medical Times*

The London Standard, Monday 21st June 1858

331

HISTORICAL NOTE

This is a work of fiction, but it is based on a real event, the epidemic of cholera which befell Broad Street in Soho, London, in late August and September 1854. It was the most rapid and deadly cholera epidemic this country has ever witnessed, killing over 500 people in ten days, in a small community. Some sufferers went from well to dead within a matter of hours.

Dr John Snow, a real person, at the time renowned as a pioneer of anaesthesia, worked all his life to prove that cholera is transmitted through water, rather than in the bad airs or "miasma" which was the commonly held view at the time. He first worked with cholera as a surgical apprentice in the Killingworth mine, where he became convinced that the close proximity between the miners' excrement and where they ate and drank during their shifts was responsible for the rapid spread of cholera through their ranks.

He worked with cholera patients in the 1831-2 cholera epidemic, and he studied patterns of disease in London in the 1848-9 epidemic. In 1854 he conducted his "grand experiment", painstakingly comparing the rates of cholera in houses south of the river Thames which were supplied by two different water companies, one sourced in an area of the Thames which was polluted by sewage, and one which had moved its supply above the tidal reach. From this he deduced that cholera was waterborne. He had not completed this work when the

Broad Street epidemic occurred. He saw this localised outbreak as a chance to test and further develop his theory. He worked tirelessly and methodically, collecting data and walking the streets gathering information about water supply and sanitation arrangements of victims and their relatives to try to deduce the source of the epidemic. He concluded that the water of the Broad Street pump was contaminated with cholera.

Although he did manage to persuade the authorities to remove the pump handle in Broad Street, it took much longer for his theory of cholera transmission to become accepted. He continued to refine and develop his work on the Broad Street epidemic long after it had ended; and he published a second and much larger edition of his work *On the Mode of Communication of Cholera*, which documented his work in south London, and included his work in Broad Street. This was published at his own expense, in January 1855.

Reverend Henry Whitehead, also a real person, was a believer in the miasma theory and was initially sceptical of Snow's ideas, but became a convert to his theory. During his work in the streets of Soho conducting enquiries for the St Luke's Vestry Committee, he retraced and expanded on John Snow's door-to-door enquiries and came to wholeheartedly support Snow's theory. Furthermore, it was Henry Whitehead's notice of the case of baby Lewis who died at 40 Broad Street, reportedly of "diarrhoea", just before the start of the epidemic, which provided Snow with the crucial index case and the cause of the outbreak.

As part of his work, Snow plotted the cholera deaths

on a map, which was presented after the end of the outbreak to the Vestry Committee enquiry, and also in his book. This "spot map" is now a famous depiction of his investigation. However, the waterborne theory was not widely accepted until the last major cholera epidemic in London in 1866, when Lankester worked once more with Henry Whitehead, and the medical profession finally acknowledged that John Snow had been correct.

Frank, Cassandra, the Bates family and the other characters are fictitious except for the Lewis family, the Eley brothers and their mother, Sir Benjamin Hall and, of course, Florence Nightingale. She did indeed work in the hospitals mentioned at the time, before she famously went with her lamp to nurse soldiers in the Crimea in October 1854. Edwin Chadwick was also a real person, although his altercation with John Snow at the lecture is fictional.

I have taken a few liberties in compressing the timescale of the investigation; as alluded to, in reality it was into early 1855 before all the links were made and the proof gathered. An investigation by the Sewer Commission and the Paving Board, responsible for the well under the Broad Street pump, initially reported no specific defect. However, in April 1855, it was deemed that the previous examinations of the well had been too superficial, and more excavations were carried out to the cesspool and drains at 40 Broad Street and the pump well. This discovered that the cesspool was forcing sewage to back up rather than flow out, and the cesspool and the drain into which it emptied were lined with loose and decaying brickwork. This resulted in the surrounding soil being impregnated with effluent. Crucially, the brickwork of the pump well was only two and a half feet away from the drain. Therefore, this provided clear evidence of the route of contamination of the Broad Street pump well by the discharges in the cesspool from the baby at number 40.

Historians may say that the removal of the pump handle came too late to stop the outbreak, which was already dying out by the time the handle was removed on 8th September. However, it is sobering to think that the 8th September was the very day on which Constable Lewis, baby Lewis's father, came down with cholera, and from which point his wife was again discharging the washings from *his* soiled bed linen back into the cesspool. Therefore, if the handle had not been removed the epidemic would, in all likelihood, have resurged and killed more people.

John Snow is today credited with being the forefather of epidemiology, the science that studies patterns of disease to help elucidate cause. His was real "shoe leather" epidemiology, consisting of detailed house-to-house enquiries to ascertain facts, and then objective analysis and mapping of his findings to deduce cause. Working at a time when knowledge of disease causation and microbiology was in its infancy, he was truly ahead of his time in applying the principles as he did. It was another thirty years before Koch identified *vibrio cholera* as the bacterium which causes the disease.

Students of medicine around the world learn about John Snow and the Broad Street pump, in what is considered a seminal investigation. The general practitioners and apothecaries who tried to help are not remembered, and sadly, neither are the hundreds who died in the epidemic. They are merely a passing sentence in the record book, just bars on a map. Nor is it widely known that John Snow himself died, only four years after the epidemic, in 1858: even after all his work, his theory was still not widely accepted in his lifetime. It is testament to his dedication and tenacity that the story still fascinates over 150 years later.

It is a sad fact that, worldwide, there are still an estimated three to five million cases of cholera and over 100,000 deaths from cholera every year. Today, in epidemic, it is almost exclusively a disease of developing countries. It is shocking that even in the twenty-first century, cholera still kills: not now from lack of knowledge about transmission, but from a lack of facilities for clean water and sanitation. Considering how the world has changed beyond all recognition since 1854, John Snow would surely be horrified if he was still alive today.

It is also sobering to think that even now, with the wealth of medical and microbiological knowledge available to us, there will ever be new and emerging diseases which we are not equipped to treat. The past few decades have seen the emergence and threat to humans from HIV, bird flu and more recently, Ebola, which still threaten populations. We can only imagine how much more terrifying the threat of seemingly unpreventable, untreatable disease was back in Snow's time.

Today, Broad Street has been renamed Broadwick Street and a memorial stone marks the site of the original pump. A replica of the pump stands a short way away, with a plaque commemorating the epidemic. The pub on Broadwick Street has been renamed the "John Snow", an ironic tribute to a man who espoused temperance all his life. Almost every building has been replaced since Snow's day and it is only by closing your eyes that it is possible to imagine what it might have been like in that hot summer of 1854.

SELECTED BIBLIOGRAPHY

On the Mode of Communication of Cholera, Second edition, much enlarged. December 1854: John Snow MD in Snow on Cholera: A reprint of two papers by John Snow MD, (New York, The Commonwealth Fund, 1936)

On the Mode of Communication of Cholera, 1849: John Snow, (London, Churchill)

Cholera, Chloroform and the Science of Medicine: A life of John Snow by Peter Vinten-Johansen and others (Oxford University Press, 2003)

The Ghost Map: Steven Johnson (Penguin, 2006)

The Medical Detective: Sandra Hempel (Granta Books, 2006)

The Victorian House: Judith Flanders (Harper Perennial, 2004)

The Victorian City: Judith Flanders (Atlantic Books, 2012)

London Labour and the London Poor: Henry Mayhew (Oxford University Press, 2010)

The Great Stink of London: Stephen Halliday (The History Press, 2009)

Mid-Victorian Britain: Christine Garwood (Shire Living Histories, Shire Publications, 2011)

The Rookeries of London: Past, present and prospective: Thomas Beames (1852, new impression of second edition, Cass & co, 1970)

Homes of the London Poor: Octavia Hill (Cass Library of
Victorian Times no 6, Cass & co, 1970)

University of California Los Angeles Epidemiology
department website

http://www.ph.ucla.edu/epi/snow.html

The British Newspaper Archive online

www.britishnewspaperarchive.co.uk

The John Snow Society at www.johnsnowsociety.org

CREDITS

Map of Broad Street epidemic and photograph of John Snow reproduced with permission of Ralph R Frerichs http://www.ph.ucla.edu/epi/snow.html

Newspaper excerpts used with permission of The British Newspaper Archive www.britishnewspaperarchive.co.uk